CURSE

OF THE

DEVIL'S

TEETH

AN EZEKIEL CRANE NOVEL

J. KENT HOLLOWAY

CHARADE
MEDIA

For Jeff Rausch…
From fan to friend. You were an amazing guy. You'll be horribly missed.

PROLOGUE

You don't have to be a chicken to know a rotten egg, and the people of Boone Creek, Kentucky, had always pegged Leroy Kingston for just that. He was rotten to the core. The way it was told, old Leroy came out of his mama "cussin' like a sailor and spitting vinegar". To most people in the area, there just wasn't anyone meaner in the whole county than Leroy.

And that reputation had always suited him just fine. Truth be told, he down right liked it. It made him somewhat of a big to-do in town and he had grown up with the locals giving him a very wide berth whenever he walked into a place—especially Bailey's Pub where they'd usually give him a free pint just to get him to leave before a fight would break out. A fight that Leroy would invariably win.

So it was a really strange sight to Tim Crawford, while driving on a dark winding stretch of County Road 205 in the predawn hours of a crisp October morning, that he caught sight of Leroy bursting from the tree line in a state of absolute terror. It was just before dawn and there was very little lighting, but Tim could tell, even in the dim light, that the man's clothes were nothing more than ragged shreds of fabric and his face, neck, and hands were caked with something dark and red. Kingston's eyes were wide, like twin moons set on a crimson-hued horizon.

Immediately, Tim slammed on the brakes, bringing his rusted out Ford F-150 to a skidding halt along the side of the road. Once he was at a full stop, he put the truck in park, jumped out of the cab, and ran to Leroy, who had collapsed to the dew-dampened earth with a groan. He laid there, his limbs shaking with every labored breath.

Tim slid up beside Leroy's trembling form and wiped away the grime and gore concealing his face. The red stains turned out to be exactly what Tim had expected. Blood. And from what he could tell, lots of it too. More than could possibly come out of Leroy himself and still allow him to run out of the woods like a madman during a full moon anyway. He gave the terrified man a quick once over, confirming his suspicions that there were no serious injuries. Just a few scrapes and scratches…easily enough explained by the thorny brambles that infested the region. But the small injuries came nowhere close to explaining the amount of blood that coated his upper body.

Tim had been a hunter since he was old enough to hold a gun. He'd seen his fair share of carnage before and knew that whatever had produced such quantities of blood would not be pretty to look at.

"Leroy!" Tim shouted. He had trouble controlling the volume of his voice. His pulse, fueled by adrenaline, thumped like a bass drum in his skull, creating a thunderous hum in his ears. "Leroy, what the heck happened, man?"

Kingston only shivered, his eyes fixed skyward in a dead stare. His body convulsed wildly, forcing Tim to cradle the well-known hellion in his arms. A slight whimper escaped Leroy's lips at the sudden movement.

"Shhhhhh," Tim soothed. "It's all right. Just you relax now." With one free hand, he reached into his shirt pocket and pulled out a silver flask. He deftly unscrewed the cap with his thumb and lifted the container to the trembling man's lips. A stream of one-hundred and ten proof homemade "white lightning" poured down Kingston's gullet. He coughed once before relaxing his throat enough to allow the corn-based liquor to slide down with ease.

After a long pull, Leroy clamped his eyes shut and let out a long, deep breath. Then his eyes snapped open with a jerk and he mumbled something amid a series of whimpers.

"What's that, Leroy? I didn't quite make that out."

The bloodied face turned slowly to look at Tim; his eyes still stretched unnaturally wide.

"Jaaaaack," Leroy rasped. "One..." He took a deep, sobbing breath. "Eyed..."

Tim tensed, knowing instinctively what the next word would be. He'd lived near the Dark Hollows his entire life and knew the stories all too well. Stories that would send even the most ornery of men into fits of night terrors if he so much as thought about them before falling asleep.

"Jack."

A frigid chill washed down the hunter's spine at the mention of the name. One-Eyed Jack had returned.

CHAPTER ONE

Bailey's Pub
One Week Later
October 13
5:10 PM

F BI Crime Analyst Kiera "Kili" Brennan slammed her fist down onto the termite-infested mahogany bar inside the ridiculous little honky-tonk known as 'Bailey's'.

"I'm sick of this crap!" she yelled at the bartender, presumably Bailey himself. Her outburst was unlike her. Normally mild and soft-spoken, the frustration she was feeling was enough to drive her to tears. Instead, she opted to channel all of it into outright anger. "I've been here for two days, and no one has even lifted so much as a finger to help me find my brother. I want to know why!"

The handful of patrons occupying the pub sat up straight in their chairs, eyeing their beers. Not daring to look at the fiery redhead now making a scene in Boone Creek's one and only bar.

When she'd first learned that a bar acted as the unofficial town center of Boone Creek, a small hamlet nestled in a very secluded area of the Appalachian foothills of Kentucky, Kili had literally laughed. After all, it was right in the middle of what was supposed to be a very dry county. She had originally wondered how many state and local violations the establishment was routinely committing, and thought it was rather quaint when she'd first pulled into town.

But almost forty-eight hours later, any charm she'd attributed to the place had worn off. She was nowhere closer to finding her missing brother, Cian, than when she'd first pulled into this coal pit excuse for a town. And these backwoods hillbillies were the ones blocking her every move in her search. They just refused to talk to her. Sure, they were polite enough. Southern hospitality and all that. But the moment she started asking questions about the incident last week that occurred in a chunk of land they called the 'Dark Hollows', the entire lot of them clammed up. Every stinking one of them. Even the worthless sheriff had given her the run-around. So, it was only natural for her to be losing her cool.

She raised her hands up in the air in an unspoken apology over her outburst, took in a deep breath, and looked at herself in the warped mirror behind the bar's countertop. Her long, normally strawberry colored hair sat atop her head, tied up in a ponytail—the ends frizzier than she, or any metropolitan professional, preferred. Her lipstick was now non-existent. The expensive Fifth Avenue pantsuit that covered her tall, thin frame was wrinkled as if she'd slept in it for two nights straight; which was humorous in itself considering she'd hardly slept at all in the last five days.

Geez, Kili. Is that really you?

Since the moment she heard about her brother's disappearance, she'd dashed out of her Arlington, Virginia townhome, hopped into her Toyota Camry, and drove non-stop to Boone Creek, Kentucky—population nine hundred and thirty six. From that moment on, she'd barely paused for food and sleep. Forget about actually showering, hair, or makeup. Now, Kili hardly recognized the woman staring back at her in the barroom mirror.

"Ma'am," the rotund bar man said with a thick Kentucky drawl. His balding dome seemed to shimmer in the dim lighting of the bar; sweat beading across his brow like liquid prisms. "You need to either order somethin' or leave. Yer vexing the customers somethin' fierce."

She glared at the bar man, her eyes narrowing. "And I'm not going anywhere until someone talks to me," she said. "Why is it so hard for you people to understand? My brother is missing. Nothing's being done about that by local law enforcement. Why can't you just help me?"

"Because they don't trust strangers," came a voice from behind her. "And with might good reason, I'd say."

Kili spun around from her position at the bar to see the swarthy, rumpled frame of Jasper County Sheriff John Tyler. The big man cast a greasy smile at her as he sauntered over to the bar, his thumbs tucked tightly in his gun belt. He slapped down a five-dollar bill and nodded silently to Bailey. Understanding the unspoken command, the bartender drew a stein of beer from the tap and set it down in front of the lawman.

"Sheriff, I don't think you understand," Kili said, trying her best not to grind her teeth. "As I've already told you...I'm with the FBI and I've come here to investigate the—"

"Stop," he said, taking a pull from the mug and wiping the foam from his lips. He turned to look at her, stroking his thick, Magnum P.I. mustache with his free hand. "First of all, darlin', you may work for the FBI, but you're not an agent. I checked."

"But..."

"Second..." He refused to allow her to interrupt. "FBI's got no jurisdiction in this matter, even if you were. And third—" He took one more drink from his beer, set it back on the bar top, and started moving toward the door. "You're not really welcome here. Go home, Ms. Brennan. I promise I'll let ya know the moment we find your brother. Scout's honor."

He opened the door and turned around to face her again, flashing her another crooked smile. His teeth were dotted with flecks of black—Kili presumed remnants of snuff—along the lower gums. "Seriously. Go home. It ain't a request, sweet thing. Understand?"

Without waiting for a response, the so-called lawman stepped out into the afternoon sun, and let the door close behind him.

Irritated, she picked up the sheriff's half-empty mug, hefted it to her mouth, and downed the remains. She threw down a couple of dollars on the bar for no reason in particular, and turned to face the pub's patrons.

"Will none of you help me?" she asked, knowing the answer before the words ever left her lips.

No one spoke. Each customer sat motionless, still staring deep into their drinks, as if all the answers in the world were located within their amber contents. She couldn't be sure, but she was starting to think their reluctance was not as much about indifference to her plight as it was good old-fashioned fear. *But fear of what?*

"All right," she sighed. "I'll be at the motel if anyone changes their mind." She walked over to the door, pushed it open, and, like Sheriff Tyler had done with her, turned around to face them one more time. "I don't care what your sheriff says. I'm not leaving town. I can't. So things are going to get a lot more uncomfortable for you around here until I get answers."

She stepped out of the tavern, into the gravel parking lot, and stalked toward her car. As irritated as she was, she couldn't help taking in the pristine, pastoral scenery surrounding her... drinking in the crisp round edges of the foothills in the distance.

Boone Creek was cradled in a valley between three different mountain ridges, now painted various shades of red, orange, and yellow with the coming of fall. A gray-white haze drifted low, like a blanket of cotton draped lazily around the tips of the hills.

The town itself was tiny. Nothing more than a single two-lane road surrounded by a strip of shops and other businesses on either side. A Five and Dime Store was the closest establishment to the bar. After that, a TruValue Hardware store, a newspaper, and a doctor's office. On the other side of the street sat an old-fashioned pharmacy—a soda jerk plying his trade could be seen from the plate glass windows. A feed store, a bakery, and pawn-shop all sat idly on the east side of the road. There was even a bookstore on the far end of the strip, unimaginatively called "The Book Shop", though she couldn't imagine the place getting much business in this town.

On the far end of town, just past its single traffic light that seemed to only flash yellow, was the town's solitary motel…the Jasper Motor Lodge, where she had rented a room for the week.

She thought about the shoddy, rodent infested dive and sighed. She wasn't doing her brother any good by continuing the search in her exhausted condition. She needed rest. It was high time to take a break, get some sleep, and clean up a bit. The more she considered this, the more the idea appealed to her.

After a good night sleep, she'd head back down to the hospital and try once more to talk to the only person to emerge from her brother's expedition—Leroy Kingston was his name. From what she'd been able to put together, her brother, an anthropologist from Columbia University, had hired Kingston as a guide to lead him to some strange ruins he'd heard about while researching Appalachian folklore. The guide had escaped what-ever had happened to Cian, but had suffered a severe catatonic fit from his ordeal. Last she'd heard, the man was suffering from post-traumatic stress disorder, coupled with nightmarish delu-sions of giant monstrous spirits said to haunt the Dark Hollows. Of course, Kili couldn't know for sure if this was true. The old witch of a nurse hadn't even let her get within thirty feet of Kingston's room. She was, however, determined that that would change tomorrow. She'd figure out a way to get in there after getting a good night's sleep.

As she opened the driver's side door to her Camry, she heard the sound of a footstep in the gravel behind her, followed by the sound of someone clearing his throat. She wheeled around to see a small, squirrelly man dressed in overalls, a flannel shirt, and mud-caked work boots. A large mesh baseball cap with the words JOHN DEERE stenciled in yellow across the front, stood about two feet away from her, his arms plunged deep in the pockets of his overalls. After several awkward seconds of silence, the man, staring down at his boots, pulled out a cigarette, popped it in his mouth, and lit it.

She looked at him without saying a word. The man took a long pull on his cigarette before finally looking up at her.

"I, uh…" He seemed to be considering what he was going to say. One look into his swiveling nervous eyes told Kili that she'd been correct in her assessment of the townspeople around here. He was scared. No, terrified was probably a better word.

"It's okay," she said, trying to ease his fears. "You can talk to me. If you're being threatened, I can find someone to protect you. You don't have to be afraid."

He cleared his throat again, expelling a plume of smoke from the corner of his lips.

"Not from this," he said. "You can't protect us from this."

"What? What are you so afraid of? Tell me."

The little man lifted his cap off his head and wiped a stream of sweat glistening across his brow with his shirtsleeve. Despite the crisp autumn breeze, he was perspiring like it was the middle of the dog days of summer.

"I can't," he said. "We can't. I'm sorry, ma'am. We ain't really this hard. Heck, our mamas taught us better than this…"

"Then help me. Please."

The man cast a worried glance over both shoulders, as if fearful that someone was watching, and then leaned in toward her.

"I can't." He took one more step closer and then whispered, "But I'm supposed to tell you about the one person what can. Someone who ain't afraid like the rest of us."

Kili's heart thumped against her chest. Finally, she might catch a break in this investigation. "*Supposed* to tell me? What do you mean by that?"

"Never you mind. Fer now, just know that you need to go see the town's doctor," he said. "She'll know how to help ya find yer brother."

Kili halted at this. "Doctor? But I've met him. He doesn't know anything."

The man shook his head. "Not Dr. MacLeod, ma'am. In these here parts, he's considered a quack. Nah, I'm talkin' about the *real* doctor...the mountain doctor." He took another drag on his cigarette and continued. "She's a water witch. Her medicine is of a different sort."

Had she heard him right? A witch?

Oh for crying out loud. She forced herself to remain open to the crazy redneck's suggestion, no matter how absurd it might be. But the man was more astute than she had supposed. He had read her expression and smiled at her. For the first time, she could see that he sported a very prominent overbite, reinforcing his rodent-like countenance.

"Don't rush to judgment until ya meet her, Ms. Brennan," he said. "I know to someone like you, it might sound a bit silly, but she knows her stuff. And she's a water witch—a diviner—gifted in locating missing things. If anyone can find yer brother, it'd be her. I swear to you on that."

She nodded at him. At this point, she was willing to try just about anything. "And her name? Where can I find her?"

He threw his cigarette down on the gravel, and smashed it

with the toe of his boot. "Everyone around here just calls her Granny, but her name's Esther Crane. She lives off Old Jenning's Road, near Beacher's Grove, a few miles north of the..." He looked around, then continued in a conspiratorial tone. "...the Hollars." He gave her the address, along with rough directions on how to get there. Then his face grew even more dour than anything she'd seen so far. "But a word of warning, Miss. Granny's got a grandson. A strange one, he is. Avoid him like the plague if you can. Granny will treat ya right...but no one around here cottons much to Ezekiel Crane. He's not to be trusted."

"And why is that?" She was having a difficult time trying to be patient with the man's superstitious mindset.

The man stuck his hands in his pockets once more and shrugged nervously. "He's a seventh son of a seventh son who made a pact with the Willow Hag years ago. He's got powers. Dark powers too. Granny, she keeps him in check, but left to his own devices..." He gave an involuntary shiver. "There's no tellin' what he's capable of. Just steer well clear of him and you should be all right."

"Willow what?"

But the squirrelly man had already turned, disappeared around to the back of the pub without another word.

EDDIE JOHNSON CHIDED himself as he climbed through the bathroom window of Bailey's Pub. For the life of him, he couldn't explain why he'd agreed to talk to the FBI woman. If the others found out...Eddie shivered at the thought. Most of them would understand, but Bailey, Tom Thornton, and Sheriff Tyler would not be happy. As far as they were concerned, One-Eyed Jack and these murders were a private affair. They weren't something to be discussed with anyone—especially an outsider. The very fact that he'd pointed the Brennan woman in the right direction was enough to cause him serious problems.

"Don't worry about it," Eddie whispered to himself, closing the window and moving over to the sink. He turned on the faucet, washed his hands, and pulled out a handful of paper towels to dry them. "There ain't no way they could know I talked to her. Just go back out there, order yourself another pint, and forget this even happened."

The little man chuckled to himself as he tossed the towels into the trash and turned to the door. He was being silly. Scared for no reason. Of course, that wasn't really very new to him. Eddie Johnson had been pretty much a wimp his entire life. And no one in Jasper County seemed to respect him because of it. Which was just fine with him. The less people respected him, the more they left him alone.

He jumped as he pulled the bathroom door open to see the scowling face of Sheriff John Tyler staring at him.

"How did you—"

Before Eddie could get the question out, Tyler grabbed Eddie's lapel and pulled him from the bathroom. Ten long strides later, the two men were in the pub's main room. With a violent shove, the sheriff threw him to the ground and glared at him. The rest of the bar's patrons all glowered at Eddie, quivering on the peanut strewn floor.

How did the Sheriff get back here so soon? Eddie Johnson thought. *He left before the woman, right? He'd been nowhere in sight when I was talking to her.*

"I-I can explain," Eddie croaked behind the lump swelling up in his throat.

"Really now?" Tyler asked, squatting down to look him in the eye. "I'd like to hear that."

"So would I," came the gravelly voice of *Reverend* Tom Thornton. Thornton wasn't really a reverend—not in the traditional Christian way exactly—but he demanded the title be used by everyone in town. "We had a covenant amongst ourselves. We can't have news about what's happening in the Hollars getting out. It's bad enough that fool Kingston started spouting off about One-Eyed Jack when he came out of there. Now, we got this Brennan woman snoopin' around too. And you haul off and go talk to her?"

Eddie tried to sit up, but was abruptly stopped by the sole of the sheriff's boot pressing down against his chest. "Uh-uh," Tyler said. "Take a load off. Relax. And tell us what you told her."

"I didn't tell her nothing!"

"You spent a might long time talkin' to her just to tell her nothin', Eddie," the pub's owner, Bailey chimed in. "It's been hard enough keeping our operation up in the Devil's Teeth quiet as it is. You know that. If Asherah hadn't come up with the brilliant idea to use these One-Eyed Jack stories as a cover, the whole town would be up in arms. Six deaths, Eddie. Six. And we've worked real hard to keep 'em quiet. No one can know what happened to 'em 'til it's finished." He pulled a cigarette from a pack, and plopped it in his mouth. "For crying out loud, Eddie, we've even managed to keep Esther Crane from knowin' about what we're doin' up there."

He shook his head. "I swear to you'uns...I didn't tell her a thing," Eddie said. His voice was even more shaky than normal. "Alls I said was she should go see Granny Crane. Said that if anyone knew where her brother'd be, it would be her."

Sheriff Tyler's eyes widened. "You told her to go see Crane?"

"Just Granny! Just Granny!" Eddie's voice was nearly a shriek. He couldn't tell them the *real* reason for pointing Kili Brennan in the right direction. Couldn't tell anybody about *her*. She'd warned him not to say anything or he'd pay dearly. When it came to what he feared more—them or her, he'd take whatever Tyler and Thornton had to dish out without so much as a whimper. "I warned her away from Ezekiel though. Told her he was bad news. Told her to steer clear of him at all costs."

"You idiot!" Tyler growled, spinning around and moving toward the bar. He nodded to Bailey, who drew out a mug of beer from the tap and sat it down in front of the sheriff. "Both Cranes are dangerous, you moron. You don't think Granny will turn Crane onto what's going on once she hears about the missing scientist? You don't think they'll start to get curious once they hear about the other disappearances?"

"I didn't think it would hurt none—" Eddie tried to say, before he was interrupted by the Reverend once more.

"You didn't think," Thornton said. "That's the problem. You never think. We have too much at stake with the Devil's Teeth, Eddie. Too much to lose. Noah McGuffin's crew will make trouble for us if this thing gets out of hand. Rumors of Jack's return have already started spreadin', which will keep most people away. But it won't stop the FBI woman. And it sure as heck ain't gonna stop the Cranes."

With Tyler leaning against the bar, Eddie climbed to his feet, wobbled to the nearest table and sat down with his back to the door. "I don't know what the problem is," he said, lighting his own cigarette, and exhaling a plume of smoke. "They say Ezekiel Crane is marked—by the Devil himself, no less. He won't care none what's goin' on up in the Hollars."

"The fact that he's marked makes him even more dangerous," came a voice from behind. Eddie Johnson's heart skipped several beats when he turned to see the lean, shapely form of Asherah Richardson gliding into the room. It was as if her feet, always bare, never touched the floor.

As always, Eddie was unable to pull his eyes away from this vision dressed in a form-fitting sundress despite the chill air outside. Her dark, mocha-colored skin, smooth and vibrant, seemed to glisten in the dim tavern lights. Though of African descent, she had emerald green eyes that could devour a weaker man's soul with a single wink. While the elderly Esther Crane was Boone Creek's resident water witch and local doctor, Asherah was something else entirely.

A witch herself, of very powerful magic. No one knew for sure how she used her talents—though speculation ran rampant in the region. She was raised by Noah McGuffin, the local drug lord, after the death of her equally as powerful mother, and was brought up to be his lieutenant and spiritual adviser. Some said she was a whole lot more to Noah than an adopted daughter, while others wondered if she wasn't the one truly in charge of his criminal empire. Of course, there wasn't a person in the bar that would refuse anything she commanded. Including Eddie. After all, it was Asherah who'd instructed him to point the Brennan woman in Crane's direction.

"As a matter of fact," she continued once she had everyone's attention, "I've foreseen his involvement. He will definitely be trouble for us. Trouble for everything we've been working toward."

Yeah, thought Eddie grimly. *You've foreseen it 'cause yer playin' the whole thing like a golden fiddle.* But he held his tongue. To do anything less would result in having it removed from his head… through a hole in his neck.

The entire room stared, transfixed on the ebony beauty. No one dared move. Even fewer wanted to speak. If Ezekiel Crane was the devil of Boone Creek, Asherah Richardson was a dark goddess. She was both a mixture of intense desire and the most chilling of nightmares.

Finally, after an indeterminable number of seconds, Sheriff Tyler stepped forward, and cleared his throat. "Asherah," he said quietly with a polite nod of his head. He stood there, gazing at her and awaiting the subtle tilt of her head that signaled her acknowledgement of his approach. A few more seconds ticked by before she inclined her head once, and gestured for the man to continue. "I guess the question we're all wondering is what we should do about Crane if he gets involved?"

She laughed at this and it was like the sound of chimes in a springtime breeze. "What on earth do you think you *could* do to him, Sheriff? You and I both know...he's no ordinary man. Do you honestly believe you have a mind or will capable of stopping him should he set his mind to something?"

Tyler's face reddened at the insult. His eyebrows furrowed, but he held his tongue. Wisely.

Asherah continued. "No, John. I think it wise to leave him alone for now. He may become trouble for us, but I fear that One-Eyed Jack will be more of a danger if allowed to continue. For the moment, we can use him, but when the time comes, there's no one better suited to deal with ol' Jack than Ezekiel."

"And the girl?" asked the quavering voice of Tom Thornton. "She's not going to stop until she finds out what happened to her brother. She's just not going to let up and you know it."

The witch turned her icy glare on the Reverend and sneered. "You let me worry about that, Thomas Thornton. After all, it's your bungling that has caused this problem to begin with, now isn't it?"

He staggered backwards at the force of her accusation. "But they were diggin' at the Teeth. They were gonna find the experiment. We couldn't let that happen."

"No, but there were other ways to deal with the situation other than shooting Dr. Brennan's assistant. And as your story goes, you would have killed the anthropologist, and Leroy too, if Jack hadn't showed up. It's sloppy. Stupid and sloppy." She shook her head with disapproval. "For now, you and your... congregation...just need to keep a low profile. Don't get yourselves into any trouble. Keep your eyes on the Teeth...on our crop...and let me deal with Ms. Brennan myself. Understand?"

"And if Jack kills again?" Sheriff Tyler asked. "I'm not sure how much longer I can keep the news of these deaths secret. Right now, our experiments are responsible for six deaths. That's six more than I agreed to when you came to me with this. I can't guarantee I'll be able to keep this up much longer without drawing attention from the Cranes, or even the state police."

"First of all, Sheriff, you'll hold up your end of the bargain marvelously. I've no doubt about that." Asherah's smile was pure venom. "And second, Jack will certainly kill again. Of that, you can be certain. He's trying to raise his brothers, after all...or at least, that's what the townspeople will think anyway. But if you're really worried, the best thing you could do for now..." She paused and looked around the room at each person there before continuing. "...when the time comes, allow Ezekiel Crane to work...his...magic."

CHAPTER
TWO

Boone Creek
October 13
6:05 PM

Tim Crawford cursed as he pulled his truck over on the side of the road, and jerked the gears into park. He couldn't believe his luck. He was already running late for his daughter, Maggie's sixth birthday party.

Her birthday was actually last week. Her party was supposed to be early last Saturday morning. But they had to postpone it after he stumbled upon Leroy Kingston, and had to take him to the hospital in Morriston. The whole affair had taken the better part of his entire Saturday. His sweet little girl had been heartbroken about the party, but she seemed to have understood. Leroy's life was more important than her birthday party.

His wife, Liz, however, wasn't so mature about it. For a better part of a week, he'd been enduring her wrath over putting 'that no good heathern coonhound' ahead of their daughter's happiness. It wasn't that Liz was insensitive. It wasn't that she lacked compassion. But Leroy had caused problems with her in the past, so there would have definitely not been any love lost if he hadn't made it out of the Dark Hollows alive.

Her incessant nagging, however, had messed with Tim's nerves enough to send him on a 'little bit of a binge'. In fact, that's why he was in the pickle he was in at that very moment. He'd been sampling a bit of Walter Macy's special apple pie moonshine after work, and had lost track of time. He'd only managed to remember the party after Liz had called him, cussing him out and calling him every name in the book until he managed to stumble to his truck, and start heading home. Now, he had a flat tire. To make matters even worse, the dark clouds that had been threatening the town all day had finally decided to let loose, and a steady downpour threatened to swallow up anything without a flotation device.

Tarnation. Guess, I got no choice.

With unsteady legs, he stumbled out of the cab, pulled his cap down across his brow, and made straight for the pickup's bed where he kept a few old tires for just such an emergency.

She'll never let me live this down. I swear, she's going to tan my hide when I get home.

Grumbling, he lowered the tailgate, grabbed the best retreaded spare in the collection, and dragged it onto the pavement. The impact splashed a frigid spray of water on his trousers, eliciting a renewed string of curses as he rolled the tire around to the passenger side of the truck, and let it spiral to the ground.

A crack of thunder boomed overhead, causing Crawford to duck while trotting back to the truck's bed to retrieve the jack and tire iron. The weather was getting worse. He'd seen no lightning so far, but where there was thunder, lightning was sure to follow. He'd have to get the tire changed fast. He wasn't keen on the idea of becoming a human lightning rod with a storm like this brewing overhead.

He lowered himself to one knee and set to work loosening

the lug nuts of the flattened tire. The rain was now coming down in sheets, making his tentative grip on the iron even more slippery, which slowed him down even further.

Come on. Come on. He managed to get the first nut removed. Then the second. *Just two more to go.*

A low growl from the other side of the truck—near the wood line—ripped his attention away from his task. He glanced up, peering over the truck bed, but saw nothing. Shrugging the noise off as a stray coyote or possibly a bobcat, he returned to his work.

Another boom of thunder reverberated overhead. This time, he felt a crackle of electricity in the air, followed by a blinding streak of lightning just over the treetops. Another clap of thunder quickly followed.

Eye of the storm is gettin' closer.

With several quick pulls of the tire iron, the third lug nut swiveled loose, and dropped to the wet pavement. Carefully, he lined up the iron's socket to the final lug nut, when another growl—much louder and ominous than the first—echoed past the howling wind and rain. Worse, Crawford felt a wave of hot, fetid breath against the hairs on the back of his neck. He stiffened, unable to move. Unable to turn around.

"Come to me, my brothers," came a deep, guttural voice behind him before a monstrous pair of hands curled around his throat, and hefted him off the ground.

The Crane Homestead
October 14
9:46 AM

KILI GLANCED down at her cell phone's GPS display as she negotiated the narrow, winding country road toward Esther

21

Crane's home. The signal faded in and out as she drove up the treacherous mountain stretch, and a gleam of stress-induced sweat had begun to form on her brow. The last thing she wanted to do was get turned around in a place like this.

She shuddered as images of the movie *Deliverance* played through her mind's eye.

At least she'd had sense enough to go back to her room last night, and get some rest. It would have been a fool's errand to navigate these mountain roads in the dead of night, even with the assistance, or rather the debatable assistance, of her GPS. Now, she felt refreshed; ready to tackle her brother's investigation once again with greater vigor. And "Granny" Crane was as good a place to start as anywhere else.

Besides, if she'd attempted the drive last night, she wouldn't have been able to soak in the majestic beauty that surrounded her. The single lane road, though dangerously straddling the edge of the canyon to her left, was simply breathtaking. The finger-like branches of ancient oaks, spruce, and maple trees spiraled out overhead, creating a spider web of colors all around her. A blanket of kudzu vines draped over the steep embankment, down into the valley, forming a green sea of lush vegetation amid treetops of orange and brown. She'd already spotted three deer scurrying through the forest to her right, something she'd rarely seen at her home near Washington, D.C. And though she was, through and through, a city girl, she could definitely understand the appeal that such scenery had for so many people.

The irritated female voice of her GPS broke her from her reverie, making Kili jump and nearly causing her to steer her Camry into the pristine abyss below. "At eight hundred yards, turn right," the staccato voice said with a patronizing British accent. *And no little attitude*, Kili thought.

Gripping the steering wheel tighter, she forced her racing heart to slow as she approached the turn. She could see it up ahead. Just an insignificant dirt road in the middle of hillbilly country. Not exactly the kind of place one would expect to find a "doctor." But then again, if Squirrelly, as Kili had come to refer to her informant at the bar, had been right, Mrs. Crane was definitely not a doctor in the conventional sense.

A water witch, he'd called her. *A water witch*? Kili shook her head at the very notion. *What the heck is that*?

Another movie image flashed through her mind's eye. The green-tinted visage of the Wicked Witch from *The Wizard of Oz*; her wart-covered nose twitching as she laughed gleefully at a dour-faced Dorothy. "I'll get you, my pretty," Kili said aloud. "Yeah, right."

Ten minutes and one ridiculously long gravel driveway later, she pulled up next to a simple little one-story brick home. The place was cheerful with a meticulously manicured yard, a small duck pond off to the left of the house, and a white wooden fence that encircled the property. Several perennial flowers arose from earthen beds around the perimeter of the fence.

It was definitely not what Kili had expected from a hillbilly witch doctor from Kentucky. She'd actually pictured a decaying wooden shack, a large satellite dish, and a few rusted-out pickups propped up on cinder blocks. This place was more Martha Stewart than Ma Kettle.

Even more incongruous was the large, well-maintained, and very expensive Hummer that sat unoccupied in the drive. She let out a sharp whistle as she took in the black-on-black behemoth in the driveway. Like a contradiction in terms, an old 1970s era Ford station wagon was parked next to the luxury SUV.

As she came to a stop, she looked out her passenger window, and caught sight of an elderly woman, she assumed to be Mrs. Crane, seated casually on the front porch swing. A small boy, no more than seven years old, stood in front of her, holding his hand delicately, and wailing like a banshee. Kili climbed out of her car, opened the fence's gate, and strolled with caution toward the porch.

"Shhhhh," Mrs. Crane was saying to the boy as Kili approached. "It'll be all right. Now, you just hush for a bit."

The woman's voice was stern, but loving as she pulled the boy closer, taking a look at his hand. "I'll be with you directly, dear," she said to Kili without looking at her. "We can talk about your brother after I tend to little Jimmy here."

Kili's heart caught in her throat. How had she known she was here about Cian? Granted, it was a small town and she'd been making quite a stink about her missing brother for three days now, but she hadn't expected news of her investigation to have made its way all the way out here.

She looked at the old woman, watching her carefully as she examined the young boy's hand. "Old" wasn't exactly the appropriate word. Yes, she was definitely elderly...around seventy, maybe even in her eighties. It was just too hard to tell. She seemed almost ageless. And though she wasn't sure, Kili had the impression that the woman was spry no matter how old she was. Agile of both mind and body. Her eyes were sharp, as if she had the ability to see anything she desired if she put her mind to it. Her face, though wrinkled with age, had retained a great deal of the beauty of her youth. Her long white hair unfurled wildly around her shoulders, partially hiding the thick flannel shirt she wore. She also sported a pair of blue jeans—carpenter cut from what Kili could discern—and a pair of tan, steel-toed work boots. Definitely not what she'd anticipated.

"Now Jimmy," Mrs. Crane said. "How many times have I told you not to go hunting for honey at this time of year?"

"I know, but—"

"Don't sass me, boy. Those bees are meaner than spit come autumn and you know it."

Jimmy's eyes drifted to the wooden planks of the front porch. "Yes, ma'am."

The old woman smiled at him, reached into her front pants pocket, and pulled out a hand stitched rawhide pouch. She then reached into it, and withdrew a thick clump of chewing tobacco. Kili watched in fascination as Mrs. Crane stuffed the tobacco into her mouth and started chewing casually.

"And Ms. Candace? Where was she when you were pawing your way into that hive?"

The little boy pretended to smash something with his toe as he kept staring down, not daring to look her in the face.

"She was around. I guess."

"You guess? Boy, you and I both know where that mama of yours was. And if she don't straighten up..."

Jimmy's eyes went wide. "Oh no! No! Don't! She didn't mean nothin' by it. She just needs to unwind from time to time, is all." The boy was in a near panic now. "Don't..."

The old woman's smile broadened as she continued to chew on the wad in her mouth. "Don't *what*, Jimmy?"

"Don't..." He stuttered, as if trying to find the best way to answer her question. "Don't turn her into nothin' unnatural. Like a toad or somethin'."

Kili could hardly believe her ears. The boy's belief that the old woman was a witch was genuine. He really believed she had the power to transmogrify her enemies into animals. She barely contained the gasp that swelled up to her throat.

Mrs. Crane's eyes darted to Kili briefly, gave a knowing wink, then turned back to the boy.

"And why shouldn't I? She ain't doin' no good as a mama, now is she boy?" She stared at him, her smile still very warm and inviting despite her harsh words. After several seconds of silence, she sighed. "Okay, Jimmy. I'll not turn her. But you better let her know I have my eyes on her. Will ya do that for me, boy?"

He nodded. "Yes, ma'am. A'soon as she sobers up...I'll definitely tell her."

The woman returned the nod, her smile even brighter despite

the film of dark fluid staining her teeth from the tobacco. "Good," she said. "Now, let's take care of that bee sting, shall we?"

She reached into her mouth, pulled out the chew, and placed it firmly onto the boy's hand. Kili watched as she pressed the glob down hard. The tobacco's juices streamed in a criss-cross pattern across his wrists.

"The juice," Ms. Crane said, glancing up at Kili, "soothes the pain and extracts the poison from the bee sting. In another minute, it'll be as if he was never stung to begin with."

Kili was incredulous. The very notion seemed so primitive. Barbaric, even. The whole affair bordered on...well, child abuse if she was honest with herself. Not only had the crazy old hag terrified the boy into thinking she could turn his mother into a toad, but she was subjecting him to no telling what kind of germs and toxins by using tobacco juice on an open wound. She found herself appalled by this so-called 'doctor' and her practices.

"It's all right if you don't approve," the woman said with a chuckle. "I can only imagine what this looks like to an outsider."

Okay. The woman was just plain scary. It was as if she could read...

"And no, I can't read your mind, sweetie," she said, pulling the clump of tobacco from the boy's hand and tossing it over her shoulder without looking. Kili watched as it flew from the porch and landed in a flowerpot a few yards away. "You're just very predictable."

She released Jimmy's hand. The boy looked at it, rubbed it a second, and then beamed at the old woman. "It's better!" he nearly squealed. "Thank you, ma'am. Thank you!"

"You are most certainly welcome," she said, returning his smile before standing up from the swing and giving him a hug. When she pulled away, her hand whipped down and away from the boy's ear in a flash to reveal a dripping comb of honey.

Jimmy's eyes nearly bulged from their sockets as he eyed the tantalizing treat that had appeared out of nowhere. "Now. If'n ya absolutely must have some of this, you know where to come, right?"

The boy nodded excitedly.

"Good," she said, handing him the comb and ruffling his hair with her non-sticky hand. She turned to look at the front door. "Delores? You about finished in there?"

A moment later, a rotund dark-haired woman waddled out the front door, rummaging through her purse. "Just finished," she said, smiling. "The medicine is brewin', just like you asked. The roots are dryin' out in the stove, and I've finished transcribin' those notes you laid out for me." She padded the purse against her hip. "I'll set to studyin' them once I get home and make Max his supper."

Granny nodded, then gestured toward Jimmy. "Good. On your way, could you please make sure he gets home safe?"

Delores beamed at the boy. "Why Jimmy, I didn't even know you was here."

The boy returned the smile, the comb of honey stuffed into his mouth. Delores took his free hand, and led him to the station wagon parked next to the Hummer. The woman helped Jimmy into the passenger seat, strapped him in with a seatbelt, then got into the driver's seat. A moment later, the car was bounding down the driveway and out of sight.

"Now," Granny said, turning to Kili. She said it with the same warm, inviting smile she'd given Jimmy a few minutes earlier. "Let's see what we can do to find your missing brother."

CHAPTER THREE

Crane Homestead
October 14
10:15 AM

The interior of the little home was just as surprising as the outside. The place was cozy. A warm fire crackled in the fireplace, and the sweet aroma of apple and cinnamon permeated the house, tantalizing Kili's nose and taste buds simultaneously. The furnishings were a mishmash of modern and antique, all blended perfectly together in a way that told her great care had been taken in decorating. They walked into the den, lined on three sides with wall-to-wall bookshelves, filled to the top with old leather bound tomes, Bibles, knick-knacks, and oddly enough, an ungodly number of steamy-looking romance novels.

Kili stared at them with a smile. *An enigma wrapped in a riddle,* she mused, turning her attention back to her hostess.

"Please," Mrs. Crane said, gesturing to a very comfortable looking leather couch. "Have a seat."

Kili complied and watched as the older woman left the room

without a word. A few minutes later, she returned, carrying a silver tray with a large pitcher filled with tea and two glasses.

"I hope you like sweet tea," she said. "Unsweet is just about blasphemous around these parts." She poured the tea and handed a glass to Kili. "Land's sakes, they'd probably string a person up, and tar and feather 'em if they even tried to serve it unsweet."

She sat down in an overstuffed reading chair, took a sip of the drink, and nodded to Kili. "Now tell me...what can I do for you?" she asked, setting the glass down on an end table beside her.

Kili swallowed a mouthful of the blissfully sweet concoction herself. After a few moments, savoring the taste, she looked up at the old woman. "Well, as you already know, my brother went missing about a week ago..."

Mrs. Crane held up a hand. "Just a second dear. Don't assume I know anything," she said. "Start from the beginning."

Kili cocked her head. "But you seemed to already know what I was here for. You knew my brother was missing..."

The old woman laughed at this. "Ah, I reckon you should understand a few things. I don't get out of the house much these days. Prefer to mill around the property tending to chores. Don't get much news either, 'cept when someone comes around for some doctorin'. But even then, people know I don't cotton much to gossip and idle chitchat. So I've not heard anything about your brother."

"But how...?"

"The *Yunwi Tsunsdi*," she answered, as if that was supposed to explain everything. "I've been hearing their mumblin's of late. A bunch of regular chatterboxes, they are."

"The Yunwi S...Suns...?"

"It's pronounced *yoon-wi ta-soons-dee*. It's a Cherokee word. Basically, it means 'the Little People'," she said in a matter-of-fact tone, as if Kili should have no doubt in her mind that they were real.

Kili's mouth went dry. What was she doing here? The woman was crazy. It was as plain to see as the nose on her face. Mrs. Crane, the town's supposed witch, was a Class-A nut job and would not be helpful in locating her brother at all.

The old woman cast her a knowing look. "Don't worry, dear. I don't expect you to believe me." She chuckled at this, reaching into her pocket and pulling out an elaborately carved wooden pipe. "And it certainly ain't goin' to help us find your brother. So, please. Tell me about it...from the beginning."

She clenched the pipe tight in her teeth, and stuffed a pinch of tobacco in the bulb. "Now, go on," she said, striking a match, and lighting the pipe. "Tell me your story." She pulled in several sharp puffs from the pipe stem. "Leave nothin' out."

Kili looked at her for a few seconds before shrugging. *What could it hurt to tell her?*

"Well, there's not really that much to tell," she said. "Like I already said...about a week ago, my brother Cian and his research assistant disappeared without a trace while up in some place called the Dark Hollows. No one, including the sheriff, seems too worried about it. From what I understand, there was only a cursory search of the—"

"Let me cut you off right there, dear," Granny said, with a concerned look in her eyes. "What exactly was your brother doing up in the Hollars?"

"He was investigating some place called the Devil's Teeth, but—"

"The Teeth?" Esther Crane asked, cutting Kili off once more. "Why on earth would your brother go to that infernal place? You're skipping too much, sweetie. The more detailed you are, the more empowered I'll be to help ya."

Kili stared at the woman a few moments, trying to figure out the best way to proceed. She wasn't sure how knowing the reason her brother was up at the Devil's Teeth would help, but she figured she really had no choice but to satisfy her hostess' curiosity.

"Cian is an anthropologist investigating the link between the Appalachian people and the Celts through their shared myths. He's traveled all over the eastern mountains, ferreting out stories and clues; working toward pinpointing the origins of these old legends. Trying to discover how much of them have retained their original Celtic roots and how many had evolved over the years."

Mrs. Crane nodded in understanding as she blew out a single ring of smoke. She then leaned back in her chair, steepled her fingers together at her chin, and closed her eyes while she listened to Kili highlight much of what she knew of the research.

"Cian came to Boone Creek about three months ago," she continued. "He was almost beside himself with excitement when he heard about the Dark Hollows."

The old woman's eyes snapped open as she shifted in her seat nervously. "Go on," she said, setting the pipe down in an ashtray and concentrating her full attention on the crime analyst. "What was so special to him about them?"

"He'd heard about some kind of ruin there. A structure of some kind," Kili said. She felt her pulse quickening at the old woman's intensified interest. *Could she know something after all?* "He didn't go into much detail. Just said that the stories described something amazingly similar to Stonehenge. He came here for the sole purpose of investigating the site. He'd been researching the place ever since he got here...with the help of his assistant and a town local named Leroy Kingston."

The woman gasped at the name. "Leroy?" she asked. "Your brother took up with that coon-scrabbler?"

Kili had no idea what a coon-scrabbler was, but by the woman's tone, it wasn't very good. "Yes. Why?"

She opened her mouth to answer, but was interrupted by the

31

creak of the front door opening beyond the den. Mrs. Crane's serious countenance transformed into one of beaming joy. Her eyes seemed to sparkle with mischievous delight.

"Ah, finally," she said, winking at her. "My grandson is home. If you want to find your brother, you'll be wantin' to talk to him. I reckon there ain't no one better suited to help you than him." She stood from her chair and motioned for Kili to stay put. "Now wait here, sweetie. Just sit tight." She moved toward the den's doorway and turned back to face Kili. A look of deep concern creased her brow. "Don't worry, dear. We'll find him."

She then turned back around and walked through the door, leaving Kili alone. She barely had time to glance around the room before a tall, lean man with a thick mane of sandy-blond hair and a neatly trimmed goatee, strode into the room.

"Ms. Brennan, I presume," he said, moving toward her with his hand extended. Though his accent was thick with the same syrupy-slow drawl as everyone else in the region, his speech was articulate; each syllable enunciated impeccably. "I hope I haven't kept you waiting too long."

She rose from her seat and shook his hand. She could hardly take her eyes off him. He was, for lack of a better word, gorgeous. He was dressed in a black t-shirt under a denim button-down shirt that he wore like a jacket. The rest of his ensemble was comprised of a pair of Levi's and brown leather cowboy boots. He had bronze-colored skin that could only come from hours of working outdoors, a pronounced chin, and ice-blue eyes that resonated with the same slight twinkle she'd seen in Mrs. Crane. The palms of his hands were rough with calluses, yet he shook hers with a genteel delicacy that she assumed was a by-product of the southern hospitality she'd heard about her entire life.

"My name," he continued, gesturing for her to resume her seat, "is Ezekiel Crane. And I am very much at your disposal in regards to this unfortunate business with your brother."

She was about to offer her thanks when a sudden thought slapped at her frazzled brain.

"You knew my name," she said numbly.

"Pardon?"

"My name," she continued. The rhythmic pounding of her heart resumed its staccato thump as a sense of wariness slithered its way into her mind. "I never told your grandmother my name. She claims to have had no knowledge of me prior to today's visit. So, how did you know it?"

He eyed her for several seconds, amusement evident on his face.

"You've no doubt been warned about me?" was his only response.

She nodded. Her mouth was desperately dry; her palms, in contrast, were wet with perspiration. Though she sensed no danger from the man, she couldn't help but think he was toying with her.

"Seventh son of a seventh son," she said. "Dark magical powers. I've been told I can trust your 'Granny', but you..." She smiled at him and shrugged. "You're apparently of the devil. Or, the Winter Hag or something like that."

"*Willow* Hag," he corrected, without umbrage. "And Eddie really needs to find something else to harp on. He's like a broken record."

"Who?"

"Eddie Johnson," he said quietly. "The man from the pub that told you to seek my grandmother's help. I believe..." He paused, casting a curious look in her direction. "I believe you refer to him as 'Squirrelly'." He hesitated a second time. "Or perhaps Ferret-face?"

Her mouth dropped. This was just plain freaky. She'd told no one at all about her conversation with the man Crane was calling Eddie Johnson. She'd definitely not told anyone about the poor nickname she'd given him.

"Right on the first guess," she said slowly. She suddenly noticed that her left hand was clutching the armrest of the couch in a dead man's grip. Self-conscious, she released the armrest and eyed him up and down. "How did you know?"

The tall man let out a deep, resonant laugh as he casually eased himself from his chair, and moved toward her. He stood a full head taller than her, and glanced down into her eyes with an understanding smile.

"Don't get too excited, Ms. Brennan," he said, beaming. "There's no magic involved here, I promise you that."

"Then how?"

"I'm not really sure why this is important to the matter—"

"Humor me," she said grimly. "The man I talked to yesterday said he was told to point me in your grandmother's direction. And I want to know if you're the one who put him up to it."

Crane paused momentarily. "Really? Someone *told* Eddie to send you to Granny?"

"That's what he said."

"Fascinating," the mountain man said, absently fiddling with his goatee. "That, Ms. Brennan, is something worth looking into after we've found your brother. But in the meantime…to answer your questions, it's really quite simple. First, I saw you yesterday…talking to Eddie. Granny rarely ventures into town, but I own a business there. A bookstore."

Why am I not surprised he's the owner of the bookstore? she thought.

"I was closing up shop when I spied you and Eddie in the parking lot of Bailey's talking. It was no real effort to figure out what you were discussing…after all, you've been making a lot of noise about town, Ms. Brennan. That's how I knew your name, by the way…and before you ask, no, Granny truly had never heard about your brother's disappearance. Well, at least not from me or the locals."

"But how did you know that I called him Squirrelly? Everything else makes sense, but that's just...just spooky."

"Well, it's really not as spooky as you think," he said. "Let's see...a short, scrawny man...habitually nervous, sporting a thick bushy mustache, tiny black eyes, and a severe overbite. Why *wouldn't* you call him Squirrelly? Everyone else in town does."

"What?"

"That's right, Ms. Brennan. Eddie's nickname in these parts is generally one of several rodent-like references: Squirrel. Ferret. Weasel. They're all used, but some of the more mean-spirited bunch in this town, in some form or another, to browbeat him."

His smile softened, but was still warm, and calming as he motioned for her to follow him from the den. "Now," he continued. "We really should be on our way."

"What?" Kili asked. "Where?"

"You came here to find your brother, didn't you?"

She could only nod in response, then got up, and followed him out the door.

"Well," Crane said, striding into the driveway. "We can't do that sitting in Granny's den, now can we?"

"But...I..." Kili was unable to find the words. On the one hand, she knew Crane was her best shot at finding Cian. On the other hand, Eddie Johnson's warning had seemed so sincere. So adamant. There'd been no doubt in his mind that Crane was not to be trusted.

"Eddie's been spouting that same line of superstitious nonsense since we were children," Ezekiel Crane said, as if, like Granny, he could read her mind. "Don't pay his warnings any heed."

"Superstitious? Is that not the pot calling the kettle black? Threatening to turn people into frogs and talking to the 'Little People' isn't exactly the hallmark of a scientifically rational mind, now is it?"

Crane stopped at the passenger side door of a late model

Chevy pickup truck, opened the door, and turned toward her as she approached. His face grew stern. Impatient.

"Look, we really have precious little time for such banter, Ms. Brennan," he said. "I'm much more familiar with your brother's disappearance than my grandmother. He's not the only one who has recently gone missing. Besides your brother's research assistant, there are at least six locals who seem to have disappeared as well. Tim Crawford, the man who found Leroy Kingston, just went missing last night; his truck found abandoned on the side of the road with a pool of blood drying on the blacktop. Two of the medics who transported him to the hospital disappeared last week. The other three who disappeared also had assisted Kingston in some way after his ordeal. Leroy himself has been unable to offer authorities any insight as to what happened. He merely spouts, as you call it, local superstitions of a ghostly encounter with a being the residents in these parts call 'One-Eyed Jack.'

"Now, whether his story is true or not, Ms. Brennan, something foul is happening up in the Dark Hollows and we really have no more time to waste. If your brother and the others are still alive, they are in grave danger. If you want to find him, you'll come with me."

Put that way, Kili knew she really had little choice.

"All right," she said, with a nod. "Let's go find Cian."

CHAPTER
FOUR

G ranny stood on the porch, watching her grandson and the
pretty redhead drive down the driveway. There was
something peculiar about this city girl. Something special,
though she couldn't quite put her finger on it.

She took a sip of her tea, then lowered the glass onto the table
next to the swing, and leaned against the railing. Strange
happenings were transpiring in Boone Creek. Strange happenings indeed, and it was setting her nerves on edge. Of course, it
didn't help that the Yunwi Tsunsdi were jabbering about like
there was no tomorrow either. Though very mischievous and
jovial, they normally weren't so vocal. But in the last week or so,
she'd been unable to tune out their voices at all, though they
refused to fill her in on what had them so riled up. From what
she could tell, they were just talking nonsense, and that
concerned Granny more than anything else.

She looked out over her property and sighed, taking in the
beautiful morning, and said a silent prayer for protection for her
grandson and Ms. Brennan. She was sure they were going to
need as much prayer as she could muster before all this was
over.

But her prayers were interrupted by the sudden sound of glass, bones, and metal tinkling on the southernmost edge of her property. She turned toward the sound, and scowled.

The chimes.

It wasn't the sublime, relaxing symphony of a gentle breeze, but rather a harsh, clashing of mismatched sounds. Dark sounds. Dangerous sounds. She'd placed the chimes—and others like it —throughout the property as warnings against dark spirits, malevolent hexes, and evil things best left unmentioned. The rising crescendo of the nerve-grinding noise coming from the south, told her something very bad was approaching her homestead and she didn't like it one bit.

Slipping back inside, she grabbed her medicine bag and a broom, then slipped a fully loaded Colt 1911 .45 pistol into a holster on her bed. She then moved out the back of the house, and strode toward the southern treeline. She walked directly up to the set of chimes hanging from a low branch on a maple tree, reached out a hand, and silenced the noise with a touch.

The woods beyond her property were quiet. No birds singing. No pattering of tiny feet as squirrels leapt through the tree limbs. No wind to trigger the chimes. Even more unsettling, the constant chatter of the Little People had seemed to die down to the unintelligible hiss of whispers.

"I know you're there," Granny said. "No use hidin' in the shadows."

There was a rustle of long dead leaves, then the area of the woods directly in front of Esther Crane grew dark, as if all light was being sucked into emptiness, never to be seen again. She could still make out the forms of the trees. But where there had once been red and orange leaves shining in the morning sunlight, now there was nothing but long straggling branches, bent at the tips in a rictus of death.

A human-like form materialized amid the darkness, though

Granny couldn't make out any details. The thing growing in the shadows never stayed in any one form for too long anyway.

"Well, deary," the form said in a sweet, grandmotherly voice. Granny could detect the slightest trace of honeysuckle nectar in the air around her—an illusion of the worst sort. "Been too long since we last had a chat. Too long indeed."

Granny turned to look back at her house, unwilling to show any respect for the creature that haunted her woods at that moment.

"There's a reason for that." Granny swept the broom up onto her shoulder, and leaned against the maple tree. "You're not welcome here. You're never welcome here, Hag."

The Willow Hag cackled. "And yet, I'm here nonetheless. Yes, here nonetheless." There was a sound like she had taken a deep breath, but Granny knew better. The thing in the shadows needed no air to breathe. "Been spending some time admiring your grandson lately. Since his return home. Grew into quite the handsome man, he did."

"You leave Ezekiel alone." Granny wheeled around and glared into the darkness. She raised the broom in a defensive stance, and spat on the ground. "You have no more claim to him. Not since siccin' Eli Smith and that ill lot on him. Not since his brother paid the price for it."

The Willow Hag clucked. "Pish Posh. Water under the bridge, deary. Water under the bridge." She paused. "But he has grown quite powerful, has he not? Strong in body, mind, and spirit, I'd say."

Esther Crane gritted her teeth. It was bold of the Hag to wander this far out of Briarsnare Marsh. Especially in the full light of day. She was up to something, and Granny didn't like it one bit.

"I'll ask you again, witch. What's your business here."

"Simple. I've come to tell you that I'm followin' through with my promise to your grandson. He might be a no-count liar...a reneger of vows...but that don't mean I don't keep my word."

Granny tried to swallow the lump building in her throat. "What is that supposed to mean?"

But the Willow Hag pretended not to hear the question. Instead, the shade of her head tilted up toward the sky, and she gave it a bit of a shake. "My, oh my. That lil' redhead. Mm-mmm. She's somethin' else, ain't she? Sweet Ezekiel sure has a soft spot for the pretty ones, don't he?" She cackled again. "And this one...she's just not another pretty face either. I know you've felt it. There's something different about..."

"She's under our protection," Granny nearly growled the words.

"That may be the case. For now. But I do wonder what it'd be like to take Ms. Kili Brennan under my wing for a bit. See what might happen, eh?"

"I'm telling you..." She raised the broom above her head, but the darkness had already faded from the trees. The sunlight once more poured into the woods, bringing life to the leaves and branches once more. "I'm warning you," Granny said aloud, certain the Willow Hag could still hear her. "Leave that girl, and my grandson, alone. Or you'll have me to deal with."

THEY RODE in silence for the first five miles, as Crane drove farther up the winding mountain road with practiced precision. He didn't seem to be the slightest bit nervous about driving the tight squeeze he found himself having to navigate. He simply kept his steely eyes fixed straight ahead; his thoughts hidden from Kili.

"Where are we going?" she finally asked, to break the unnerving silence more than anything else. "I'd assumed that we'd be going to the hospital to talk to Kingston. After all, he was the last to see my brother."

Without answering, he popped open the center console, extracted a can of Copenhagen, and slipped a small pinch into the pocket between his lower lips and gums...all with his right hand while his left was still firmly planted on the steering wheel. He then glanced over at her briefly from the corners of his eyes.

He caught Kili staring at him.

"Pardon me," he said, stuffing the can into his right hip pocket. "A rather nasty habit, I must admit...but one that I've struggled with overcoming my entire life. I've traveled the world several times over in my life, Ms. Brennan. But apparently, it's true what they say. You can take the boy out of the mountains, but can't take the mountains out of the boy. No matter how hard he may try."

"I, uh, am sorry I was staring. You just didn't seem to be the type to..."

"To have a weakness for tobacco?" He gave a soft, melancholy chuckle over this. "An unfortunate side effect of nurture versus nature, I'm afraid. My grandmother is a wonderful woman. She raised me well and loved me and my two remaining siblings like her own. But she's from a different era. One that knows nothing about the negative effects tobacco can have on human physiology." He paused for several seconds, lost in thought.

"You have siblings?" she asked, trying to change the subject, but feeling instantly embarrassed at the inane question. *Seventh son of a Seventh son, Kili, you dolt. Of course, he has siblings.*

He gave her a weak smile, but his eyes betrayed something dark running through his mind as he pondered how to answer her question.

"I do," he finally said. "But only two now. My six older brothers and my parents died in car accident when I was still a boy." The pickup slowed and then made a sharp right turn onto a gravel road. He then continued. "One younger brother and a younger sister are still alive...though I haven't seen either of them in years."

"I'm sorry," she said, not really knowing what to say.

"It's quite all right, Ms. Brennan. Now, to answer your question about where we're heading..." He brought the truck to a complete stop, threw it in four-wheel drive, and turned left onto a suspiciously ominous hunting trail. "We're heading to the Dark Hollows," he said, easing the wheels of the truck over a rotten old log that blocked their trail. "Better to check things out here while we still have daylight. We can talk to Leroy later tonight if necessary. Now, please. Tell me more about your brother and his research...as well as what you know about the day he disappeared."

She went on to explain Cian's research. His fascination with the common links between the Appalachians and those of her own ancestors, the Celts...about his obsession with a Stonehenge-like structure he'd been told about nestled somewhere in the Dark Hollows. How he and his research assistant, Miles Marathe, had set out to find this local Stonehenge, and mine for its secrets.

"The last time I talked to him was the day before his disappearance," she said, her eyes staring vacantly out the driver's side window. "He'd told me they'd found something. Something amazing."

"Did he tell you what it was?"

She shook her head. "No. He said he didn't want to jump to conclusions. He had to analyze the site more thoroughly before he told anyone about it."

Crane was silent, focusing on the rough terrain of the hunting trail they were traversing. After a minute, he spoke. "And this research assistant. I've not heard anything about him. The only one to come out of the Hollows was Leroy."

"I'm assuming he's with my brother. He's missing too."

They said nothing else for another twenty minutes when Crane pulled the truck to a stop and climbed out.

"Here we are," he said, after discreetly expelling the tobacco from his mouth.

"Where exactly are we?"

"We're at the closest point a person can drive to the Hollows," he said, reaching into the bed of the truck and withdrawing a backpack. He opened it, retrieved a thin strip of roughly hewn wood, three small packets of sugar, and a hunting knife. He then strapped the knife to his belt, stuffed the packs of sugar in his shirt pocket, and handed her the backpack. "It's not that heavy," he said. "If you would be so kind as to carry it for me, I'd much appreciate it. I really need as few distractions as possible for what I'm about to do."

She took the pack and slung one strap over her shoulder. She watched as he pointed the stick directly into the air and muttered a few unintelligible words.

"What are you doing?" she asked.

"Shhh." His eyes bore straight up into the sky, focused intently on the tip of the stick. Then, slowly, his arm lowered; the point gradually turning slightly to his right. East, if her bearings were correct. She followed his gaze, attempting to discern what he was looking for, but soon gave up when all she could see beyond the tree canopy was a single raven sitting on a high branch, looking down at them.

Soon, however, Crane motioned for her to follow him, and they stepped into the thick vegetation of the Appalachian woodlands.

CHAPTER
FIVE

K ili glanced down at her watch. It was nearly twelve-thirty in the afternoon. They'd been wandering through the woods for the last hour and a half, and she was exhausted. She was also confused. Ezekiel Crane had not offered any explanation for what he was doing…walking aways, stopping, pointing that silly stick into the air, then bringing it down, and moving once more in a new direction. And still, the only thing she could see was the raven, as if was following them along their hike. The entire ritual made no sense and in her mind, they were wasting too much time.

"I think we need a break," Crane said, the sudden sound of his voice startling her. "You look tired."

"A little," she admitted. She found an overturned tree, removed the pack from her shoulder, and sat down. Pulling off her boots, she instantly felt soothing relief to her battered, trail-weary feet. She leaned back, absorbing the cheerful cries of the various unidentifiable birds flitting through the trees around her. It was just so peaceful here. Quiet. Relaxing. Occasionally, she caught the sound of something, presumably acorns or other debris, falling from the autumn-painted treetops above onto the forest floor. A group of large, gray squirrels chattered merrily, their oversized bushy tails twitching as they leapt from the thick web of branches in play. She took in a deep breath, absorbing all the sights and smells.

It was so hard to imagine that her brother had disappeared somewhere nearby. The place just seemed so magical...like something from a storybook. She couldn't envision anything sinister ever happening here.

"If you'll open the pack, you'll find some bottles of water," Crane said, crouching down in the center of the clearing, and pouring out the contents of one of his sugar packets.

She rummaged through the backpack and produced two bottles, throwing one to Crane. She opened hers, and downed the contents of her own bottle in three gulps. She then wiped the excess water from her chin, and nodded at the small pile of sugar on the forest floor.

"What's that?" she asked.

"This?" He pointed at the mound, pulled out his can of dip, and sprinkled a few drops of tobacco in a circle around the sugar. "It's an offering. To the Yunwi Tsunsdi."

"The Little People?"

"I believe your kin would have referred to them as the Fae. Faeries. Elves. Tricksters all of them. We're about to enter the Dark Hollows. Territory said to be haunted by their kind. The sugar and tobacco assures them we are not there to cause trouble."

"You can't be serious." As the words slipped from her lips, she was conspicuously aware that her mouth hung open in disbelief. She couldn't fathom someone in the twenty-first century actually believing in such hoodoo. "Mr. Crane, you appear to be an educated man. Intelligent. Articulate...especially for around here." He let out a laugh at the last statement. "How on earth could you possibly believe in such things?"

He spread another circle of tobacco around the sugar mound,

and stood to his full, six-foot two-inch height. He then dusted his hands off on his jeans and took a swig from the water bottle.

"Ms. Brennan," he said, obviously amused with her skepticism. "As the Bard so eloquently put it, '*There are more things in heaven and earth, Horatio, than are dreamt of in your philosophy.*'

"You must understand...I'm not like my grandmother. I've never personally seen the Yunwi Tsunsdi. Never talked to them, per se. And like you, my educated, rational mind would rather they not exist—life is far simpler if the only things that exist are those we can see with our own eyes, right? But my kin have prowled these hills for six generations. And the Cherokee who befriended them were here countless generations before *them*. They knew this land and the things that dwelt in it better than anyone else on earth. So if they passed down stories of the Little People through the years, I'd be a fool to ignore their warnings, now wouldn't I? Besides...why should we unnecessarily stir up a hornets' nest if we can avoid it?" He pointed back down to the sugar mound. "That's just a precaution. In case Shakespeare was right."

"And that stick you've been waving around all afternoon? I suppose you're going to tell me that's *not* a dowsing rod?"

He cocked his head to one side as he held up the piece of wood. "A dowsing rod?"

"Yes. A *dowsing* rod." She emphasized the word, letting her growing irritation and frustration flow from her lips. This whole thing was ridiculous. The man was playing games with her. "I can't believe you're doing this. This is nothing but one big joke to you, isn't it?"

The ever-present mirth on his lips drained away. His face grew stern—almost harsh. "Ms. Brennan, I can assure you...I take what happened to your brother, as well as the others that disappeared, with the utmost seriousness. There is somethin' foul a'brewin' in these parts." The man's normally impeccable elocution faltered as he grew increasingly agitated with her accusations. "I aim to get to the bottom of it...whether you're with me or not.

"Now, I know it may seem strange to you. All of this. What I do. But it gets results. I promise you that." He pointed the stick straight into the sky once more, brought it down to eye level, and then looked over at her. "Now. We approach the Dark Hollows. You may come with me if you like. Stay here. Or leave. But whatever decision you make, you will not question my integrity in this matter. If my instincts are correct, there is much more at stake here than your missing brother."

Having said his piece, Crane carefully stepped over the sugar mound, and stalked off into the thick wall of trees that led into the primeval world of the Hollows. Kili, after taking a deep breath, picked up the backpack, and followed him while what sounded like children laughing far away in the distance.

FIVE MINUTES after Ezekiel Crane and Kili Brennan moved deeper into the woods, a lone figure moved into the clearing in which they had so recently rested. The entire rest area was closely scrutinized with special attention given to the small pile of sugar with the two concentric rings of tobacco.

Satisfied with the examination, the figure stood, and eradicated the confectionary offering with a grime-crusted bare foot. *Good*, their stalker thought, smiling mirthlessly. *She will be pleased*.

With nothing else to see, the figure moved silently into the entangled confines of the woods, ecstatic at the prospects that lay ahead.

CHAPTER
SIX

A nother thirty minutes crept by until Ezekiel Crane stopped, raising his hand to bring Kili to a halt as well. Besides dipping into a downward slope as they approached the hollows, the woods around them had gradually become denser, blocking out nearly all the light of the sun. Only pale slivers of light pierced the veil above, offering mere snippets of illumination for them to walk. She was beginning to understand why the area was known as the Dark Hollows. She'd never seen a murkier, more ominous place in her life.

The trees just seemed dead all around her; their decaying trunks hollow and diseased. Only the tallest of them, able to reach the nourishment of sunlight, created a thick canopy of red and orange leaves above. Gnarled branches swayed overhead in a steady breeze, like the razor sharp claws of some fierce multi-armed beast looming over her, and ready to pounce. The forest floor was littered with refuse—pine needles, dead leaves, and a few skeletal remains of several small animals.

If the mountains until this point were a scene taken from a children's storybook, the Dark Hollows were ripped right out of someone's nightmare.

"Hold on a second," he said, crouching down to examine something on the ground. He once again mumbled inaudibly, then reached into the dirt and picked the object of his interest up with his thumb and forefinger. He held the thing up to Kili. "A worker ant. Best hunters in the world."

She looked at him dumbfounded. "What does that have to do with finding Cian?" she asked, irritation lacing her words. "We're wasting time!"

He glanced over his shoulder at her. "Patience, Ms. Kili," he said. "This little critter is going to help us find your brother."

Once again, she couldn't believe what she was hearing. The whole ordeal was bordering on the ludicrous. Sticks and bugs did not lead people to missing things. There was no magic. People couldn't talk to animals or the trees. And there was no such thing as faeries and elves. She realized, to her complete dismay, that she'd made a horrible mistake. Squirrelly had been right. He'd warned her, but she'd been blinded by her obsession to find her brother. She'd been willing to do anything...and that, she was afraid, was going to be her undoing.

Kili, what have you done?

The smile drained once more from the man's face as if he could sense the turmoil building up inside her.

"Don't worry," he said. "All will be explained in time. Just trust me a little longer, okay?"

In truth, what choice did she really have? She was stranded with nowhere to go. She would have to put her faith in this mad mountain man until she could safely return to civilization.

When she nodded her agreement, Crane's smile returned. He then turned his attention back to the tiny ant still clutched in his hands, its six powerful legs scrambling frantically as it tried to escape his grip. He brought the insect up to his mouth and whispered something to it, then lowered it to the ground, and released it. Kili watched as the ant reunited with a stream of others marching along the forest floor to the south.

"You mind at least telling me what that was about?" Kili asked, her hand placed firmly on her hips.

"All in good time, Ms. Brennan. All in good time." He took another drink from his water bottle, and recapped it. "By the way, we're very close now. But, I must warn you. The signs are not good. I'm afraid that when we finally arrive at our destination, we will find Death there...waiting."

"Signs?" she asked, a lump growing in her throat at his words. "What signs?"

"I honestly don't want to say too much until we find it." He looked at her, his face suddenly grim. "But I must ask...do you, Ms. Brennan, have a gun?"

The lump seemed to double in size at his question. Her heart thumped against her chest in an increasing crescendo. One hand absently moved toward the small of her back where the .380 caliber Walther PPK her father had given her for her twenty-first birthday rested in its holster. "Why? Why do you ask?"

His eyes followed her movement, and he smiled.

"Good," he said, tucking the stick into his back pocket, and turning toward the south. "Keep it handy. We're being stalked."

And without explanation, the tall man stepped forward, and beckoned her to follow. As she complied, she pulled her weapon from its holster, chambered a round, and clutched it tight in her right hand.

SHE SMELLED it long before they found it. The double-team sensation of vertigo and nausea assaulted her as the pungent perfume of death wafted through the surrounding woods. A malodorous blend of methane, ammonia, and something she couldn't quite identify drifted up on the currents of the breeze. The unmistakable stench of decay.

"Dear Lord," she gasped, bringing her free hand up to her

mouth. Her racing pulse kicked into overdrive as the possibilities of what still laid hidden among the thick underbrush around them. Were they too late? Was her brother dead? Had all this been in vain?

"Easy, my dear," Crane said softly in her ear as he placed a steady, but gentle hand on her shoulder. She hadn't even realized he'd crept up that close to her. His wraith-like movements were unsettling to say the least, yet she found herself taking great comfort in his soothing words. "All is most certainly not lost."

She looked at him. Her eyes wide. "How do you know? That smell...someone is dead out here."

He nodded, sympathy etched across his brow.

"Yes, Ms. Brennan. You are correct. Even more so, the smell is distinctly human. Animal decomposition produces an entirely different kind of odor. It has to do with the creature's diet and the different forms of bacteria lining the stomach walls more than anything else. But though we are about to discover the remains of a human being, it doesn't mean that it is your brother. Remember, there are more people than just Cian missing from Jasper County."

"Yeah, unless we find them all." She tried to hold back a sob at the thought. A stream of tears had already begun to flow unbidden down her cheeks.

"We won't," he said, stepping away from her, and carefully treading across the debris-covered ground. He moved a few feet away, bent down, and scrutinized something unseen. He turned left, brushed away a cluster of branches that had fallen, and suddenly let out a low whistle.

"What?" Kili asked, wiping the straggling tears from her eyes. "What did you find?"

He glanced at her, his eyes dark. "Prepare yourself," he said. "Ordinarily, I'd rather you not see this. But it's imperative that you look...to verify my theory. I believe, Ms. Brennan, that we have found your brother's research assistant."

A paradoxical relief washed over her at his words. On the one hand, she prayed it wasn't Miles. On the other, it would be far worse for her if it wasn't. She let out a breath, steeling herself for what she was about to witness, and holstered her gun once more in the small of her back. No use accidentally firing the weapon in a fit of despair if Crane was wrong.

She moved forward, coming up behind the tall, lanky mountain man, and peered around his shoulder. The sight nearly floored her. Bile rose to her throat as she turned away from the macabre tableau, and forced herself to take in slow, deep breaths with her mouth.

"It's best to breathe through your nose, Ms. Brennan. Breathing through your mouth only makes it worse."

Though the odor was just as sickening as the image now imprinted on her mind's eye, she complied with his suggestion, and found the steady rhythm of breathing helped to ease her nausea under control.

"Ms. Brennan?" Crane asked, placing his hand once more on her shoulder. She knew the unspoken question he was asking, and knew he needed an answer.

"It's Miles," she said between gasps of air.

"Are you sure?"

She nodded. "Cian is rather stocky. Short. No more than five-foot six. Miles Marathe was closer to your height. Well over six feet tall, and lean." She tried to swallow, but the ever-increasing lump in her throat prevented that normally autonomic function of her physiology. "Unless this matches the description of one of the missing locals, that's definitely Miles."

Crane turned back to the bloated corpse sprawled out in a bed of fallen boughs. His face was unrecognizable, most of the flesh having been stripped away by insects, carrion, and other animals. A swarm of flies, ants, and beetles buzzed furiously over the body, feasting on the rancid flesh. Crane crouched down, dug into his pockets for a set of latex gloves, and slipped them on.

"You always carry gloves with you when you go into the woods?" she asked, finally pulling herself together enough to watch him.

Ignoring her question, he reached out and shifted the congealed clothing hanging from the dead man in tatters.

"What are you doing?" she said, grabbing his arm and yanking him away from the body. The ever-present raven cawed, seemingly out of anger for her rebuke. "You can't touch that. We have to wait for a crime scene unit...the Medical Examiner. We can't contaminate the scene any more than we already have."

His smile had returned once more, though darkened slightly by the gruesome scene they now found themselves in.

"Ms. Brennan," he began.

"And stop with the Ms. Brennan crap," she said. "Kili. Call me Kili, please."

He nodded at this. "We'll compromise. I'll call you Ms. Kili. Okay?"

She reluctantly shrugged an affirmative, and he continued. "Ms. Kili, listen. This is Boone Creek. There are no crime scene units around here. The nearest State Police Station is nearly three hours away. Every second we wait is critical to your brother's survival."

"But surely you guys at least have a coroner or something. Can't we at least wait for him?"

"All right," he said, standing up, and holding out his hand. "My backpack please."

She handed it to him, and watched as he rummaged through it before pulling out a rather expensive looking camera.

"You are, of course, correct. We should at least document the scene before I conduct my examination." He snapped a few shots with the digital camera, backed away, and took more pictures at a wider angle. "But haste," he continued as he took more photos, "*is* essential for a variety of reasons."

"Are you referring to whoever it is that's been following us?"

He nodded. "Not to mention the downpour we're about to get. Except for last night, it hasn't rained here since your brother's disappearance. After last night, we're going to be lucky to find any trace evidence on the body of any use. Another storm now would make it certain."

She looked up into the thick canopy above, but even though she couldn't see much, there was enough sunlight peeking through the branches to make his last comment preposterous.

"Rain? I, uh, don't think we have to worry too much about that. It seems to be a pretty clear day. Besides, I took a look at the weather report this morning. They said we'd have clear skies for the rest of the week."

He snapped another picture and laughed. "Sure. And meteorologists are known for their *accurate* weather forecasts."

"Well, big shot...tell me. Why do you think it's about to rain?"

He stopped, put the camera back in the bag, and pulled out a notepad. He then began sketching the scene out as best he could.

"Because my nose is itching." He made the comment without an ounce of humor.

"What? Your nose is itching?"

He glanced over at her with a wink. "Isn't yours?"

Now that he mentioned it, she realized it was. But she figured it was simply a psychosomatic response to his suggestion. Besides, even if her nose was itching, it certainly didn't mean that rain was coming. Still, she decided to ignore the comment.

"So what about this mysterious person who's been following us? What itched to tell you that?"

He let out an abrupt chuckle. "No itch. Just good hearing."

"And where are they now?"

He leaned in to her, drawing close to her ear. "Very close," he whispered. "Watching us as a matter of fact." He pulled away, and started sketching again. "But I wouldn't worry too much about it. I know who it is," he said aloud.

"Who?" she whispered.

"Later," Crane said. "Right now, we need to examine Mr. Marathe here before the rain comes."

She rolled her eyes at his insistence on the rain, but decided to leave it alone. Besides, she had other issues to deal with at the moment. "We still need to wait for the coroner or something. I don't care how you people do it out here in the sticks, but with my brother's well-being on the line, I demand that we do it right."

"As do I, Ms. Kili. As do I." He gloved up yet again, and crouched beside the body one more time. He reached out to unbutton Miles' shirt once more, exposing his bloated torso... several jagged wounds slashed their way up his chest in a gruesome spectacle. Panicking, Kili reached out, and grabbed his wrist again.

"Crane!" she growled. "I'm warning you."

"Ms. Brennan," he said, using her formal name. "It's all right." He pulled his arm out of her grip. "You see, I *am* the Jasper County Coroner."

"What?" *This day just couldn't get any weirder.*

"That's right. I'm the duly appointed coroner of Jasper County. Or rather, I should say, I'm the deputy coroner." He proceeded to open a few more buttons of the deceased's shirt before continuing. "Granny's actually the elected coroner around these parts."

Without elaborating on this, he reached into the pack resting on the ground beside him, pulled out an antique magnifying glass, and began examining the chest wounds.

"Hmmm. Intriguing." He said it casually, as if he'd forgotten about the red-headed crime analyst standing directly behind him.

She waited for him to explain, but he never did. Instead, he pulled out a plastic evidence bag and a pair of tweezers from his backpack, and picked up several tiny specks of what looked like dust from the corpse. He dropped whatever it was into the bag, sealed it, and placed it in his pocket. He then began his scrutiny of the body again, working his way up the chest, and focusing intently on the neck. From there, he moved up to Marathe's head, which was still partially covered in leaves and bracken. Carefully, Crane wiped the debris away to discover that the top portion of the man's skull lay completely bare...his hair and scalp removed from the skull. Kili could see a jagged fissure snaking its way across the brow—evidence of a fractured skull.

"Oh, my God," she said. "Has he been...scalped?"

Crane eyed her over his shoulder without answering, grim-faced, then turned back to his examination. After several minutes of this, he pulled away from the body, stood up, and reached into his pocket to withdraw his cell phone. Punching a single button, he placed the phone to his ear and waited.

"Tyler," he said after several seconds. "It's Crane. We've found the research assistant."

He paused as the Jasper County Sheriff growled obscenities in the other end of the phone.

"Be that as it may, Sheriff, you need to get up here now. It appears, upon initial inspection, that Mr. Marathe may have been murdered." Another pause. "Yes, exactly. And do please notify the Sanford brothers that we'll be needing their transport vehicle. I'll be conducting an autopsy later this evening."

Sheriff Tyler said something inaudible.

"That's right. Thank you, Sheriff." He hung up the phone, and looked at Kili. "Now, we have some important work to do while we wait." He then wheeled around to his right and shouted into the woods, "The first order of business is to ask you some questions, Bear!"

Kili spun around, trying to figure out who Crane was talking to, when a large, burly man stepped out into the clearing.

"And how the heck did you know it was me?" the man asked with a huff. He was quite possibly the largest man Kili had ever seen, sporting a thick, bushy black beard that accentuated his bright, hazel eyes. He wore the brown uniform of a forest ranger and large black boots. "I was being extra careful, too."

Crane smiled, but held up his hands to keep the man at bay. "Careful Bear," he said. "This is, after all, a crime scene. We can't have you traipsin' all over the evidence, now can we?"

Kili noted that Crane's drawl seemed to increase as he spoke to the giant of a man, his speech pattern shifted almost back to that of the region.

"Ms. Kili, meet Jerry 'Bear' Boone," Crane said. "Bear, this is Kili Brennan."

"The FBI agent?" Bear asked, his eyes widening with what looked to be child-like wonder. "Never met me a real G-man before, though my granpap used to run into them all the time back durin' his 'shine runnin' days."

"I'm not exactly an agent. Just a crime analyst. Trying to find my brother—"

"I hate to interrupt," Crane said, "but I'm curious, Bear. Why are you here?"

The large man's face flushed, nearly changing three different shades of red. "You know good and well why."

Crane seemed to consider this for a moment before nodding. "And you didn't announce yourself earlier because?"

He blushed again, his eyes lighting up with mischievous pleasure. "Wanted to see if you still could...um..." He looked over at Kili and back at Crane. "You know."

"Use mountain magic?" Crane asked.

Bear nodded. "You were gone a might long time, Zeke. Thought you might have forgotten yer ways while you were traveling the world getting' yerself educated." He paused, a look of concern on his face. "But I should tell you, I came by yer sugar offerin' to the Wee People. Someone had trampled it fierce. From the looks of things, it wasn't too long after you'uns had moved out."

Crane's brow furrowed at the news. "Interesting," he said. "Most intriguing."

"That's the other reason I was stalkin' you," Bear said. "Wanted to keep an eye on ya. Weird thing is…the only tracks I seen came from you two. There was no third set anywhere as I could detect."

"Very curious indeed." Ezekiel Crane looked over at Kili. "Bear's one of the best trackers around. If he can't find signs to track, that's an impressive feat of our mysterious offering vandal." He turned back to Bear, apparently unconcerned. "Now tell me…as a Ranger, as well as, um, your other avocation, you know the Hollows better than anyone." He pointed over to the body. "Do you know anything about that? Any strange goings-on around here that you can recall? Anyone besides the anthropologist and his entourage lurking about?"

The big man stared impassively at the corpse, as if he'd seen such sights on a regular basis. But Kili thought she caught something strange flash in his eyes for a brief moment. Something like fear.

He shook his head. "Nope. Nothin' unusual that I recollect. But that don't mean nothin'. The Hollars' a mighty big place. And on the night her brother disappeared, I was up yonder on Waver's Ridge…nowhere near around here."

"Well, Mr. Marathe was not killed here," Ezekiel Crane said. "His body was dumped. He was killed somewhere else, and placed here." He stepped past the body, and pointed at the ground. "See? Drag marks. Coming from the west."

Kili peered around the corpse, looking at where he was pointing, but could see nothing. If there were drag marks to be seen, she certainly couldn't make them out.

"Well, I'll be," Bear said with a whistle. Apparently, he had no problem seeing them.

Crane looked at the big man. "Tell me...what do you know about the old stone ruins in the Hollows?"

Bear's face went white. "You mean the 'Devil's Teeth'...the Injun holy grounds?" He shuddered as he spoke the words. "You don't want to be messin' with those, Zeke. Nothin' good can come from it."

"I'm afraid we have no choice. Dr. Brennan was investigating the ruins when he disappeared. To find him, we'll have to take a look at the stones."

The man nodded. "All right then," Bear said. "I can guide you up there. But not now. It'd be dark by the time we got there and that's no place to be after dark."

"Why not?" Kili asked, genuinely interested.

The burly man glared at her. "Because, darlin', that's when One-Eyed Jack roams the Hollars. That's when he does his killin'."

CHAPTER
SEVEN

The Dark Hollows
October 14
7:00 PM

By the time they returned to Ezekiel Crane's pickup, rain was pounding against the metal roof of the cab in diagonal sheets. They had left the crime scene in the irritated hands of the sheriff, two deputies, a body transport crew, and a volunteer firefighter who acted as a part-time crime scene technician for the sheriff's office. Bear had chosen to remain at the scene as well, in case help was needed to move the body across the rugged terrain.

Kili slouched in the passenger seat of the truck, drenched and shivering as she watched the streams of water roll across the window. She looked over at Crane, who'd been silent since filling Sheriff Tyler in on the case. She didn't know much about the people of Boone Creek, Kentucky, but she did know one thing—neither Ezekiel Crane nor John Tyler liked each other much.

"So how did you know it was going to rain? I mean really?"

Kili asked, attempting to break the tension more than anything else.

He cracked a weak smile. Something was bothering him, but Kili could not figure it out. The man was already an enigma as it was, and though she could sense tension between he and the sheriff, she didn't believe his sudden melancholy had to do with any rivalry between the two. No, it was something entirely different.

"I told you, Ms. Kili," he said, gripping the steering wheel tight as he slowly drove along the tenuous, mud-soaked hunting trail. "My nose was itching. It's a sure fire indicator for rain."

She nodded at this, not really believing him, but deciding to let it slide for now.

"And finding Miles' body? I suppose you're going to tell me that dowsing rod of yours and that ant led you right to him?'

He gave her a sideways glance. "Absolutely. Though, I never said the stick was a dowsing rod. That was your own presumption." He brought the truck to a stop, and pulled out onto the blacktop road that would lead them back to town. He then continued. "The stick was nothing more than a stick."

"What?" Kili asked, bewildered. "What in the world could a stick do to help you track down a decomposing body in the middle of the woods?"

"You'd be surprised what a good, whittled stick can do in a pinch," he said. "In this instance, I was using it as a crude theodolite...similar to those used by surveyors. You might or might not have observed the carrion flying high overhead upon entering the forest?"

Her face flushed as she shook her head. She'd been so determined to locate Cian, she hadn't really seen much of anything except for that strange raven that had seemed to follow them throughout the day. And it appeared to have no interest at all in anything but the two of them.

"Well, there were a large number of birds circling overhead," he said. "But I also knew that once we entered the Dark Hollows, we would be unable to spot them due to the tree canopy above. So, as we progressed on our hike, I began mentally creating landmarks using the device that would help me to triangulate a more approximate location once we entered the heavier vegetation." He beamed at her before turning his attention back to the road. "Simple science, Ms. Kili. Simple science."

"And the ant? How did you use the ant?"

"Ah, the ant," he said with a laugh. "In death investigations, the first thing you learn is that insects are our friends. They might be disgusting, if not a bit unnerving, but they are an invaluable asset in any murder case."

She waited for him to continue, but he didn't. He simply looked straight ahead, regained his more dour expression, and drove toward town.

"And?" she finally said.

"And what?"

"How did the ant help you in finding Miles?" Her voice held an unintentional bite to it.

"Oh, well, the particular ant that I picked up to show you had nothing at all to do with helping me track down the victim," Crane said, his voice soft and reflective. "It was his brothers...his colony...that I was more interested in. You see, when a corpse begins to decompose, the chemicals that normally comprise the body begin separating. Two of those chemicals are sugar and alcohol, which, by the way, are like crack to ants. The stream of marching ants heading into the Hollows told me there was a large source of food somewhere up ahead, and all we had to do at that point was follow their trail."

Kili stared at him with incredulity. *There is no way that worked.*

"No way," she said, shaking her head. "You're lying to me. I've studied at Quantico. Though I'm not an agent, I'm familiar enough with modern forensics to know that that's just not how it works."

He glanced over at her again with a shrug.

"Suit yourself," he said, his straight white teeth practically sparkling beneath his smile. "I used mountain magic to find him then."

Kili didn't know whether she wanted to laugh or scream. The man was intolerable. Then, a sudden thought struck her...one that took all fight out of her. *Cian.*

"Mr. Crane," she said quietly. "Will we find him? Alive, I mean?"

He stared silently out the window for several moments before nodding.

"Yes, ma'am. I think there's more than a good chance we will. If we're fast enough that is."

They were approaching the single traffic signal in town and Kili felt the truck start to slow as Crane came up on the intersection of Main Street.

"And why do you think that? What gives you such confidence that Cian is still alive?"

"Simple," he said, pulling into the gravel parking lot of an old diner; its ancient neon sign flashing HANDY ANDY'S DINER. "The reason I'm confident he's still alive is that we only found one body today. Mr. Marathe was dragged to a secondary site. If your brother was dead too, the killer would have dumped them both there. That much, I am certain, Ms. Kili."

He pulled into a parking spot, and turned off the engine. Kili glanced around. A handful of cars and trucks, and three semis with coal-laden trailers were the only vehicles in the lot. She looked at the building. It looked as if it had been a Waffle House or an IHOP at one time, but someone had converted it into a greasy spoon.

"Uh, what are we doing here?" she asked.

"We need to eat, don't we? We have a long night ahead of us, and it would be better to grab a bite before the autopsy."

...*before the autopsy*? "What?" Kili asked. "You think eating grease covered slop is a good idea before an autopsy? Are you crazy?"

"Trust me. The Lord, after all, does move in mysterious ways." He opened the door of the truck, instantly unleashing a downpour into his cab. "Besides, their tiny little burgers are a masterpiece of the culinary arts!"

And with that, he climbed out, ran over to her side of the truck, and opened her door. "Come on," he said, shouting over the howling wind. "Granny would tan my hide if I didn't open a door for a lady, but there's only so much any man's chivalry can stand. And I don't have an umbrella."

Deciding not to argue, Kili dashed from the truck and ran immediately to the overhanging roof of the building. She waited for Crane to close her door and catch up.

"I should warn you, Ms. Kili," he said, moving toward the entrance of the diner. "You will find that, once we enter the establishment, I am something of a pariah around here."

"The Seventh Son of a Seventh Son," she said, nodding her acknowledgement.

His eyes frosted over briefly. "Not exactly," he said, opening the door to the restaurant. "But close enough."

The moment they stepped into the place, all went still...as if a giant vacuum had been turned on, sucking all the sound out the front doors. Of the twelve occupants of the diner, nine had their eyes fixed solely on her companion. Two were passed out, reeking of corn alcohol. And one, a young, attractive waitress, was busying herself counting the register. The moment she observed the hushed silence, however, her eyes shifted up and over...finally locking on Crane. She mouthed a silent curse, and stalked over to them to reluctantly take their order.

The Dark Hollows
October 14
7:50 PM

DEPUTY FRANK CRANFIELD huddled in the relative shelter of an oak, drawing in another puff from his cigarette, and cursing Sheriff Tyler. Having just joined the sheriff's office three months ago, Frank was the newest deputy on the force. The rookie. Which meant that when it came time to secure the murder scene until evidence technicians could return during the light of day, he'd been chosen to stand guard. In this downpour. With nothing but a set of galoshes and a cheap plastic poncho to protect him from the rain.

His cousin, Dustin, had been right. He'd have been much better off going to work for Noah McGuffin's organization than working for a burnout like Tyler.

"Geeze," he growled, exhaling a plume of smoke into the rain. "What the heck am I doing here?"

Like most lifelong residents of Jasper County, Frank wasn't overly fond of the idea of spending the night in the Dark Hollows either. He'd heard enough stories—knew far too much about the haints and other spirits that called the hundred and fifty acres of dead wilderness home—to ever have volunteered for the detail on his own.

He shuddered at the thought of the haints. From what his granddaddy had told him, most of the things that haunted the Hollars pretty much left the living alone. But the haints? They thrived on carnage. Fed off of fear. Amused themselves by leading unsuspecting humans to get lost in the woods, then kill them in the ghastliest ways imaginable.

What were those protections Granddad taught me? His mind rifled through all the old tales, trying to piece together those old nuggets of wisdom that would keep him safe should the haints come his way.

Of course, if anyone asked him, Frank would have told them exactly what he thought of the corpse that devil, Crane, had found earlier that day. If Ezekiel Crane hadn't killed him, then it was probably some of his unholy haints what did it. Everyone knew Crane spoke to the Dead. Knew he had ways of summoning them...force them to do his bidding. The deputy had long ago dismissed tales of One-Eyed Jack as mere campfire stories to scare kids. Crane, on the other hand, was the real deal. The real threat to Boone Creek, if not all of Jasper County.

Why couldn't he have just stayed gone? He shivered against the cold, but considered his train of thought further. When Crane had disappeared some fifteen years before, it had been the greatest thing to happen to their peaceful little town, since the town's founder, Daniel Boone, had set up camp here during his famous expeditions. Ever since Eli Smith and his Leechers ran Crane off, everything had pretty much run smooth. No crazy, supernatural murders. No terror-inducing hauntings. No dark witchcraft to curse the God-fearing citizens. Boone Creek, for all intents and purposes, had been just like any other town in south-eastern Kentucky. Which meant that except for the occasional drunken brawl at Bailey's or unsanctioned meth labs exploding, it was a pretty decent town to raise one's kids.

Frank let out another curse. *Then,* he *had to come back and bring his curse with him.*

The embers of his cigarette burned his forefinger, and he tossed it to the ground with a shout. "Dang it!" He stomped the cigarette out with his shoe, and immediately lit another one.

A twig snapped behind him, causing him to jump with a girlish scream. He spun around, using the oak as a shield, while fumbling for his sidearm. Once secure in his shaking hands, he raised the revolver up.

"Who's there?"

There was no answer.

"Is that you, boss?"

The only sound was that of the rain pounding against the branches above.

"Crane?" Then under his breath, "Oh, I hope it's Crane. I'd love to put him down once and for all."

"You, my dear," came a smooth, feline voice behind him, "aren't worthy to lick Ezekiel Crane's boots."

Frank turned around again to see the mocha-skinned form of Asherah Richardson stalking toward him.

"Ms. Richardson," he said with a squeak to his voice.

He couldn't take his eyes off of her. The rain traced the sweet feminine contours of her body, soaked into her light cotton sundress, and revealing far too much of her sensual form for even the most loosely modest of women. She, on the other hand, glided closer. A cat-eating-a-canary smile painted on her face.

"You have a lot to say about Ezekiel Crane, don't you?" she asked, tilting her head to one side, as she slithered up to him, and wrapped one wet arm around him; drawing him close as if she was about to kiss him. "I've been hearing you mumbling about him for a while now."

Frank fumbled for the correct words to say. Like most people in Boone Creek, he was familiar with Asherah and Crane's scandalous relationship in the past. Knew that, despite the horrific way in which their relationship ended, Asherah could be maliciously protective of him. To say the wrong thing now could prove disastrous for him.

He opened his mouth to answer, then closed it again. Swallowing hard before offering a nervous shrug. He'd decided it was his best option.

Her snow-white smile broadened at this, and she took a single step back. "Wise answer. Ezekiel Crane is worth a thousand of you, Deputy. You'd be even wiser to remember that."

With another gulp, he nodded his understanding.

"Now," she said, clapping her hands and spinning around

toward the place where Marathe's body was found. "We have work to do."

Frank, his legs wobbly beneath him, stepped forward. "Work?"

She glanced up at him with a wink. "You're going to help me remove any evidence that might still be lurking about." She leaned up and kissed him on the cheek playfully. "You're not going to tell anyone I was here. And oh! You're going to do it with a smile on your face."

CHAPTER
EIGHT

Handy Andy's Diner
October 14
8: 13 PM

"So tell me about this *One-Eyed Jack*," Kili said, watching the waitress walk away with their order in hand. The woman, though polite in her own way, had regarded the two of them with a nervous disdain...her hands had been shaking the entire time she jotted their orders down on her narrow notepad. When she disappeared into the kitchen, Kili turned her attention back to Crane. "I keep hearing about him or it or whatever, but no one will explain anything to me."

The downpour continued its deluge outside, now accompanied by crackling streaks of lightning and pounding thunder. From the looks of things, it wasn't going to lighten up any time soon, and Kili figured now would be as good a time as any to get answers to the ever-increasing number of questions that had been rattling around inside her head.

Crane, for his part, looked at her from behind an upturned

glass of water. He guzzled the liquid without answering, then set the glass down on the table with a sigh.

"A local legend," he explained; his face once again downcast. "As old as anyone can remember. Older, in fact, than the white man's presence in the New World."

Kili glanced around the dining area as Crane spoke. All eyes flitted back and forth between the two of them; every customer tensed for anything. If there were any on-going conversations at all, it was probably hushed whispers about them.

"You see, legends say that before the white man came, there were giants in these parts. Ancestors of the Cherokee, Chawktaw, and even the Huron tribes. There were thirteen of these giants, who were the guardians of the land, and the protectors of the Native Americans of the region. But these weren't human giants, Ms. Kili. They were nature spirits...similar in many ways to the Little People."

"Only in reverse," Kili said, grinning.

He nodded with a sallow smile of his own. "The stories go that eventually, after a certain amount of peace began to exist among the tribes, these giants began disappearing from the land. By the time the white man arrived, all thirteen of the giants had returned to the Spirit World. The Native Americans were practically defenseless against the expansion of Manifest Destiny. They were hunted, slaughtered, and scalped for bounties by French explorers making their way west."

Kili remembered a history professor of hers explaining how, despite what pop culture might say to the contrary, 'scalping' had not originated with the Native Americans. Instead, it had been learned from French adventurers and trappers seeking their fortune in the New World.

"One day," Crane continued, "the chieftains of the various tribes in the area ceremonially called upon the Spirit Giants to protect them. They were answered by only one warrior—one that the French eventually came to call *Jacque de L'un Oeil* or 'Jack of the One Eye'. Apparently, Jack was a fierce spirit warrior. A cyclopean giant that tore through the French explorers, and English settlers like a whirlwind, massacring them in droves with his mighty tomahawk, made up of a full grown oak for a handle and a monolithic stone for a blade. Eventually, the settlers struck a deal with the Indians and a friendship was soon formed. After that, there was no longer any need for Jack, so he departed once again, into the spirit world."

Kili sat, absorbing the story with surprising interest. She'd never been one for legends and tall tales. That was her brother's obsession. But there was just something—something far back in the more primitive recesses of her mind—that drew her to the story. Something ethereal; an inexplicable desire to learn more.

The waitress, her nametag reading "Candace", returned to their table, carrying two plates filled with four tiny cheeseburgers, fries, and pickles on the side. She set them down on the table with a huff, and walked away without a word.

Ignoring the cold shoulder, Kili turned her attention back to Crane. "So what does One-Eyed Jack have to do with my brother? With any of this? It's a great story and all, but I don't see how it helps the investigation any."

Crane took a bite of a burger, and set it back down on the plate. He chewed several times before swallowing, then looked back at her.

"Well, remember the monolithic stone I said made up the hatchet blade of his weapon?"

She nodded.

"Well it was one of thirteen similar stones, used by the giants when doing battle. Before disappearing from the land, the giants had plunged their tomahawks into the ground—a symbol of 'burying the hatchet' and peace among the tribes. The stones were set into a circle, and soon became known as 'The Devil's Teeth' by the settlers because they looked like a set of gigantic stone teeth jutting out from the earth. Anyway, legends say that this megalithic structure, the same one your brother was apparently investigating, was a gateway to the Spirit World. A door to the land of the Giants."

Kili tried to swallow, but discovered her throat was parched. She had sat silently, listening to the tale in rapt attention. Though she knew it was just a fairy-tale, it just sounded so amazing. So wondrous. No wonder Cian had been captivated by it. She reached for her glass of Coke and took a swig, easing the dryness.

"So why does Leroy Kingston think this One-Eyed Jack has returned?" she asked. "I mean, even if he believed the story, why would one of these giants come back to the Dark Hollows?"

Crane shrugged. "That is, in fact, an excellent question," he said in between bites of a French fry. "And one that warrants further investigation."

Candace the waitress approached their table; her brow creased with worry. It was the first time Kili took the time to get a really good look at her. She was in her early thirties with a nice figure that was accentuated nicely, believe it or not, by her waitress uniform. Her bleached blonde hair was cut short, hugging the back of her neck. Though she had a few scars from obvious bouts of acne from earlier years, her face was pleasant, though a bit angular. She had brown eyes behind long dark lashes, and her thin lips were highlighted with cherry red lipstick. Kili had the impression that this was a woman who might turn heads in a town like this.

Candace refused to look Ezekiel Crane in the eye as she placed the check on the table and asked, "Can I get you'uns anythin' else?"

Crane grinned up at her. Despite the woman's frigid disposition toward him, his smile was friendly and sincere.

"Indeed you can, Ms. Staples," he said, taking the check from the table and glancing at it discreetly. He reached into his back pocket and fished out an eel skin wallet. "If you'd be so kind, would you mind telling us about your relationship with Dr. Cian Brennan?"

Kili and Candace both gasped at the question. The waitress' eyes widened with both embarrassment and anger. Kili's, on the other hand, widened for reasons entirely different. There was just no way her brother would ever become involved with this... this...trailer-trash of a waitress. Cian had much better taste than that.

"I—I don't know what yer talkin' about," Candace protested, her cheeks flushing. "Dr. Brennan was a customer, sure, but we never...ya know."

"Come now, Ms. Staples. We've no time for games and lies." Crane leaned forward conspiratorially. His eyes narrowed as he looked up at her. "You know I have ways of findin' out the truth of such things." He smiled at her again, but this time, his grin held no warmth. "Which would you prefer? To be open and honest with us now? Or for me to discover the truth on," he paused, "my own."

The waitress sputtered for breath. Her saucer-sized eyes stretching even farther into a caricature of fixed terror. Candace Staples, like so many others in Boone Creek, was horrified of this man. Kili couldn't help but wonder why. *He is odd, sure...but nice enough*, she thought. *So why does everyone start shaking in their boots when they're around him?* The fear that these people had would have bothered her a great deal more if he wasn't using it to help track down her brother. But Kili resolved to find out the truth about Ezekiel Crane when all of this was over.

"Please, no," Candace said, taking a step back. Crane's hand flashed out, grabbing her wrists, and anchoring her in place. His eyes burned up at her. She went rigid, unable to move even if he wasn't still clutching her wrist.

Kili glanced around the diner. Though all eyes were on them, no one dared move to assist the stricken waitress. One burly trucker tensed in his booth, ready to come to her rescue, but was waylaid by the stern hand on his shoulder by a man at an adjoining table.

Ezekiel Crane paid no attention to any of it. His full concentration was focused on the waitress. The eyes of both were locked viciously on each other.

"It was nothing. I promise. Just a fling, that's all." The proclamation spilled from her lips in a tidal wave of words. "We were just havin' a good time. A couple of friends. Sometimes with benefits. He was lonely. I was lonely. He was just a nice guy... that's all. I promise. I don't know nothin' else." A stream of tears cascaded down her cheeks as she spoke. "Please. Oh, please. Don't...don't..." She was unable to finish her plea before she began bawling.

Crane released his grip, but kept his stare fixed on her.

"Ms. Staples, your exquisite acting skills are very impressive," he said, his face now an apathetic mask. "And though I do believe you truly are frightened at what I am capable of; I also know you are not telling me everything. You're hiding something from me and I can assure you, I will discover what it is."

"Mr. Crane," Kili said, reaching out and taking hold of his wrist. "Stop. The poor girl is terrified."

"Don't be fooled, Ms. Kili. Though she's not an evil woman, Ms. Staples here has quite a reputation. She's as cold and heartless as a glacier." He opened his wallet, and began rummaging through the bills. "I believe you ran into her son at Granny's house just this morning as a matter of fact."

Jimmy. The boy with the bee sting. Granny's warning to him about his alcoholic mother. This was her?

"And I can assure you, if your brother was involved with her, it was anything but casual. Right, Ms. Staples?" His warm smile had returned as he rose from the booth and placed a twenty-dollar bill on top of the check. "Keep the change, but know this...you and I are not finished here."

The waitress could only stand there, more tears pouring

down her face, which was now as pale as a February snow. Despite what Crane had said about the woman, Kili couldn't help but feel bad for her…for the way he had treated her.

But before she could offer an apology on his behalf, the tall lean man helped her from the booth, ushered her out of the diner, and into the drizzling night.

CHAPTER
NINE

Morriston, Kentucky
October 14
10:03 PM

T he cab of Crane's truck was silent as they drove through the rain-drenched streets, slowly making their way toward the county seat of Morriston, where the Jasper County Hospital was located. With the exception of Crane explaining that it would be a few hours before Marathe's body was ready for autopsy, and that they should use the opportunity to pay Leroy Kingston a visit, neither of them spoke.

The uncomfortable silence provided the perfect opportunity for Kili to stew over the encounter at Handy Andy's diner and the waitress, Candace Staples. The fear Crane elicited in not only Ms. Staples, but the restaurant's patrons—and everyone else, for that matter—concerned her. There was something very dark lurking in the shadows of Ezekiel Crane's past, and Kili once again found herself wondering if she'd made the right decision by involving him in her investigation. Granted, she'd uncovered more information about her brother today than she had in the previous days before, but she couldn't help wondering about the emotional cost her investigation was having upon the people of the town.

She considered all this while staring passively out the passenger side window, the rhythmic thump of the windshield wipers lulling her mind into a stupor. Realizing she was about to doze off, she sat up in her seat, adjusted the seatbelt around her shoulder, and yawned; willing herself awake. It would not be wise, she decided, to let her guard down while in her mysterious host's presence. There were just too many things she didn't know about Crane, and she knew she'd be foolish to trust the man until she discovered the dark secrets he was keeping from her.

As the truck passed the green street sign welcoming the two to Morriston, Kili cleared her throat, preparing to break the thirty-minute silence—as a means to shake herself out of her lethargy more than anything else. She had a thousand questions she was dying to ask Crane, but knew that any personal queries about his past or the townspeople's opinion of him would be met with the evasive sidestepping of a master politician. So, she opted for something a bit more conducive to their current investigation.

"So tell me," she said, not taking her eyes off the road. "What did your friend Bear mean when you asked him why he was up in the Dark Hollows?"

"To what, exactly, are you referring? Bear said quite a few things in that conversation."

"Well, when you asked him about it, he simply said you *knew* why he was up there, and that was it. You didn't probe any further. I guess I'm just looking for a scorecard here. Why was he up there if it wasn't within his duties as a ranger?"

"Ah," he said with a soft chuckle. "I sometimes forget you've not been in town very long. Haven't yet been told of the Boone Family Treasure as it has come to be known in these parts."

"Treasure?"

"Indeed," Crane said, his smile practically shining with amusement. "Our friend is not just a forest ranger. He's also our resident treasure hunter...from a very long line of treasure hunters, I might add. You see, Bear is a direct descendent of Daniel Boone." He paused, letting her take it in. "It's actually not uncommon for many Kentuckians to trace their lineage back to the great frontiersman, though most are lying through their teeth about it. Bear's claim, on the other hand, is quite authentic."

"But what has this got to do with treasure or the Dark Hollows?"

"It's simple. Boone's family has been plagued for generations by a tantalizing little secret of their progenitor. It appears that while making his way through the Appalachians, he stumbled on a patrol of British soldiers carrying the payroll for their brothers-in-arms. An altercation ensued, Boone and his men quickly dispatched their opponents, and they secured the rather hefty chest containing the King's gold." Crane made a left turn down what appeared to be a service street and continued his narrative. "Unable to carry the chest for the rest of his expedition, Boone opted to bury it, and planned on returning later to reclaim it. However, as the legend goes, he never did. He supposedly buried it somewhere up in the Hollows, and Bear's family has been hunting it ever since. And that, Ms. Kili, is exactly what he was doing up there when he stumbled upon our trail. But both he and his entire family have faced such ridicule over the years by the locals here, he doesn't like to admit to still searching for it...which is why he was loathe to actually voice his vocation when questioned."

Kili considered the tale a few minutes in fascination before a thought struck her. "But couldn't that make him a suspect?" she asked. "What if my brother accidentally stumbled on the treasure? That would be a pretty huge find. One that would definitely get him as excited as he was when we last spoke. What if

Bear found out and decided to—I don't know, take matters into his own hands?"

Crane steered the pickup into what appeared to be a loading area of the hospital, pulled up beside the large white building, and turned off the engine. Then, he looked over at her and nodded.

"It's a possibility," he said. "And one that I've already considered. Though I must admit, it would be very uncharacteristic of him if he did. Despite his size and foreboding appearance, Bear is one of the gentlest souls I've ever encountered. While most in Boone Creek have regarded me with suspicion and ire my entire life, he has always been rather friendly toward me. Still, it's worth keeping him in the back of our mind as he guides us to the Devil's Teeth tomorrow."

And with that, Crane opened the door of his truck and climbed out. The rain had slackened to a mere drizzle. Kili opened her own door and followed him to the back of the pickup where he was busy sorting through his pack. Without a word, he rummaged through it, pulled out a small rawhide pouch attached to a leather cord and draped it over his neck.

"What's that?" Kili asked, pointing to the pouch.

Instinctively, he clutched it in his hand and grinned. "My medicine bag," he said, releasing it again to search through the backpack once more. Soon, he came up with another object that he quickly pulled over his head. A rabbit's foot—not one of those tiny cheap novelty ones died pink or yellow, but rather a large furry foot attached to a leather thong.

Kili couldn't help laughing at it. "Really? A rabbit's foot too? You expecting bad luck or something?"

His face darkened as he glared at her under his rain-soaked blonde hair. "So far, Ms. Kili, it appears that we've had nothing *but* bad luck during this investigation, wouldn't you say?" His face softened a bit. "A little *good* luck would be pretty nice right about now. However, the foot isn't for luck. It's for something else entirely."

She waited for him to elaborate, but true to form, he refused to explain the enigmatic comment, and continued his search through his pack. He withdrew a few more odds and ends, including a long nylon string, and smiled at her as he closed the backpack up and stuffed it once more into the tool box in the back of the truck.

"Ah, now to find a persimmon tree," he said, holding up the string, wheeling around, and striding over to the side of the hospital with Kili right on his heel.

"A persimmon tree?" she asked as they rounded the corner and into a beautiful garden surrounding a patio area filled with picnic tables, stone benches, and a whitewashed gazebo over-looking a small koi pond. Kili figured it was a common area that patients would use for some fresh air and sunlight—maybe a place to sneak a smoke or two. "Why are you looking for one of those?"

Crane ignored the question, glancing around the garden proper until he found a stand of trees clustered in the northeast corner. As she followed his gaze, she was surprised to see the raven there, perched among its branches.

Don't be silly, Kili. That can't possibly be the same bird.

Pulling the string he'd retrieved from the bag taut in both hands, Crane strode over to the tree with the raven, and wrapped the cord around the trunk. "Put your finger here and hold it," he said, indicating the place on the string loosely tied off. When she complied, he pulled out a slip of paper and a pen, scribbled something on it, and tucked the sheet inside the string. He then, pulled out a pocketknife, cut off a few patches of tree bark, and stuffed them in his "medicine bag". Once done, he finished tying it off, stepped back to appraise his handiwork, and let out a satisfied sigh. "There. That should do it."

She stared at him, her hands on her hips. "That should do

what exactly?" she growled, annoyed with always being three steps behind when it came to the man.

He threw her his most charming smile yet and said, "Break Leroy's fever, of course." He gave her a gentle clap on the shoulders as he beamed, then stepped around her and headed toward the loading bay area of the hospital once more. Dashing up the six narrow steps, two at a time, he lightly rapped three times on the locked service entrance, stepped back and waited. By the time Kili caught up to him, the thick metal door creaked open, and an elderly black man poked his balding head out of the entrance. His eyes widened when he saw Crane.

But his reaction to seeing the mountain man was nothing like Kili had expected. Instead of ducking swiftly back inside and barring the door, he shoved it open, let out a howl of joy, and embraced Crane in a swarthy bear hug.

"Ezekiel!" the man shouted; his voice a bit louder than was probably necessary. The jovial black man was wearing the distinctive blue uniform of a security guard, his paunch hanging over his belt in a rumpled mess. "I heard you were back in town! It's plum good to see ya again, my friend."

Crane returned the smile, holding the man's hands tight in his own. "It is wonderful to see you too, Mason. It's been a very long time."

Mason cackled at this. "I'll say. It's been since...what? Since you saved Rose?"

Crane stepped back, his face blushing slightly from what appeared to Kili to be embarrassment, then he cleared his throat. "Oh, Mason, I'd like you to meet a friend of mine," he said, abruptly changing the subject. "This is Kili Brennan. Kili, I'd like you to meet a dear friend, Mason Ellis."

The security guard turned his attention to Kili, his smile broadening even wider, giving the rotund man a cherubic appearance. His joyous spirit was nearly contagious, and Kili could hardly contain a giggle that threatened to escape her lips at the smiling man. She reached out a hand, and said, "Glad to meet you, Mr. Ellis."

He looked down at her hand, an air of surprise on his face, then batted it away before taking her in a warm embrace.

"We don't cotton to ceremony around here, Ms. Brennan," he said, squeezing her tight. "A friend of Mr. Ezekiel's is a friend of mine."

After several surprisingly comfortable seconds, Mason released his hug, and turned back to Crane. "Now, what can I do fer ya? I know you'uns didn't come all this way out here to chew the cud with me."

Crane nodded. "Perceptive as ever, though spending time with you is one of the more enjoyable past times I could think of...but I'm investigating a death in the Dark Hollows. You have a patient here—a witness—and I need to speak with him."

Mason's face suddenly darkened. "Leroy," he said. "You're talkin' about ol' Leroy Kingston."

"Is that a problem?"

The security guard thought silently for several seconds before shaking his head. "Now I know why you came to me first," he said with a soft chuckle. "Nurse Rollins wouldn't let you anywhere near Kingston, even if his very life depended on it." Mason looked over at Kili. "Think's Zeke here's got some dark juju, and would probably try to stake him in the heart with a tongue depressor if she thought she could pull it off." He let out another cackle.

Kili wanted to ask the man why he didn't have the same reservations about her companion, but couldn't get the words out before Crane spoke up. "Do you think you can get us in to see him?"

"Won't do ya much good. He's crazier than a polecat in a room full of perfume," he said with a shrug. "But I can definitely get ya in."

And without any further ado, he gestured the pair inside, and followed them into the basement corridor of the hospital.

"Ms. PAMELA," Kili heard the old security guard say to the charge nurse sitting at her station in the central junction of the Intensive Care Ward. She and Crane listened with their backs against the wall in an adjacent corner. "I hate to be a pest, but my back is a'killin' me again. Could I get you to take a quick gander at it?"

There was a brief pause, then the irritated gravelly voice of a woman who obviously smoked way too much responded. "Mr. Ellis, how many times do I have to tell you—working here doesn't give you the right to free healthcare. I have patients to attend to."

"I know…I know, but I was so busy helpin' my Rose with her garden this morning. Pulled my back out of whack somethin' fierce, and weren't able to see a doctor before my shift. It ain't too busy tonight, Ms. Pamela…couldn't ya just take a quick look?"

After a few seconds, Kili heard an exasperated sigh, then, "All right. Let's go into Examination Room 3." There was a rustle of paper and clothes, then the gentle click of a door closing from around the corner.

"Come on," Crane whispered, grabbing her hand. "We haven't much time." They moved out into the open space of the ICU and stole quietly to the room Mason had told them they'd find Kingston. Without pausing, her companion turned the knob of the door, and slipped quietly into the darkened room with Kili close behind. Once both were inside, he closed the door, and turned to face the bed in which Leroy Kingston lay.

Though Kili wasn't sure what the guide had looked like before the encounter, the visage she beheld lying prone in the hospital bed nearly took her breath away. To use an expression she'd heard on more than one occasion since coming to Boone Creek, he looked like death warmed over. The man was tall. That much she could see from underneath his bed linens, but he was also gaunt—almost skeletal. His hard, sunburned face seemed emaciated. His cheeks sunken. Though he was clearly uncon-scious, his haunted eyes stared, unblinking, up at the ceiling. Bandages clung to his skin across his forehead, arms, and neck and she got the distinct impression there were plenty more hidden protectively under the covers.

Without a word, Crane moved over to the right side of the bed, and placed a hand across the catatonic man's brow. "Hmmm," Crane muttered. "He's worse off than I had anticipat-ed." He moved over to the end of the bed, extracted the patient's chart from a cradle mounted to the frame, and examined it for several seconds. "It seems his injuries were superficial. The doctors seem to think his condition is purely psychological in nature, though they *have* detected some sort of infection in his respiratory system."

"What kind of infection?" Kili asked.

"They're not quite sure. Tests have been inconclusive, but it's playing havoc with his breathing. They've had to put him on a ventilator with a pure oxygen mix on at least four occasions."

Crane moved back to Kingston's bedside, drew open the small medicine pouch hanging from his neck, and pulled out two slivers of the tree bark he'd cut from the persimmon tree. He then crushed the pieces up by hand into a near powder, and sprinkled the stuff on Kingston's forehead.

"Why are you doing that?" Kili asked.

Crane mumbled something under his breath, then looked over at her. "Tree bark from the persimmon I tied the string around—it will reduce his fever and hopefully make him coherent enough to speak to us."

She gawked at him, unsure how to respond.

"Tree bark, Ms. Kili, has a long history of healing properties.

As a matter of fact, for a long time, it was the active ingredient in aspirin, which—"

"Which helps to reduce fever," she said, with a nod, once again perplexed by the man's unorthodox methods. "But don't you think the doctors haven't already been giving him aspirin? Do you honestly think that crumbled tree bark is going to do any good where real medicine hasn't?"

He shrugged with a laugh. "Well, that's why the string and the piece of paper with his name written on it were tied to the tree," he said, as if that explained everything. But without giving her an opportunity to comment further, he moved around to the other side of the bed, leaned forward, and whispered something into Kingston's ear.

A few breath-holding seconds later and the man suddenly stirred. It wasn't much. A mere flutter of an eyelid. The gentle twitch of neck muscles. But Crane had definitely elicited a reaction from Leroy Kingston, which was more than she could say for the doctors of the Jasper County Hospital.

"Leroy," Crane said in a soft, calming voice just above the man's ear. "We need to speak with you. We have some questions."

Kingston's head rolled slightly, away from Ezekiel Crane's soothing voice.

"Leroy, I'm afraid I must insist," Crane said, gently turning the guide's face to look at him. "I know you are scared. Know your ordeal is not something you'd rather relive..." He held up a finger, and let it hover a few inches from the headboard of the bed, then began softly tapping at it in a slow, steady beat. "It's all right, Leroy. Just concentrate on the tapping. Focus on it. Let it envelop you. The tapping is a shelter, Leroy. A place of refuge."

Tap. Tap. Tap.

"Do you hear it? Do you hear the tapping?"

Leroy nodded, his eyes still fixed in a blank stare at the ceiling.

"Good," Crane said. "Leroy, your fever is breaking even as we speak." *Tap. Tap. Tap.* "You'll begin to feel much better shortly, and with it will come a sense of overwhelming peace. Tranquility. Safety." *Tap. Tap. Tap.*

Kili stared at the scene in silence. Her companion seemed to be trying to hypnotize Kingston to get the information out of him. More hocus pocus. Another ridiculous approach to use on an investigation. She had always prided herself on being a free-thinking, open-minded woman. But her short time with Ezekiel Crane was stretching the limits of her own tolerance.

Suddenly, Kili realized the room had grown completely silent. Crane was no longer talking. No longer tapping his finger against the headboard. Even the sound of Kingston's EKG monitor seemed muffled. But there was one sound that seemed so out of place in the stark hospital room. So strange and unearthly that Kili had to concentrate to be sure she was actually hearing it.

The sound of children laughing.

It's almost eleven o'clock at night. Who lets their children play at this time of night? They should be in bed! Of course, she supposed, it could have been someone's television playing too loud in their hospital room. That made the most sense.

She looked over at her companion to see if he noticed the sound, but if he did, he gave no indication. Instead, he withdrew the notepad and pen from his back pocket, and handed them to her brother's guide. Correction—Crane placed the notebook on Kingston's lap, and wrapped the man's right fingers around the pen, setting it down on the open pad.

"Now Leroy, I'm not going to ask you to say anything," Crane whispered in his ear. "But I remember your momma, God rest her weary soul, had once told me how much you love to draw. You still love to draw things, don't you boy?"

Kingston gave a slight nod at the question.

"Good. Because I want you to draw this pretty little lady

standing at the foot of your bed a picture." Crane pointed over to her, directing Kingston's empty eyes over to her. "See her? Well, I need you to draw a picture of what happened to her brother... the man who hired you as a guide through the Hollows. Can you do that?"

Another nod, then, almost imperceptibly, the man's hand started moving slowly over the sheet. His eyes still fixed on the ceiling, the pen began to fly over the page in rushed, jagged jerks of Kingston's wrists.

"I wasn't aware that hypnosis was something a person typically picked up in the mountains," Kili said in a hushed voice, watching the catatonic man scraping away with his pen.

Crane kept his full attention on his charge, but answered her anyway. "That's because I learned how to do it at Oxford."

Once again taken aback, Kili scrambled for the words to respond to his surprise answer. "As in the university?" she asked weakly.

He awarded her with a quick glance up and a winking grin. "What? You don't think they take hillbillies? I was—" His voice trailed off the moment he realized Kingston's scribblings had ceased, and turned his attention back to him. "Are you finished, Leroy?"

Another staring nod.

Tentatively, Crane reached out, and took hold of the notepad. Kingston's grip suddenly tightened on it, his wild eyes jerking to look directly at Crane. He opened his mouth to speak, but no words came out.

"It's all right," Crane said, resuming his gentle tapping of the headboard. *Tap. Tap. Tap.* "It's all right. Everything is fine. You're safe."

But Kingston maintained his white-knuckled grip on the pad of paper, his arm shaking with either exertion or fear.

Tap. Tap. Tap.

"Leroy, please. Let go."

Then, without warning, the crazed man began wailing at the top of his lungs. His arms and legs flailed wildly in all directions. Crane was able to snag the notepad just as Kingston's hand shot up, and grabbed him by the throat. Crane's hand clutched at his assailant's wrist, trying to wrest it free. Kili flew to the side of the bed, grappling with the screaming man's arm, trying desperately to pull him off her companion.

"Jaaaaaack!" Leroy screamed, glaring maliciously at Crane. His strength was beyond anything Kili would have imagined possible from someone so frail. She found herself powerless to stop him from crushing her companion's windpipe.

Then, the door to the room flew open, and the thin, angular form of a haggard looking nurse stormed into the room. "What is going on in here?" she yelled above the din. But when she saw Ezekiel Crane, locked in a death grip with her charge, her eyes widened in immediate suspicion. "You!"

Immediately, Kingston released his iron-strong grip from around Crane's throat and leaned back into his pillow. His eyes once more locked fully on the ceiling. It would have seemed as if his outburst had never happened except for the wide red marks across Crane's neck.

Regaining his breath, and his composure, Crane straightened up his shirt, re-fastened a few buttons that had come loose in the struggle, and turned to face the nurse.

"Ah, Ms. Rollins!" he said with a smile as if nothing at all happened. "How good to see you this fine evening."

She glared at him for several long seconds, before raising an accusatory finger at him. "Devil! Child of the devil is what you are," she said. "What witchery have you done to him, Crane?"

He tucked the notepad into his shirt pocket, and took a step forward. Nurse Rollins instinctively took one step back, her hand clutching something chained around her neck. Kili presumed it was a crucifix or something similar.

"I've done nothing but alleviate Mr. Kingston of his fever," he said. "When we leave, you will discover that it's completely gone."

She mumbled a curse under her breath, then pointed to the door. "You need to leave right now. I would call security, but I have a feeling it wouldn't do any good with that no count Ellis."

"Fine. We were just leaving anyway." Crane walked over to the door, and gestured for Kili to follow. Then he turned back to the nurse. "But a word of advice, Ms. Rollins. If you hold this against Morris, I will look very poorly on you in the future. *Very* poorly."

Her trembling mouth opened to protest, but then closed. Her cruel, watery eyes widened at the implications racing through her frazzled mind. But without waiting for her to respond, Crane strode out the door and down the hallway to the hospital's elevator.

BY THE TIME they made it back to the truck, the rain had picked up once more, and the two were drenched and shivering when they climbed into the warm confines of the cab. Crane quickly started the engine, and turned up the heat before turning a knob by the steering wheel to power on the overhead dome light.

"You ready to see what our very ill friend drew for us?" he asked, reaching into his shirt pocket to retrieve the notepad.

Kili nodded, taking in deep breaths in an attempt to slow her racing heart.

Wiping the water from the cardboard front of the pad, he opened it up and glanced down at the pen marks scrawled across the page. His eyes narrowed, taking in every nuance of every line. A grim expression creased his face as he gazed at it. After several minutes, he handed the pad to her.

"I'm afraid," he said, an unmistakable air of disappointment in his voice, "that your brother's situation may be more dire than I had first thought."

Kili slowly looked down at the page and gasped. The image emblazoned onto her mind's eye was worse than anything she could have imagined.

Mr. Crane, it seemed, was the proverbial master of understatement.

CHAPTER
TEN

Jasper County Morgue
County Road 309
October 15
12:30 AM

The Jasper County Coroner's Office was located in an abandoned Baskin Robbins about seven miles northeast of Boone Creek. The ice cream shop, one of several businesses that tanked in a small shopping center four years earlier, had been purchased by the county to act as its morgue for two reasons. First, it had a reasonably-sized walk-in freezer to store bodies. Second, it was seven miles from town, and therefore, inconspicuous to the residents of both Boone Creek and Morriston. Pressed for a third reason, some of the county commissioners might say that it was to keep Ezekiel Crane as far away from the population as possible.

None of this, of course, bothered Crane himself, who preferred his solitude whenever possible. It wasn't that he was a hermit or anti-social, but rather was content to spend his time in inner contemplation and a distraction-free environment. It also allowed him his privacy when practicing his particular brand of death investigations.

"The subject is a thirty-seven-year-old Caucasian male," he said into a digital voice recorder as he examined the corpse draped across the autopsy tray. "Height, six-foot two-inches. Weight, one hundred and seventy pounds." He proceeded to dictate his observations of the external examination as usual, highlighting the devastating trauma of Marathe's chest cavity, as well as the partial decapitation of the man's skull. He paid special attention to the strange granules he'd found on the man's clothes at the dump site; finding even more of them lining the adipose tissue of the chest.

Several minutes later, after the body was photographed from various angles, he took a scalpel and made the standard 'Y' incision down the chest—being sure to cut around the lacerated bridging of the chest injury. Once completed, he took more photographs of the inside of the chest cavity, collected more of the alien granules, then proceeded to cut through the rib cage using a pair of tree loppers.

During the more menial portions of the autopsy, Ezekiel Crane pondered the case he was currently working on. The missing anthropologist and the mystery of what he'd discovered up at the Devil's Teeth. He pondered the other missing residents of Jasper County, and wondered why Sheriff Tyler and his ilk had tried so hard to keep the disappearances a secret—especially from him. As far as he knew, Tyler had no idea that Crane had caught wind of the missing people and he planned to keep it that way until he knew more about what was going on in his community.

Then, there was the enigma of Kili Brennan. On the surface, she was exactly as she appeared to be—a concerned sister of a missing scientist. Loyal. Trustworthy. A decent human soul who showed great concern for Candace Staples when he'd given her the witcher's third-degree. That said a lot about the girl, in and of itself. But there was something deeper to the FBI analyst. Something even she probably wasn't aware of.

First, she'd seen The Raven. She didn't seem too concerned about it. Probably just thought it was a normal everyday bird. But on more than one occasion, he'd caught her staring at it. A feat, as far as he knew, that could only be accomplished by three other beings on the planet. So the question was, how had she been able to see it. It was *his* harbinger. His...albatross, for a lack of a better analogy. So how had she managed to...

He paused his current line of thought as something small and metallic caught his attention within Marathe's chest cavity. Reaching in, he thumbed away a few pieces of fat, and withdrew a round pellet.

"Hmmm."

He dropped the pellet into a plastic tray, and continued to rummage around the chest's interior until he had found several more.

"Buckshot." Marathe had been shot, apparently in the chest with a shotgun. But it was strange that he'd seen no pellet wounds to the body. Just the huge gaping hole in the chest— which, despite the movies, isn't how a shotgun wound normally looks. Besides, the chest wound looked like it had burst from the inside out. And he'd found nothing within the skull to suggest he was shot in the head. Like, the chest, it seemed to have simply exploded from the inside out. So what were the buckshot doing in the assistant's chest?

The mystery was becoming even more enigmatic the further Crane dug, and he was no fan of mysteries. He preferred having the answers, not chasing questions.

The set of chimes he'd hung near the entrance of the morgue began to ring in a chaotic unholy cadence. He spun around, brandishing his scalpel, and gasped.

Her vision was exactly as he remembered it. Long, kinky brown hair draped over slender shoulders. Emerald green eyes that seemed to radiate in the florescent lighting of the exam room. Her form-fitting, sheer sundress—the left strap hanging down over her shoulder, and drawing the eyes to the light brown perfectly smooth skin of her cleavage. As usual, she wore no shoes as she strode further into the room, a luscious smile playing across her face.

"Hello, Ezekiel," Asherah Richardson cooed. Her voice was like a mixture of melting butter and molasses. "You've been gone for far too long."

Crane stared back at her, but remained absolutely still. Absolutely quiet.

"I'm hurt actually," she continued, gliding up to him, and tracing a single finger down the front of his shirt. Her perfectly white teeth beamed up at him playfully. "You've been back for almost six months now, and you haven't bothered to come see me. Haven't bothered to call. Not even an email?"

Carefully, he took hold of her wrist and pulled it away from his chest. "You'll pardon me, Ash, if I don't harbor the same 'good ol' times' nostalgia as you in regards to our past...um, association," he said coolly. His initial surprise at her appearance had quickly subsided, and he'd once again regained his composure. "Now, my dear, as you can see, I'm rather busy. What is it I can do for you?"

Asherah's face morphed into a faux pout. "You're not happy to see me?"

"What do you want, Asherah?" Crane asked, his voice harsher than he'd intended.

She stiffened. "Watch your tone with me, Ezekiel," she hissed. "Remember...I'm not one of the locals that you can send into a sniveling mess with a menacing glare, and a snap of your fingers. After all, I taught you everything you know."

It was Crane's turn to smile now. "That's not entirely accurate. Though I'll admit...you are, at least, partially responsible for the fear these people have of me. Now please, get to the point of this visit, or I should be required to ask you to leave."

"The point, Ezekiel, is that I would like to help you with your, um, little investigation here."

"And why is that?"

"For old time's sake?" She brushed the palm of her hand over his right cheek.

He crossed his arms, and raised an eyebrow at her.

"Or perhaps having One-Eyed Jack running around is just bad for business. Noah's not happy about it. The sheriff's not happy about it. And the town's people are about to lose their ever-loving minds about it. It's a powder keg waiting to happen."

Crane considered it a moment, then shook his head.

"I'm not entirely convinced you're not somehow behind this, Ash. If One-Eyed Jack truly has returned—and I'm not entirely convinced of that yet, by the way—it sounds exactly like something you'd be part of. It brings just the right amount of chaos into our little town to tickle your rather morbid fancies." He paused. "Look, I know you, Noah, Thornton, and a few others have something going on up in the Hollows. Not sure what it is, but I do know it's something dangerous, stupid, and..."

She raised her hand and smacked him across the jaw. "My plans are my own, Ezekiel Crane. They may be dangerous, yes. But never stupid. And believe it or not, my love, my little operation in the Hollows is completely altruistic. Something, I think, you'll be quite pleased with when completed."

Crane's face still stung from Asherah's slap, but her words stung worse still. The last time she'd uttered a similar declaration, his life, and the life of his brother, was changed forever.

"Ash," he said. His voice quiet and reflective. Gentle, even. Despite their history, he could not deny the old longings were still there for her. "If you truly care for me, don't do anything we will both regret. Not again."

She smiled up at him, rose up on the tips of her toes, and kissed the spot she'd just struck. "Don't worry, Ezekiel. I'm truly on the side of the angels now. I swear, this will make you proud of me again."

With that, she spun around, and glided from the room without another word. As the front door opened, Crane could just make out the harsh cawing of The Raven just outside the building, and he shuddered at the thought of whatever was coming next.

Jasper County Lodge
October 15
12:57 AM

THE SHRILL RING of the telephone jolted Kili awake from her over-soft hotel room bed; her pulse quickened against her temple from the sudden interruption. Exhausted from both the physical and emotional turmoil she'd experienced the day before, she'd been dead to the world, and the unexpected intrusion to her slumber pushed her nerves into overdrive.

She looked at the bright red digital numbers of the clock on the nightstand—almost one in the morning. She'd only been asleep a couple of hours. Ezekiel Crane had opted to drive her to the motel after leaving Kingston's hospital room, stating that Miles' autopsy would be long and tedious—not to mention something that she simply might not want to witness. She hadn't argued, and stumbled into her room after watching him drive off. She'd pretty much passed out the moment her head hit the pillow.

She was actually a little surprised she'd been able to fall asleep so easily given that Leroy Kingston's bizarre sketch was now permanently burned into her memory, like a shadow emblazoned onto a wall after a bright flash of light. Bizarre really wasn't the right word for it. Disturbing, macabre, or even terrifying were perhaps better ones. The scene depicted in the shaky, jagged scrawl had been one of a giant mouth stretched wide into space. A ring of long, pointed fangs jutted out, closing in on three stick-like figures. One figure was sprawled out on a bloated, wet tongue—something looking like blood pouring from his body. Another stood two sizes larger than the others, a dark one-eyed cloud hovering over him with what had appeared to be a hammer or an axe raised high above. The third figure was trying to escape the teeth, but was surrounded by a cluster of similar, though smaller clouds grasping at his arms and legs...as if they were attempting to prevent him from absconding. And surrounding the entire image was a frame of bones and skulls, fire blazing in their empty sockets.

Kili and Crane had sat in the truck for about an hour, trying to peer through the madness that had bred the primitive piece of art. On the surface, it had seemed clear enough. The teeth were simply representing the megalithic structure her brother had been investigating—the Devil's Teeth, as the locals called it. The three figures were Kingston, Miles, and Cian, though neither could quite understand why one was drawn to a greater scale than the others. But it had been the cloud that had perplexed Crane the most...that seemed to give him a greater urgency for the case. When pressed about it, he'd simply stated that in all the years that stories of One-Eyed Jack had circulated, he'd never once been depicted in such an amorphous state. No legends ever conceived him to be some formless cloud hovering ominously overhead.

Kili wasn't sure, but she almost detected a sense of panic welling up in the strange man's eyes as he had gazed at the sketch.

The phone screeched against the silence once more, causing her to start.

Groggily, she glanced over at it once more. The only person who would call her at this hour, she figured, would be Crane—perhaps with some new piece of information about Miles' death.

Stretching from her place in bed, she picked up the phone's receiver. "Hello?"

There was silence on the other end, save for a series of quick shallow breaths, and the faintest trace of childlike giggling in the background.

Again with the kids?

Kili propped herself up on her elbow, and white knuckled the phone. "Hello?" Her voice was a little more alert and forceful this time.

A throat cleared. It sounded female.

"Who is this? What do you want?"

"I—I didn't do nothin' to your brother," the woman on the other end of the line finally said. Her speech slurred and trembling, Kili realized it was the waitress from the diner. "Don't let him do..." She paused, took a deep breath, and continued. "Don't let him witch me or my boy. Please. I didn't do nothing."

Candace Staples sobbed. She was scared. Frenzied. And Kili knew that all of it was because of Ezekiel Crane. The man certainly commanded a great deal of fear in the townspeople here, but for the life of her, Kili still couldn't figure out why. It was the twenty-first century for goodness sake. Who believed in magic anymore? She was beginning to feel sorry for the woman. Crane had been unnecessarily cruel to her at the diner, and Kili couldn't help but wonder if some of it might not have been personal.

"It's okay," she said. "I won't let him hurt you."

Candace let out a sniffle, then cleared her throat once more. She inhaled sharply again, and Kili thought it sounded as if the woman was smoking. The metropolitan snob in her speculated on the *what*, but chided herself for being overly judgmental.

"Thank you," Candace said with a sob. "That man's the

Devil, ya know. You should stay away from 'im if you care about yer soul."

Kili sighed. "So I've been told. Numerous times, actually. Now, is there anything else you need? It's late. I'm tired, and I have a long day ahead of me tomor—"

"We need to meet," Candace blurted. "Right now, if possible. You need to understand—me and your brother—we had ourselves somethin' special. I loved him with all my heart. I never woulda done nothin' to hurt a single hair on his head."

Kili winced at the waitress' words. She still found her brother's involvement with her to be just too farfetched to believe. But she decided not to press the issue now.

"All right, but why is it so important that we meet right now?"

Another deep breath on the other end. Then a very slow exhale.

"Because I have news. Somethin' you need to know." Her voice continued to tremble, though the sobbing had subsided. "Can't wait 'til tomorrow. Too many eyes and ears around during the day. Plus, Crane. I don't want him anywhere near me. If you want the information, you'd best come see me now."

She didn't like the thought of meeting the woman like this— so melodramatic, it almost seemed staged. Like something out of cheap noir film. But in the grand scheme of things, what choice did she have? For better or worse, Crane seemed to think Candace Staples knew more than she was admitting about Cian and his disappearance. And despite the fact that she had only just met him, Kili was beginning to trust the mountain man's instincts about the case. He might be a little eccentric, if not a bit theatrical, but he sure had located Miles' body pretty quick.

Of course, it also occurred to her that the reason he was able to find her brother's research assistant so ably was because he was the one who put him there. No, Ezekiel Crane had not been scratched off her own suspect list just yet, but for now, he was lower on the list than Candace.

"Where do you want to meet?" Kili asked.

"Bailey's Pub." Her response was a little too quick. "It's closed now. No one's around. But I have a key. We can talk in private there."

The more Candace spoke, the less Kili liked what she was about to do. "Fine," she said, scrambling out of the bed. "I'll be there in..." She glanced at the clock. "...fifteen minutes." Kili was about to set the receiver back into its cradle, but added, "And Ms. Staples, this better not be a waste of my time."

"Trust me," she said with a sniffle. "It's not." And then the line went dead.

Kili hung up the phone, and quickly got dressed. She moved over to the bathroom sink, put her hair up in a ponytail, and slid a baseball cap on her head. By now, she was beyond caring how presentable she was anyway.

"Okay, Kili," she said, looking at herself in the mirror. "Let's go have a chat with your brother's *girlfriend*."

Then, moving over to the nightstand, she pulled out the drawer and withdrew her Walther .380. "But there's no way I'm going to meet her without backup."

CHAPTER
ELEVEN

Bailey's Pub
October 15
1:23 AM

K ili stood at the closed door of the pub, and took a deep breath. It had started raining again, and the wind was currently picking up momentum, whipping the dead leaves littering the parking lot in tight little swirls at her feet. The tail of her hair blew around her face as she reached a shaking hand inside her coat to ensure that her weapon still rested in its shoulder holster for the tenth time since leaving the hotel. Something about this whole thing just didn't make sense. Wasn't adding up. She could understand Candace's desire for a private meeting—away from Crane especially—but not like this. There had been something in their conversation that did not sit well, and it was putting her nerves on an even greater edge than before.

Well, Kili, there's not much you can do it about it, she thought; willing her heart rate to slow. *If there's even a chance the woman knows something about Cian's disappearance, you've got to take the chance.*

Inhaling the damp, cool air once more, she pushed the bar's door open, and walked inside. The place was dimly lit with a single overhead light, hanging above a small table in the center of the room. The pale illumination cast a puke yellow glow over Candace Staple's nervous form, who eyed Kili, and gave a furtive nod.

"You came alone?" Candace asked, lighting a cigarette with a trembling hand.

Kili moved toward the table, and returned the nod. "Of course." She pulled out the chair opposite Candace, and sat down. "Now, let's talk. What do you have to tell me?"

The woman stared at her, two trails of mascara streaked down her cheeks, evidence of where tears had run through her pancaked makeup. Her eyes furrowed with a look of fear, and possibly remorse.

"I'm sorry," she said, wiping away another tear.

"For what?"

Candace's eyes shifted, looking somewhere past Kili's shoulder. The sound of a door locking echoed behind her, followed immediately by the clicks of several firearms being cocked. Before she could move, Kili felt the cold steel of a gun barrel pressed tight against the back of her neck.

"Don't do nothin' stupid," hissed a harsh male voice from over her shoulder. "Now, I reckon yer probably carryin'. You'd best just sit tight 'til Candy here searches you."

Kili sat frozen in her chair as Candace glided around the table, a tight grin creasing her face. The little hussy had been playing her like a fiddle. The tears. The apology. The pleas to keep Crane away from her. All of it had been a lie. One look in the waitress' cold brown eyes told her that she was enjoying this —a little too much perhaps.

Candace patted her down, came to the holster nestled inside

her jacket, and extricated the .380. She handed the weapon to the man behind her, and continued the search. After another minute, she looked up, and shook her head. "That's it."

For a moment, all was deafeningly silent in the bar. The sound of the rain striking at the pub's tin roof, the rumble of distant thunder, and a single nervous cough from somewhere behind her were the only noises she heard.

"Good," the man finally said. "Okay, sweet thing, I want you to stand up." The gun pressed tighter against the skin of her neck—a reminder that she had no choice in the matter. Kili complied, raising her hands in the air, and sliding from her chair in one swift motion. "A'right. Now turn around....real slow like."

She did as she was told to see eight figures standing in a semi-circle in the dimly lit bar...all shrouded in dark hooded cloaks and balaclavas obscuring their faces. Two figures wearing ski masks stood erect at the door, shotguns resting casually against their forearms. The others dotted the room, hugging the shadows as best they could, and attempting to present a shadowy nightmarish image for her. But despite the weapons they were brandishing, Kili found herself more amused than frightened. She knew that no matter how hard they attempted to hide their identities, each person in the room at that moment had more than likely been there the day before when she'd demanded information from an apathetic crowd. Though she wasn't sure of the exact nature of this little encounter, she knew it was designed more to frighten her than anything else. At least, she hoped so.

She stood unmoving, looking each person in their shadow-shrouded face. She stopped when her eyes came upon one figure considerably shorter, and thinner than the rest. He seemed to be trembling uncontrollably under the folds of a cheap set of graduation robes. Probably the one who'd coughed a few seconds before.

"Eddie Johnson," she said, throwing the smaller man a stern, maternal glare. "What do you think you're doing?"

The hooded weasel went rigid for a brief second, and glanced around frantically. He then took a single step back, and turned his cowled face toward the peanut-strewn floor.

"What's all this about?" she said, wishing she was confident enough to handle the rest of the motley band as easily as she had Squirrelly. "For your information, you are illegally holding an officer of the Federal Bureau of Investigation…a very serious felony." She turned her gaze to Candace and scowled. The woman merely shrugged coolly, and moved over to the closest man to Kili…the one who'd held the pistol to her head. She then slid her arms around his waist and pulled close to him.

"You don't scare us," Candace said with a cruel smile. "Without that devil, Crane, around, you ain't nothin'. And you sure as heck ain't no Fed."

The man with the pistol, a .357 from what she could tell, shoved the waitress roughly away, and stepped toward Kili.

"Here's what's gonna happen," he said. "Yer gonna drop this little investigation, and go on home. Yer gonna forget about your brother, and move on."

Kili stared at the man incredulously. Was this guy for real? Did he really think she would just drop everything on his say-so and leave town? *Leave town*…the memory stopped her in her tracks. He'd also called her *Sweet thing*.

"Sheriff Tyler, is that you?" she asked.

His only response was to lift the weapon in line with her head. "This ain't no game, girl," he said with a growl. If she'd shaken him up by discovering his true identity, he wasn't going to let her know it. "This whole affair ain't none of yer business. One-Eyed Jack, the Devil's Teeth…all of it…is Boone Creek's problem. Not yours. You're stirring up a hornets' nest around here, and we'll be the ones left to clean up the mess long after you're long gone." He paused. "I promise. The moment we find out what happened to your brother, you'll be the first to know."

Kili's mouth went dry as she stared at the gaping hole of the gun's barrel. This wasn't funny anymore. They weren't joking. If she didn't forget about finding Cian, she might end up just as "missing" as him. That thought struck her hard, and she couldn't help wonder if her brother had had a similar "town hall meeting" himself.

"You...you know I can't leave," she said, trying her best to keep her gelatinous legs from folding underneath her. The realization that these people were dead serious about putting a stop to her investigation had rattled her far more than she would have expected. "He's my brother."

"Who is more than likely dead," another voice said harshly from the shadows.

"Be smart, young lady," said a third, slightly kinder voice. "Yer not welcome in these parts. Get out while yer able."

Without a word, every single hooded figure leveled a weapon at her...a sign that they had no interest in negotiating. She would either comply with their demands or she would die. It was as simple as that.

This can't be happening, she thought. *It's unreal. This kind of thing just doesn't happen.*

She had no idea what she was going to do. She could, of course, agree to leave, and then simply return, but knew that would be futile. She'd find herself in the exact same situation again if she stayed...or worse, she might not even have the luxury of threats next time. She could, of course, renege, and then call a few friends of hers with the Bureau—but without evidence to support the threats, there would be nothing they could do. And the case still didn't fall under the FBI's jurisdiction. Of course, she could flat out refuse their demands, which would likely result in her death, making that option the least appealing of all.

No, the only real option she had was to agree to their terms. But how could she? How could she give up on Cian so easily? Crane believed he was still alive. Leaving now could condemn him.

"John, look at her," Candace said with a sneer. "She ain't gonna leave. She'll keep on diggin'. It's bad enough she's usin' Crane, but she's gonna stir up One-Eyed Jack even more if she keeps pokin' around. He'll come into Boone Creek. Kill us all."

The man gripped the revolver tighter as the waitress spoke. It looked as if he was unsure of himself...as if he was trying to decide what to do next. But Candace wasn't finished. She leaned in closer, her lips pressing up against his hood in a seductive whisper.

"Me and you both know there's only one way to deal with this." She glared at Kili. "Her brother deserved what he got, and so does she."

A mixed wave of fear and rage roiled around in Kili's mind, battling for dominance. She didn't know whether to cry or pounce on the little slut with all her fury. Involuntarily, her fingers clenched together, balling into a tight fist.

"Tsk tsk, Ms. Brennan," Sheriff Tyler drawled from underneath his hood, hefting his pistol for emphasis. "I wouldn't do that if I was you. Candy here might be a bit cold-hearted, but I'm beginnin' to suspect she's right in this respect. Though I'm of a mind to believe her motives ain't entirely noble—after what yer brother did to her, who can really blame her—but I honestly don't see you taking our little pow-wow here to heart." His shoulders shrugged from inside his robes. "Now what are we supposed to do about that?"

"John, what the heck are you sayin'?" someone asked. "You ain't seriously thinkin' about—"

"Never you mind what I'm thinkin' at the present, Nat," Tyler said, his gun still trained on Kili's head. "We all agreed to this... agreed to do whatever needed doin'. Somethin' in the Hollar is riled up, whether it's ol' One-Eye or not. Our lives, and the lives of our kin are in danger, and the way I reckon it, it's all her brother's fault." He glanced over at Candace briefly, and turned back to Kili. "Now I really am sorry about this, but I honestly don't know no other way."

He pulled the hammer back on his revolver, and steadied his aim, exhaling deeply as he prepared to fire.

Then, the entire building shook with a blast of thunder roaring overhead. The front door burst open, and a gust of wind whipped through the bar, kicking up dust and debris along the floor as it passed. In unison, all eight of the hooded figures, as well as Candace, wheeled around to see a foreboding shadow filling up the doorway. A collection of gasps and one sniveling squeal erupted from several of the onlookers. A streak of lightning flashed, illuminating the exterior of the building for a brief second, and every single soul went rigid at the sight of Esther "Granny" Crane leering at them, a smoldering wooden pipe clenched in her teeth, and a thick hickory staff held tight in her hand.

The old woman's eyes burned at the onlookers.

"*They* told me what was a'goin' on here," she said, unmistakable menace in her voice as she exhaled a plume of smoke. "But I didn't believe 'em. Nearly called the whole lot of 'em liars." She stepped into the bar, letting the door slam thunderously behind her. "After all, I never thought in a million years you idjits would be this plum stupid."

She took another step into the interior of the bar, and slammed her staff down on the floor. Immediately, a crack of thunder erupted above, and the single overhead light flashed out, plunging the bar into darkness. A series of shrieks echoed around the room, but were stifled a second later when the power came back on...this time bringing with it every light in the bar showering the entire establishment with brilliant illumination.

No one moved. Each man's weapon was all but forgotten as Mrs. Crane's narrowed eyes scanned the room.

If Ezekiel was an instrument of the Devil to these people, Esther Crane was a vengeful angel of the Almighty, ready to bring judgment on the wicked. Where they feared the grandson, they stood in reverent awe of the old woman. Complete respect, admiration, and yes, fear of a different sort as well. She was clearly the matriarch of this community and no one, not even the pugnacious sheriff or the drunken harlot, would dare question her authority.

She stalked across the room, the robed and fatigues-wearing figures parting as she passed like Moses and the Red Sea. As she approached Kili, her wrath-filled eyes softened, and a warm, comforting smile spread across her face.

"Are you a'right, dear?" she asked, holding out her left hand to her. Her right still gripped the staff tight.

Kili nodded, unable to speak, but taking hold of the proffered hand. Seeing the woman this way, in this context—the respect she commanded, the thunder and lightning, and the fearless ferocity of her entrance—Kili knew that this was no ordinary lady, and she found herself admiring the elder Crane a great deal more than before.

The old woman beamed before wheeling around to face the others. She glared at each one of them, as if her ancient eyes could pierce through the shadow of each hood to stare directly into their souls. After every last one of them stood trembling in her presence, she spoke. Her voice was not particularly pleasant.

"Now," she almost growled the words. "I'm takin' Ms. Brennan out of here. Do you'uns have any objections?"

She paused, waiting for anyone to speak up. When they didn't, she began moving back toward the door with Kili in tow.

"Good," she said as she strode past them. She came to the door, but turned to face them before opening it. "But just one more thing. This sweet lady is *my* guest—and therefore, under my protection. Not Ezekiel's. If you so much as look at her funny, you'll be insultin' me, and I know none of you'uns want that. Right?"

To the man, each shook their head in a wary negative. Mrs. Crane merely nodded and opened the door, gesturing for Kili to step out of the bar. She complied, and the old lady followed.

Oddly enough, the rain had already stopped by the time the two walked out into the open air. A steady gust of wind still whipped past their heads, but the downpour and thunder had abruptly stopped.

"They didn't hurt you, did they?" she asked, squeezing Kili's hand tight as they walked through Bailey's gravel parking lot.

"No. Just scared me more than anything."

"Well, that ain't nothin' a good swig of my homemade Apple Pie whiskey can't cure," the old woman beamed, directing her toward the large Humvee parked diagonally in the lot.

"The Hummer...it's yours?" Kili asked.

"Well, of course it is." Granny moved around to the passenger side, and opened the door for Kili, then moved to the driver's side and climbed in. "Who'd you think it belonged to? Ezekiel?"

Kili merely nodded as she pulled the seatbelt over her shoulder and locked it in place.

The old woman practically cackled. "Ha! That ol' fuddy-duddy of a grandson wouldn't be caught dead in somethin' so 'pretentious', as he calls it." She started the engine, and pulled out of the lot. "Though it was his fortune what paid fer it."

She said the last with a proud smile, and wink at Kili as they drove toward the Crane homestead.

CHAPTER
TWELVE

Boone Creek
October 15
2:15 AM

C andace Staples staggered out of Bailey's Pub at a brisk, but unsteady gait, determined to walk off the rage burning in her gut—not to mention the Wild Turkey she'd been consuming since her encounter with Ezekiel Crane earlier that night. The brief four-block hike back to her car might do her some good, she thought.

Sheriff Tyler had, of course, offered to drive her home, but she knew exactly what that meant...knew precisely what that Neanderthal intended for his act of chivalry, and she wanted no part of it. After all, there was nothing in this world that John Anderson Tyler could offer her. Besides, she needed time to herself to stew over the way the others had cowered in front of that creepy old hag...how they caved to her every demand like she was the queen or something. Just like they always did.

But then, what had she expected? Nothing in this coal pit of a town ever changed. It was why she wanted so desperately to pick up, leave, and never look back.

The one gleam of hope she'd had in recent memory was the arrival of the anthropologist, Cian Brennan, to Boone Creek. He was going to be her one-way ticket out. Her plan had been simple, yet perfect in its simplicity. Get to know the redheaded doctor, lure him in with the pleasures of the flesh, and make him fall in love with her. A few love charms and potions she'd picked up over the years wouldn't hurt either, of course.

And it had all worked so perfectly too. Her feminine wiles, and no little raw sexual charisma, had worked its own kind of magic. Or so she'd thought.

Then, the night before Cian's "disappearance", they'd gotten into an argument. He'd always had some hesitation about getting too serious with her. Some hang up about being from two different worlds—two different cultures. In essence, he thought he was just too good for her. She knew that. Everyone in town did. But the night before he disappeared, he'd gone from vaguely apprehensive to absolutely furious with her. Somehow, he'd found out about the final stage of her plan. The *coup de gras*. The sure fire way she knew would hook him. He'd confronted her, in front of God and everyone about how she was intentionally trying to get pregnant to trap him into taking her with him when he left. He'd been furious. He'd practically laughed in her face in front of everyone at Bailey's, and said he never wanted to see her again.

The uppity jerk, she thought as she swayed toward the empty parking lot of Handy Andy's. She'd parked it near the woods behind the old diner, which in hindsight, might not have been a very good idea considering how much trouble she was having walking. *Who did he think he was? He thought he was so much better than me. So much above me. Well, my! How things have changed, haven't they, Cian?*

Candace allowed a cruel, vindictive smile to creep up her

face as she fumbled inside her purse for her car keys. It served him right, what happened to him. Using her the way he did. Getting what he wanted from her, and just discarding her like yesterday's rubbish. Now, she was sure, he was getting his comeuppance, and the thought pleased her more than she would have ever imagined.

She stumbled over to the driver's side door, but before she could insert her keys into the lock, they slipped from her alcohol-numbed fingers onto the gravel. With a curse, she carefully stooped down and picked them up. As she rose, her world suddenly whirled around her in a wave of dizziness. She closed her eyes tight to shut out the alcohol-induced vertigo, but it just made things worse. Her dinner slowly made its way up her throat and she retched, trying to keep the food down. The effort only made the drunken haze worse. Without preamble, she fell forward, face first, onto the parking lot, and drifted slowly out of consciousness. All was growing black. But just before her mind teetered toward oblivion, she had the most unpleasant sensation of something hovering above her immobilized frame...something that seemed to chuckle malevolently at her. A chuckle all too familiar.

KILI SULKED in the passenger seat of the Hummer as Esther Crane drove expertly over the snaking mountain road that lead up to her home. She couldn't get her encounter at the bar out of her mind. It had all been so surreal. So bizarre. What were they hiding? What didn't they want her to discover in her search for her missing brother?

"You look exhausted," Mrs. Crane said, keeping her hands firmly on the ten and two o'clock positions of the steering wheel; her thumbs gently moving back and forth on the faux leather.

Kili glanced at the dashboard clock. Its green glow revealed that it was approaching three in the morning. No wonder she was exhausted...she'd gotten only a couple of hours of rest. However, for the moment, sleep would have to wait. There's no way she'd be able to relax enough to sleep now. Besides, in a few hours, dawn would break, and she and Crane would make their way up to the Devil's Teeth, the Stonehenge-like monument her brother had been researching before he disappeared. She wasn't about to miss that for the world. Too much was at stake, and she knew there'd be plenty of time to sleep later.

"I'll be fine," she said, smiling at the elderly woman. "A few cups of hot coffee, and I'll be as good as new."

Mrs. Crane nodded at that. "They didn't scare you off?"

"No way," Kili growled. "If anything, they just pissed me off." She paused for a second, then gazed at the old woman. "Who were they? I know Tyler, that waitress, and Eddie Johnson were there, but who else? And why did they go to all that trouble—disguising themselves with those ridiculous getups—to frighten me away?"

Granny chuckled. "They're a bunch of drunken peckerwoods, is what they are," she said. "And I'd say most of 'em were just scared. Superstitious, the entire lot of 'em."

She paused for a few seconds, as if thinking, then listed those she suspected had been part of it.

"Let's see, I'm pretty sure there was Nathaniel Morrow... people just call him Nat. He's a coal miner and widower...father of six. A decent enough man, when he is sober anyway.

"Also, I think I spotted Tom Thornton. He's the foreman with Tegalta Mining. Nat's boss, actually. He's the son of a disgraced Baptist preacher who got mixed up with some pretty unsavory— some rather dark things. Tom's no better than his daddy. He even started his own little 'church' up in the mountains a few years back. Not sure who it is they worship up there, but it sure ain't the Lord. Some say they've taken to worshipping the old spirits that still dwell in the darker corners of the hills around here."

Kili laughed. "And that's weird for you, how? Aren't you a witch? You talk to faeries, don't you? What's so different?"

The old woman's face drew stern, her eyes narrowed for several seconds before softening again. "I forget you ain't from around these parts," she finally said. "There's a big difference in what I do and what they do. First of all, I worship no one but our Lord and Savior. We're a God-fearin' Christian people around here...no matter what it might seem. And my 'witchery' is little more than an exceptional understandin' of the world He created. Some might call it science if they'd open their minds up enough to take a decent gander at what it is that I do. That's the way, Ezekiel sees it, anyway.

"As for the Yunwi Tsunsdi...you're right. They are not of the material world by no stretch," she said. "A more ornery lot of spirits would be hard to find. But they also ain't 'evil' neither. They's God's critters too, and they bow down to Him when it's all said and done, though I ain't sure they know anythin' about grace. But the things Thornton and his ilk bow down to up in his old church...they's the type what ain't got names. At least none that we mortals can remember anyhow. Even the Yunwi Tsunsdi refuse to speak of 'em...once you name somethin', after all, you call 'em to ya. And that, my dear, is somethin' no one with any God-given sense wants to do."

Kili sat silently, absorbing what she'd just heard. It just sounded so unbelievable. The old woman seemed so wise...so worldly. How could she believe in such nonsense? Even worse, how could she *not* see that her way of life was little different than those of Tom Thornton and his church?

Still, despite the hypocritical paradox in Granny's tirade, it sounded like Thornton might have been a pretty good candidate to add to her suspect list. If his church was as evil as she was being led to believe...worshipping some strange, dark gods...

then maybe there's some sort of connection between them and the Devil's Teeth, a place that was supposedly just as old and dark.

Letting out a breath, she decided to move back to the topic at hand. "Okay, who else was there?"

"Well, let's see," Granny said as she turned onto her long, dirt driveway. "If I'm not mistaken, and I rarely am, I'd bet my bottom dollar that old Noah McGuffin was there too."

"Noah McGuffin?"

"Yep. Boone Creek's resident, um, how do I put this? Pharmacist would be the nice way of sayin' it."

"You mean a drug dealer?"

She shook her head. "No, not exactly. More a supplier than anything else. His pa got him started few years back growing weed. Recently, from what I hear, he's moved on to other things. Prescription pain meds like Oxycontin. Dabbles in Zanax and some other nasty stuff too. Rumor has it, he's been sick of late. Sounds like it might be serious, but it hasn't affected his operation at all with his adopted daughter running the show."

"And he's partnering with the sheriff to scare me away from my investigation?"

Mrs. Crane belted out a hoarse laugh. "That ain't exactly the only thing those two are partners in, dear. John Tyler couldn't care less about McGuffin's business...just so long as he gets a cut in the profits." She paused for a second, then added, "And as long as he gets re-elected too...which is something Noah can definitely make happen, if he has a mind to do it."

Kili was thinking about this as the Hummer pulled up next to the Crane home. The sky over the horizon was almost a purple black. The moon was hidden behind a brace of dark clouds, allowing the constellations to explode with dazzling light above.

"Well, why would McGuffin care if I went looking for Cian?" Kili finally asked as they both climbed out the SUV. "I mean, it's not like I'm interested in his drug running operation."

"Well, McGuffin's property...especially his, um, less-than-legal property, runs up into the Hollars. From what I understand, the Devil's Teeth rests right in the middle of one of his fields," the elder Crane said.

They made their way up onto the front porch, when a familiar sound caught her attention. She stopped, whirling around in search of the playing children.

"Ms. Brennan?" Granny asked, placing a hand on her shoulder.

Kili turned back to look at the older woman, bewilderment on her face. "Sorry. I keep hearing these kids laughing. Heard them at least three times today before now."

Granny placed her other hand on Kili's free shoulder, and turned her to face her. The woman's face was grim. Concerned. "When did it start, dear?"

Kili shrugged. "Uh, I don't know. I guess when Mr. Crane and I were about to step into the Dark Hollows." She felt her legs shaking. The way Granny was looking at her—as if trying to peer deep inside her heart and soul—was unnerving her. "Then, later at the hospital when we saw Leroy Kingston. And finally, on the phone...when Candace called to set up that meeting."

The old woman nodded. "And you say the only thing you hear is children laughing? Nothing else? No words? No singing?"

Kili shook her head. "I don't think so." *No singing? What is that supposed to mean?*

Granny continued to stare at her for several uncomfortable moments before her warm smile returned. "Ah, it's probably nothin'. Just you bein' tired and concerned for yer brother, is all." She gestured toward the front door, and they walked inside the cozy house in silence. Kili noted that the door wasn't even locked, and found herself envying the simple life the old woman had made for herself here in the mountains.

Once inside, she was again directed to the living room where she plopped down onto the sofa, pulled off her shoes, and kicked her feet up on a nearby ottoman.

"I so need some sleep," she said with a yawn. But she knew that even if she had time, it would be no easy task for slumber to come. She had too much to think about. The strange ethereal laughter she kept hearing. Thornton and his cult. And McGuffin. He was a fantastic suspect to consider as well. After all, Cian would have been conducting his research right in the middle of "Pot Central". The drug dealer would have had ample reason to want her brother to disappear.

Mrs. Crane smiled at her. "I'll go make you a cup of hot coffee," she said. "Ezekiel will be home soon, and will want to get started up to the Devil's Teeth at dawn. It won't do for you to be dog tired when he gets here."

Once Granny was out of the room, Kili closed her eyes, and drifted off into a dreamless sleep.

CHAPTER
THIRTEEN

C andace Staples awoke with a pounding headache, and no idea where she was. The rich, earthy scent of the outdoors greeted her hypersensitive nostrils before she even had the strength to crack open an eye. Whatever she was laying on felt soft and spongy against her aching back.

Why was her back in so much pain though? What had she done to it?

Probably slept on it wrong, she thought, bringing a hand up to her face, and wiping a small stream of drool from the corner of her mouth. At least, she hoped it was drool. Her vertigo-inducing haze told her she was still quite intoxicated. So, she supposed, whatever she wiped from her mouth could have been just about anything.

It wasn't the first time she'd awakened in a strange place after a night of too much whiskey. By now, she was getting used to the mysteries she'd invariably incur when she was drunk. All part of the 'joyous wonder' of alcohol dependence, she liked to tell people.

Okay, Candy. Time to get up, and make your way back home.

With a sigh, she cracked her eyelids open, and looked up. It was still dark. Crickets and other insects chirped and buzzed all around her. A vast canopy of trees sprawled overhead, like a needlepoint of wood erected to offer her shelter from the elements.

Geeze, I must have wandered off into the woods behind the restaurant, and passed out. Candace chided herself for being so stupid. The woods had never been one of her favorite places to be. Especially at night. There were just too many icky things with teeth lurking around for her tastes.

But despite her desire to get out of the forest and back home as soon as possible, Candace found herself unable to move. Her muscles were just too tense. The pain in her head and back were too severe to allow for any sudden movements. So, she decided to take in the sights around her to acclimate herself.

The first thing she noticed upon her second inspection was the thirteen huge stones that loomed around her. Thirteen, gigantic, moss-covered, flat stones. Stones displaying strange, primitive symbols painted in bright red and orange. Symbols of animals and strange creatures. Swirling things and giant birds. Macabre skull-like face drawings, and other terrifying things. But that wasn't the worst of it. The stones also resembled a series of jagged teeth jutting up from the earth's soil like a gaping mouth swung open to swallow anything that walked into it.

A wave of panic crashed down on her nerves with the realization at what she was seeing.

Dear Lord, she attempted to say against a set of paralyzed vocal cords, but it was useless. She couldn't get a single sound to escape from her clenched throat. *The Devil's Teeth. I'm inside the Devil's Teeth!*

She tried to rise, but her muscles wouldn't budge; as if they were lashed down to the soil with iron cords. She raised her head and examined herself. No, there were no ropes or other bonds keeping her in place, but still she couldn't move. And it was slowly dawning on her that whatever was keeping her immobilized had nothing to do with her blood alcohol content. It was something else. Something unseen. Something menacing just outside her periphery.

Her heart thumped in her chest as she unsuccessfully heaved against her invisible bonds. It was useless.

She turned her head and glanced down at the ground in hopes of getting a better grasp of her situation. She was lying on a plush blanket of bright green moss with several strange looking mushrooms sprouting up in bright, multi-colored clusters. The bedding was as soft as velvet and wondrously comfortable against her bare skin—so calming. Relaxing. Despite her dire circumstances, the organic mattress on which she rested beckoned for her to roll over, and go back to sleep.

My skin! The thought of her bare skin touching the lichen snapped her out of the lulling slumber that called to her. She glanced down at her body again. She was completely nude. Not a strip of clothing covered her thin frame. *What's happening? How did I get here?*

There was no way she could have stumbled drunkenly all the way to the Dark Hollows. It was nearly thirty miles away from the diner. Much farther on foot, traversing the rugged mountains. She couldn't have possibly walked here. And what about her clothes? Had she stripped herself or were they removed by someone—or something—else?

She felt certain that it had been someone else. Her dazed mind sliced through the haze of her memory, sorting through the broken images of the past few hours, trying to piece everything together. She remembered leaving Bailey's, and collapsing near her car. Nearly passing out. She remembered a presence standing above her, and laughing. A laugh that seemed vaguely familiar to her. An ominous, deep-throated chortle that tugged at the primal reptilian brain in the back of her mind. A dread that rushed through her veins when she thought about it even now.

Where have I heard that laugh before? Surely, only in her most disturbing nightmares. It hadn't sounded like anything a human could make. And yet, it had to be. *Right?*

She decided it best to take a better look around, and the only way to do that would be to sit up. Slowly, she willed herself up onto her elbows. The effort was enormous, but she finally managed to do it despite feeling as if the gravity within the ruins had increased five times greater than normal. Finally leaning up on her elbows, she pulled her legs around, and positioned herself into a crawling position. She attempted to raise herself fully to her feet, but the effort was beyond any strength she had left.

So she resolved to crawl her way out of the Teeth. She knew she had to get away no matter what...even if she was forced to do so on hands and knees.

She looked around to gather her bearings, but soon realized it was impossible. She was surrounded on all sides by thirteen monolithic stones that looked to be about twenty feet tall each. Beyond that was an impenetrable wall of thick vegetation made up of both a large patch of Noah McGuffin's marijuana crop and the haunted woods of the Dark Hollows.

There was no way to escape—naked as she was—through the rough terrain. Even if she managed to scrabble out of the ancient ruins, there was no way to find her way back to Boone Creek. She'd dropped her purse in the parking lot of the restaurant when she passed out, and hadn't found it upon awakening, so she didn't even have her cell phone with her.

Trying hard to forget these unnerving thoughts, she began moving slowly along the soft, moss covered ground, making her way toward what she assumed was the northern most stone. If she remembered correctly, the town lay due north from the center of the Hollows. It was as good a direction as any to start.

She crawled several feet, feeling her way with trembling hands, when suddenly she found herself in open space, and falling headlong into a shallow pit. She hit the bottom about three feet down, jarring teeth and bone, but otherwise uninjured. Carefully, she turned over, and used her hands to push herself from the dirt floor of the pit, only to feel a heavy cylindrical object half-buried in the soil.

Instinctively, she reached for it, and brought the thing up to her face for a better look. It was long and smooth, dark brown in color; then she screamed. Her muscles went rigid in disgust as she realized what she was now holding. With a squeal, she threw the object to the ground. *A bone! A human bone!* To an arm or a leg, she didn't know for sure. She looked down at where her hands rested firmly on the freshly dug soil, and began to make out the shape of other bones, then with a little sifting of the dirt, a skull.

I'm in a grave!

But it was a grave for no human she'd ever seen. The skull she'd uncovered was monstrous—easily three times as large as any human she'd ever seen. Just as the realization struck her, a plume of phosphorescent green mist arose from the desecrated remains, engulfing her in a suffocating haze. She scrambled to extricate herself from the pit, but the strange cloud clung to her with unseen, clasping claws.

Panicked and with every ounce of her being, she pushed herself off the ground, and scrambled hand over feet out of the grave. Once free, she crawled—clawing her way over the mossy ground—to get as far away from the ghastly apparition as possible. Two feet. Three feet. She glanced over her shoulder, but the cloud of green was expanding. Moving toward her with savage purpose. Four feet. Five. Then, exhausted, her elbows buckled under her, and she crashed to the ground with a groan. She rolled around, waiting for the thing to envelop her once more, but when she looked, it was gone.

In its place, however, stood the shadowy figure of a man. He was standing mere inches away from the open grave, and Candace squinted to make out whatever features she could. But the light was just too dim. For all she knew, he was merely another phantasm come to carry her soul to hell for the things she'd done in this rotten, contemptible life.

As if fulfilling her own prophecy, the figure stalked toward her, bent down, and grabbed her ankle. She kicked and screamed, but nothing she did had any impact on her tormentor. Instead, he pulled her back toward the hole in the ground from which she'd just escaped. Back toward the open grave with the huge, malformed skull and bones. With a final jerk at her ankle, she plummeted back into the ground. She rolled over, looking up at her abductor, but it was as if a shroud of darkness hovered inexplicably over his features, obscuring her view.

"Brother?" the shadowman said. His voice seemed pained. Scared. Maybe even hurt. "Is that you?"

Brother? Candace thought. *Oh, God! I'm dealing with one of them psycho killers!*

Though she wasn't hopeful, a small part of her wondered if she might reason with him. Make him see he'd kidnapped the wrong person. It was a slim shot, but she had to try something.

"N-no," she said; her voice quivering. Tears streaked her face. As much as she tried, she was unable to turn off the waterworks. "I'm n-not your...your brother. My name is Candace. A girl."

The figure cocked his head to one side.

"P-please," she said. "Help me."

"Candy?" the man said. His voice sounded almost childlike. "What are you doing here? You're not supposed to be here. They'll kill you if they find you here. Like they did Miles. Like they tried to do with me."

Candace's heart pounded in her chest. The voice was familiar again. So familiar. But something wasn't right about it, though she couldn't quite put her finger on it.

Soon, however, the figure took a single step forward—into a single beam of moonlight breaking through the trees above. Candace gasped.

"Cian?" she asked, a well of hope bubbling up at the sight of her former lover. But, like his voice, something was different about him. He seemed taller somehow. Maybe even a bit misshapen. Then, Candace realized it was probably just a simple trick of the light and her own frazzled senses, and her hope returned. At least his face—his sweet, freckled face—was still the same. "Is that you?"

The man smiled at her, his thick mane of bright red hair seemed to shine within the white glow of the moonlight. His tattered clothes hung limp around his portly frame. Candace had never been so glad to see him in her whole life. She was even willing to forgive him for dumping her so callously last week.

"Of course, it's me, Candy," Cian said, his smile fading quickly to one of gut-wrenching sorrow. "But you're not supposed to be here. They're coming, Candy. My brothers are coming and so are those who want to control them."

"Cian, what are you talking about?" Panic surged anew through her veins. Something was wrong. The man was confused. Maybe even insane. "I'm scared. Just take me home. Please?"

"They're coming, Candy! Run! I can't hold them much long—"

But the man's words were cut off from his own screaming lips. Candace watched in horror as Cian's face stretched into an impossible angle, shaping itself into something...someone else. The grotesque transformation reminded her of something her boy, Jimmy, might do with a glob of Silly Putty, but this was so much different.

The anthropologist's face distorted and convulsed. His rich head of red hair shifted and shimmered, transforming into a flowing mane of sandy blonde. His face now sprouted the telltale signs of a stubbly goatee and mustache. And suddenly, Candace was staring into the cold, unnerving eyes of Ezekiel Crane.

"No!" she screamed. "No! What is happening? This can't be real!"

Crane grinned maliciously at her. "Oh, but it *is* real, Candace Staples. It's very very real," Crane drawled. "But you're not supposed to be here. They are coming. My brothers are finally coming, and woe to any who stand in our way."

"What does that mean?" she said. "What are you talking about?"

"You should have told me the truth," Crane said, glowering down at her from the lip of the grave. An ancient tomahawk suddenly materialized in his hand. "I told you. I told you I had ways of discovering the truth, but you didn't listen."

Candace pushed with the heels of her feet, inching backwards until she was pressed against the grave's wall. But the tall, lanky devil of a man lowered himself into the pit with her. Tears streaked down her cheeks as she sobbed. "Why? Why are you doing this to me?"

"It's not me, Ms. Staples," Crane said, hefting the weapon above his head. "It's him. One-Eyed Jack. And soon, he'll be reunited with his brothers once more."

"Please." It was all she could say between sobbing gasps. She clenched her eyes shut, wishing beyond hope to awaken from this horrible nightmare. "Please."

"It is time," said another voice entirely. She cracked her eye open to see something entirely different than Ezekiel Crane looming over her. The apparition had shifted once more and the sight that now greeted her tear-soaked eyes was something from the stuff of nightmares. Malformed. Massive. Easily twelve feet tall, and maybe half as wide. It was neither human nor animal. Not physical, but not quite spiritual either. It was a giant creature with one, glowing green eye set into a black void of a face.

"It's time for you to return to the land of your ancestors, Candy," the creature said, with no malice or anger in its voice. There was very little emotion at all to it really. "To make room for those who will walk the earth again."

And the spectral form of One-Eyed Jack, raising his toma-hawk above his head, was the last thing Candace Staples ever saw.

The Crane Homestead
October 15
5:30 AM

KILI BRENNAN WAS nudged awake by the indecipherable whispers and giggles of a small child at her ear. She opened her eyes, but the only person standing in front of her was the old woman, holding a plate containing a steaming mug of coffee and handful of biscuits with blackberry jam. She groggily glanced at her watch.

5:30 AM.

Geeze, she thought with a simultaneous yawn. *How long did I sleep?*

"Thought I'd let you get some rest," Mrs. Crane said. "But Ezekiel called. His autopsy is finished, and he's on his way home now. Thought it best to give you some coffee to wake you up, but wasn't sure what you wanted in it. So I brought you some sugar cubes and creamer." She placed the tray on the coffee table in front of her, and then sat down in the overstuffed chair to Kili's right.

Kili prepared her drink to her taste, and took a sip. It was nearly as euphoric as the sweet tea she had the day before. But despite the caffeine, there was just something in it that seemed to ease all her tension. With each sip, she began to feel better than she had in days.

"Tell me about Ezekiel," Kili finally said, setting the mug down, and taking a bite of one of the moist jam-covered biscuits.

The old woman beamed at the mention of her grandson's name.

"Oh, such a special boy," she said. "Bright as the noonday sun. Gifted beyond my wildest dreams. No finer man will you ever meet on this side of creation, I think."

Kili nodded at this, then cocked her head nervously as she prepared to ask the difficult question that had been gnawing at her since her first encounter with the enigmatic mountain man. Fortunately, the old woman anticipated the question.

"You want to know why the townspeople feel the way they do about him," Mrs. Crane said, her smile disappearing slightly, replaced with a pained look. "I suppose it's a fair enough question... and one better suited for Ezekiel to tell you when he's ready." The elder Crane paused for a second, then sighed. "But, because I don't reckon I can expect you to trust my grandson without a little trust in return, I will say this...my grandson is a Seventh Son of a Seventh Son—normally a station of high honor around here. They are revered. Lauded as great spiritual men, and able to cure all sorts of ailments. Ezekiel was destined to fulfill that very purpose...until the car crash what kilt his pa—my son—and his ma and six older brothers." Her eyes closed as she spoke, as if soaking in some bittersweet memory. "I won't go into detail, but needless to say, all but one younger brother and sister were killed instantly. Ezekiel had stayed home...playin' hooky from church. And that's how it all started."

Kili stopped chewing her biscuit. "That's it?" she asked. "That makes no sense. Why would everyone fear him because of that?"

Esther Crane shook her head mournfully. "I said that's how it started, dear. Not how it ended," she said. "For whatever reason, the townsfolk found it peculiar that Ezekiel hadn't been in the car that day. I never knew why. But their suspicions about him only grew with time. By the time he was thirteen, they'd all but accused him of having something to do with his family's own death. It didn't help matters that he'd developed a deep-seated relationship with Asherah Richardson. A black girl, orphaned at birth, and raised by that rascal Noah McGuffin. A white boy in love with a black girl in these parts...well, you can imagine the scandal.

"But it certainly didn't help none that she started takin' up with black magic, just like her mama. And was completely open about it, I might add. Poor Ezekiel then became guilty by association. If Asherah practiced black magic, then it was only natural to assume my grandson did too."

"Did he?" Kili heard herself asking before she realized how insensitive the question was.

Mrs. Crane seemed to think about it for a moment, then gave a slight nod. "Maybe. He's never said actually. But I suspect he may have dabbled in it a bit as a teen." She took a sip of coffee, then gave an even more confidant nod. "No, I know for a fact he participated in at least one dark magic ritual. One I'd forbade him to do. But Asherah, twisted by her own rearing and love of chaos, convinced him otherwise. He went ahead with the ritual —a summoning spell of the darkest kind—and..." Her voice trailed off. A single tear escaped from one corner of her closed eyes and swept down her left cheek.

"And?'

Granny opened her eyes, and looked back at her. "And he's never been the same since."

Kili absorbed the information, then spoke. "And the townspeople found out about the ritual? That's why they're so afraid of him?"

The older woman nodded once more. "Among other things. They believe he's cursed, Ms. Brennan. Marked."

"Why would they think that?"

"Well, fer starters, because he is. Ever since that night...that ritual...Death has followed my grandson like a coon dog after table scraps his whole life. Throughout his life, people he's become close to have simply died. Some of the strangest deaths you've ever seen too. Sometimes, the deaths have been people that had wronged Ezekiel in some way. People who've hurt him in the past."

"So the people are afraid of him because of that? Because they think he has the power to bring death down on them?" Kili asked.

Mrs. Crane let out a soft chuckle. "Oh, that's just one of the reasons they're so afraid of him, dear. Just one of many. You should hear the stories told 'bout Ezekiel Crane. They even say he can speak to the Dead as easy as he can speak to you or me."

Kili sat on the couch, staring at the old woman; unaware that she was holding her breath. After several seconds, she cleared her throat, attempting to wrest control of her atrophied voice.

"And can he?" she asked. She couldn't believe she was seriously asking the question. "Speak to the Dead, I mean?"

The elder Crane took a sip of coffee before answering. "Maybe. Maybe not. Ghosts of all kinds haunt the hills and valleys of the Appalachians, Ms. Brennan. Lots of stories about the dead walking amongst us, and the precious few what are gifted to talk to them. But he's never told me one way or another if he's one of them, and I don't reckon he ever will." She let out a short cackle at some internal joke, then continued. "Between you and me, I think he kind of likes the mystery of it all."

"The mystery of what?" came a voice from the hallway. A second later, Ezekiel Crane strode into the living room, his jacket slung over his right arm. He bowed slightly at Kili before bending over to give his grandmother a kiss on the cheek. "What are we talking about?"

"Oh, never you mind," Granny said, winking over at Kili.

She stood from her chair, and gestured for Crane to sit. "Now that yer home, I'll finish makin' breakfast so you'uns can be on your way as soon as possible." She walked out of the room without looking back, but continued. "Besides, I think the two of you have important matters to deal with."

CHAPTER
FOURTEEN

E zekiel Crane and Kili finished their breakfast—a feast of biscuits and gravy, country ham, eggs, grits, and oatmeal —climbed into the truck's cab, and made their way back toward the Dark Hollows.

Crane had been even more quiet than normal all through their meal, and had seemed coldly unconcerned about her encounter with Sheriff Tyler, Candace, and the others the night before at Bailey's. He'd even refused to talk about the autopsy until they were on their way, out of deference to Granny. Now that they were finally settled into the warmth of the pickup's cab, Kili could contain herself no longer.

"Okay," she said, shifting in her seat under her safety belt. "Spill. What did you find out?"

He shrugged. "I'm afraid, I'm even more perplexed than before the autopsy," he said, keeping his eyes fixed dead ahead. The sun was only now creeping up over the fog-shrouded mountains, and much of the road was still cast in deep shadow. "Much of it, we already knew. Mr. Marathe was killed by severe trauma to his chest and abdomen…but the mechanism behind those injuries is giving me some trouble." He paused, placing a pinch of snuff between his lip and gums with one hand, then added, "When I'd first seen them at the scene, I'd believed they could have been made by a hatchet of some kind or a tomahawk, but now, I'm not so sure."

"How come?"

Crane nodded. "It's difficult to say. First, I found pellets from a shotgun in his abdominal wall. Buckshot. However, the injuries are too irregular for such a gunshot wound. While spread would account for a wider area of trauma for a shotgun injury, it would still be a round pattern. This injury was not. It's more like the flesh tore apart rather than perforated. That fact makes me think the chest, as well as the skull trauma, were caused by something else."

"Like what?"

"That, my dear, is the *question*. It almost seems as if..."

"Don't say it."

"...as if it was caused by something incorporeal. Something immaterial."

"I just told you not to say it," Kili said. "Come on. You don't honestly think that the spirit of One-Eyed Jack materialized out of nowhere, and hacked Miles to death with his ghostly toma-hawk, do you?"

"Well, while I don't think the buckshot killed Marathe, its presence seems to preclude anything supernatural," he said, turning the wheel sharply to the right to drive onto the now familiar hunting trail they'd traversed the day before. "Also, if it *was* One-Eyed Jack's weapon of choice, I hardly think there'd be anything of the victim left to examine." He threw her a quick smile. "A twenty-foot hatchet blade, even a spectral one, isn't exactly conducive to leaving a body intact, now is it?"

"Good point." She leaned back in the seat, propping her feet up on the dashboard, and absorbing this information. "Did you find anything else?"

He discreetly spat into a Styrofoam coffee cup, and nodded.

"Do you remember those granules I found on the clothing and skin of the body?"

She replayed the scene in her head before nodding. "You mean those dust particles?"

"Exactly," Crane said. "Only it wasn't dust or dirt of any kind actually. They were spores."

"Spores?"

"Yes. Some sort of fungal spore. A microscopic examination was inconclusive. I wasn't able to identify the genus of the fungus, but I'd say that when we find the murder scene, we'll find the fungus."

She took that in, then asked, "What about the scalping? Anything unusual there?"

"The scalping injury, I believe, was post-mortem. Though the head is notorious for bleeding out, even after death when head trauma is involved, he showed very little bleeding at all," he explained. "But once again, there's no evidence of the instrument utilized in the mutilation."

She looked at him, but he didn't immediately elaborate. He appeared to be deep in thought. "And?" she finally asked, goading him to continue.

"Oh, yes. Well, the trauma appears similar to the other injuries. Almost spontaneous." He pulled the truck up to about the same place he did yesterday, and parked it. Another vehicle, a mud-encrusted Jeep Grand Cherokee with KENTUCKY PARK SERVICES stenciled on its side, sat several yards ahead. The burly figure of Bear Boone, wearing the same park ranger uniform from the day before, leaned casually against the tailgate, waiting for the two to join him. An old-fashioned corncob pipe was clutched tight in the man's teeth. Crane waved at him from the cab, then climbed out, and moved to the back of his truck. He continued speaking in a hushed whisper as he grabbed two backpacks, and handed the lighter one to Kili. "But whatever caused the head injury appears to have come from the inside out."

The two started walking toward Bear with slow, deliberate steps.

"What?" Kili asked quietly. "How is that possible?"

Crane shook his head. "I honestly don't know yet. I have a glimmer of an idea, but don't want to say anything until I have more data. Not until I've either confirmed my theory or the results come back from the lab."

Kili laughed. "You do love keeping me in the dark, don't you?" she said as they approached the large man, now extending his hand to shake Crane's.

"I do indeed," he said, then took the proffered hand, and grinned from ear to ear. "Bear, it's good to see you again."

The big man smiled back, but was a bit more subdued than Crane. "Just wish it was under better circumstances, Zeke." He let out an involuntary shiver. "I don't reckon I've slept a wink since lookin' at that poor dead feller last night. It done gave me the willies and I ain't afraid to admit it."

Crane clapped a hand on the larger man's shoulder. "Rest easy, my friend. All I need of you is a guide to the Teeth. Once you get us there, you won't have to stay."

He nodded in response, and then beckoned for the two newcomers to follow. They hiked through the woods for the better part of two hours, stopping occasionally for water and rest. Kili noticed that, though they were now in the thick of the Dark Hollows, they did not pass by the spot in which Miles had been discovered. She couldn't help wonder if it was an intentional oversight on Bear's part.

Eventually, as they hiked, the vegetation abruptly changed from various oak and maple, a few spruce, and even a small grove of weeping willows to a very familiar looking field of plants with five leaves spread out as if waving to them in the breeze.

Noah McGuffin's marijuana crop, Kili thought, trying hard to hide her smile. There had to be acres of the stuff, growing like a vast field of corn, planted in multiple rows. *Geeze, what a set up.*

Without warning, Bear Boone came to a stop, holding up his hand. "We've got to be careful from here on," he said. "Ol' Noah likes to booby trap his crops to keep thieves and the Law out of his hair." He paused, looking warily along the ground through the row they were now standing in. "Watch your step. Keep a gander out fer trip wires. Spikes. Anythin' that don't belong."

"You mean besides the thousands of pounds of pot growing in the middle of a forest?" Kili asked, laughing.

"Yeah, besides that," Bear said, apparently not getting her attempt at humor. Then he took a step forward, and waved for them to follow. "Step where I step."

And with that, the three made their way through the maze of illegal crop in slow, careful strides.

THE FIGURE WATCHED THEM PASS; amused with just how oblivious they were to his presence. He had hoped that by stomping out the blonde man's offering to the Yunwi Tsunsdi yesterday, he would have prevented them from coming this far into the Little People's territory. Crane's presence was dangerous, and could destroy the ritual brewing that would summon his brothers back to the White Man's world. He couldn't let that happen. Too much was at stake.

The three trespassers suddenly stopped. The big man started speaking to them, probably describing the dangers they might encounter in the field. They needn't have bothered. He'd already disabled all the traps, though in hindsight, he wondered if that had been such a good idea. It might have prevented them from reaching their destination. The most sacred of places.

The female suddenly laughed. The figure tensed. The laugh

was so familiar. He hadn't gotten a really good look at the woman yet, and now that the voice seemed so recognizable, he could think of nothing else but discovering her identity.

The figure stood up from the branch of the oak on which he was perched, grabbed hold of the limb above his head, and hoisted himself up. Slowly, he clambered up farther in the tree, careful not to rustle the dying leaves around him, and give away his presence. Satisfied after climbing two levels higher, he laid down on the thick branch, and looked down at the three interlopers.

And it took every ounce of his considerable newfound strength to contain the gasp of surprise that threatened to erupt from his gut.

It's her, he thought. His limbs began to shudder uncontrollably at the woman's visage. *It can't be. It's impossible.*

But as he continued to stare at the trio, his mind spun with visions. Prophecies yet to be fulfilled. And all manner of dark creature lurking in the shadows of the underworld. *They're coming. My brothers are coming. But so are they who are much worse. Time is running out.*

A single unconscious tear rolled down the figure's cheek as he watched the pretty red-headed woman and her two companions move once more through the crops. He couldn't believe what he was going to have to do. She was the key. Somehow, deep down inside his soul, he knew. She was the key to everything.

CHAPTER
FIFTEEN

The Devil's Teeth
October 15
8:45 AM

Twenty minutes later, Crane, Kili, and Bear broke through the thick forest of pot and came to a clearing approximately one hundred and fifty yards in diameter on a steep incline. The branching tendrils of the forest on the other side of the clearing still kept the sun from washing its warm light fully to the ground, creating a strange otherworldly haze all around them.

But the odd ambiance of the place was the least of Kili's concerns at the moment. Her mouth swung open at the sight of the massive stone structure resting ominously on top of the hill.

It was exactly as Cian had described in his emails and phone conversations with her. So similar to the ruined megalith of Stonehenge in Salisbury, England. Her eyes fixed onto the thirteen gigantic slabs of stone forming a circle at the hill's crest. There was no evidence of the cross slabs that would have rested on top of the others, creating a sort of doorway, as Stonehenge had, but it was eerily similar in its construction.

How had the stones been brought here? Who had built it? Why? When? What connection does this place have to the one in England, and how is it possible that such a connection would even exist? All of these questions, and countless more, flashed through her mind in an instant.

No wonder Cian had been so fascinated, she thought. *It is absolutely breathtaking.*

The sound of incessant cawing caught her attention, and she looked up to see the old familiar raven perched on the slab just above Crane's head. Its knowing eyes glanced down at her with indifference, then cawed again as if trying to say something to her.

"Ms. Kili?" She heard Ezekiel Crane's soft-spoken voice, breaking the spell. "Are you all right?"

She could not pull her eyes away. "Huh?" she mumbled. "Oh, yes. I'm fine. J-just, um, taking it all in…"

Her voice trailed off as she stepped toward the colossal structure. The stones were indeed nearly twenty to twenty-five feet tall, covered in thick vines of kudzu, and shimmering in velvety green moss.

She stepped even closer, vaguely aware of Crane's presence next to her as she came to the closest slab, and leaned in for a better look. The stone appeared worn and jagged, but she couldn't help but get the impression that if cleaned and polished, she might be looking at a block of solid marble. Underneath the mossy coating, she could just make out a series of strange pictograms painted in fading colors. The shapes and what they represented was beyond her ability to fathom.

"This is…absolutely…amazing," she said, fearing that her words sounded slurred…so enthralled she was with the archaeological find. "It's…it's…"

"Ms. Kili!" Crane's voice sounded sharp. Exaggerated. She

turned to stare absently at his ruggedly handsome face. "Ms. Kili, I do hate to bring this up, but we're here for a different matter altogether than to appreciate this fine piece of history." She was aware that she'd barely heard the man, but for some reason, she just didn't care. What could be more important than this? "We're here, in case you need reminding, for your brother, Cian."

The sound of her brother's name snapped her out of the entranced state the place seemed to induce. Of course. It was the whole purpose of this expedition. The very reason she'd come. To find her brother, not his work. So why was she so captivated by the Teeth? So mesmerized? Almost lackadaisical toward her brother's plight? There was something *very* wrong within these ruins, but she couldn't quite put her finger on it.

"You're right, of course," she said, with a nod. She glanced around, but saw no sign of their guide. "Where's Bear?"

Crane stared at her, a look of concern furrowing his brow.

"We sent him on home as soon as we arrived," he said. "You don't remember?"

"Oh, yeah," she said, looking past Crane's shoulder at the next stone slab in line. "I'd forgotten." She took a deep breath, and turned her concentration away from the tableau. "Okay. Let's get started. What are we doing here?"

Crane had already pulled off his pack, and withdrew a pair of handkerchiefs. He handed her one. "Tie this around your face," he said, doing the same, and looking like some sort of bandit from an old western.

"What's this for?"

He hesitated for a moment, looked around, then said, "You don't smell it?"

She shrugged. "What am I supposed to smell?"

His eyes narrowed slightly before he said, "Death. It's here."

Kili's mouth went dry. She felt her legs grow weak, trembling. *Cian.*

Crane placed a warm hand on her shoulder and smiled. "Don't worry Ms. Kili. If I'm not mistaken, it's fairly recent. I don't think it's your brother." He turned back to the megalith. "Now, shall we take a look?"

She nodded, tied the bandana around her nose and mouth, and followed him into the interior of the ruins. It was like stepping onto the page of some Irish faery tale. The inside of the megalith was carpeted with a thick blanket of bright green moss and lichen. The bulbous heads of multicolored mushrooms dotted the terrain, as well as the interior sides of the stone slabs, growing up at an angle. The ring of stones appeared to form an almost perfect circle, with a massive horizontal slab resting flat against the ground in the center...like a great sacrificial altar of... the giants.

The place was surreal, and Kili found herself half expecting a troop of elves and other mythical creatures to poke their heads up out of their hiding places and say hello.

"It's stunning," she said, her voice conspicuously muffled behind the cloth over her mouth.

"Yes," Crane said. "Yes, it is."

Kili looked at him. "You're from around here. You've never been here before?"

He shook his head, his eyes scanning every facet of the ruins. "No. It wouldn't have been wise on my part to come here. The locals already have...a problem with me. If I had discarded the remainder of the taboos they had placed on me, and visited the Teeth, I dare say I would never have been able to live here in peace."

She stood quiet, taking that in for several seconds. "What do *they* think this place is? Do they really think it's connected to those spirit giants you told me about?"

"Yes. Yes, they do Ms. Kili," he said. "Or at least most of them do...though they might be reluctant to admit it. There are others that believe this place is something else entirely..." Crane stopped, his sharp eyes catching something to his right. "Something even darker."

"You mean Tom Thornton and his 'church', right?" she asked, but he wasn't there. She turned around to see him walking toward one of the northern-most stones. She followed warily, glancing over the man's broad shoulders.

She quickly discovered the object of Crane's interest. It was a pile of freshly sifted dirt, resting lazily atop the moss-covered ground.

"What is it?" she asked as the two of them stopped short of the pile.

Crane didn't answer. Instead, he slipped on a pair of latex gloves, then reached into his pack, and pulled out a small, folding camp shovel, a gardening trowel, and an assortment of brushes. He extended the shovel's handle, and carefully began digging away at the dirt. The soil was loose. Unpacked. And the work was quick and easy. After a few minutes, he switched to the trowel, scooping away small clumps of dirt until he struck something solid, but fleshy. Crane put the tool aside, grabbed a large paintbrush, and began brushing the soil away with precise sweeps of his wrists. In seconds, he had uncovered the unmistakable evidence of a human leg, the pale marbled skin in stark contrast with the thick streaks of crimson that caked it.

"Oh dear Lord," Kili said, under her breath.

The Raven cawed in response, but if Ezekiel Crane heard her, he didn't respond. He merely continued sweeping away the dirt and grime, revealing more and more of the body that had only recently been buried next to the giant northern stone. Soon, it became apparent that the victim was a nude female, hacked up along her torso exactly the way Miles had been. Jagged wounds crisscrossed along her chest and abdomen, exposing her bowels in a gruesome evisceration.

Kili's head spun at the grisly sight. The scene, mixed with the odor of blood and earth bombarding her senses, threatened to overwhelm her. She pulled the handkerchief down, its presence stifling and restrictive, and gazed down at the mutilated corpse.

"You might want to keep that on," Crane said, brushing away the dirt near the body's neck, moving slowly, methodically to her face.

"I'll be fine."

He craned his head around, his face stern as he looked at her. "It honestly wasn't a suggestion," he said, waiting for her to comply before turning his attention once more to the grave. His brush swiped away more dirt, revealing the chin, then the severe thin lips of the woman. Finally, he uncovered the rest of her face, and reeled back in surprise. His eyes wide.

"Candace," he said, standing up again, and wiping the dirt from his hands on his jeans.

Kili stood in stunned silence. It had been the last person she'd suspected.

"How? I mean...I just saw her last night," she said, her voice hollow, echoing loud inside her own skull.

Crane shook his head. "I don't know." He turned to look at Kili. "I'll admit. I didn't expect this, and it certainly does *not* bode well."

"What do you mean?"

Ignoring her question, he opened the pack strapped to Kili's back, and rummaged through it. He soon came back around with a camera, a laser thermometer, and a strange object that looked like a set of wind chimes. He scanned the ground briefly, found two sticks. The shorter, he shoved into his back pocket, but drove the longer one into the ground. He then hung the chimes onto a notch he quickly whittled at the top of the stick, and released it.

The melodic sounds of glass striking hollow metal tubes of varying lengths wafted through the ruins. The sound was rhythmic. Enchanting. Relaxing and tranquil. It seemed utterly out of place in the foreboding place.

"What is that for?" she pointed to the chimes as he started snapping away photos of the body.

"Chimes are wonderful tools of the trade. More investigators should use them in my opinion," he said, his eye squinting through the lens of the camera as he took a picture. "Legend says they draw back the spirits of the Dead, among other things."

Kili stared at him; wondering if she misheard him. She'd almost forgotten about his backwoods, superstitious ways. It was one of the most ridiculous thing she'd ever heard. *Well, besides using a divining rod, and an army of ants to find a corpse,* she thought, remembering how well those two things had worked yesterday. *But come on! What on earth could a set of wind chimes do at a crime scene?*

"And I suppose you plan on speaking to the dead if they drop in for a visit," she said, a half-hearted smile stretching up one side of her face.

He pulled away from the camera, and looked over at her. "I see you've been talking to Granny about me," he said with a wink. "Like I said, the wind chimes do a lot more than call to the Dead. Think of it as a forensic experiment of sorts."

Crane cast his attention to the chimes once more, moving over to them, and crouching down. He watched as the hanging pendulums of glass and metal swayed with the steady breeze, sending up a chorus of tinkling music. He jotted something down on a notepad, stood up, and then pointed the laser thermometer at the brutalized remains of the waitress.

"Interesting," he said, slapping the device in his hand once, and pointing its beam again. "Very interesting."

"What?"

"Her surface temperature," he said. "She's warm."

"So? From what I understand, it takes a while for a dead body to cool."

"You'd be surprised," Crane said, his voice strained. "Corpses usually begin cooling to ambient temperature immediately upon death. Base readings say the soil around Candace is sixty-eight degrees Fahrenheit. She should be pretty close to that. But her body temperature is currently reading 97.4 degrees."

"What? That's impossible," Kili said, stepping toward the grave, and crouching down for a better look.

"Careful," Crane said, placing a warning hand on her shoulder. "Don't get too close."

She wheeled around on the balls of her feet, and glared at him. "Okay, you know something. What's going on?"

He reached his hand out, and helped her to her feet. His smile seemed tenuous at best. "It's a mistake to voice a theory before we have all the facts," he said. "Let's just say there are some, um, irregularities to both of these deaths that I'm concerned about. And these thermometer readings would indicate that Candace had a very high fever when she died. Suggestive to say the least."

"Well, thank you, Mr. Mysterio," she said, turning her attention back to Candace. "Okay, let me ask you this then...do you have any clue who did this?"

He pulled his cell phone from his pocket. "I need to call Tyler," he said, ignoring her question. "He's not going to like this. He had a thing for Candace."

Irritated by his stubbornness, she snatched the phone from his hand. "Answer me! Who is doing this? Where is my brother? What's going on in this crazy hillbilly town?"

"Kili, I'm honestly not sure." He held up his hands in a submissive gesture. "I have some ideas, yes. But I don't feel comfortable voicing them right now. To do so might lead us down a false trail, ultimately making it even more difficult to find your brother later on. No, for now, it's just better to hold my tongue. At least until I have a few more pieces of the puzzle. I'm sorry."

Biting back tears of frustration, she nodded at his rebuke, and handed him the phone. Her brother's situation was becoming bleaker with every piece of evidence they uncovered. If Miles, and now Candace, were dead, then where did that leave Cian? How could he possibly still be alive? Somewhere in these primeval hills, a madman lurked with a shotgun, an antique tomahawk, and a thirst for blood. And she was no closer to finding her brother now than when she'd first arrived. It all seemed so hopeless.

Crane powered up his phone, but before he could press the button to call for the sheriff, he stopped. His gaze fixed toward the grave.

"Hello," he said, carefully stepping down into the pit, his two booted feet straddling both sides of Candace's body, and stooped down. "What have we here?"

Kili followed his line of sight, peering down into the dirt around the corpse. Crane bent past Candace's head, the telltale signs of a scalping now evident, and brushed away more dirt. A brownish-gray dome poked up from the ground like some fossilized turtle shell half buried in the dirt. She watched as her companion continued to swipe away the soil until the object was fully uncovered.

It looked like a human skull. Only it was much larger than any she'd ever seen. In fact, it was gigantic...roughly the same size as that of a regulation basketball.

"What in the world..." She couldn't complete the question. The enormity of what she was seeing struck her in the gut like a sledgehammer. *Giants. The ruins.* They were said to be linked, hand in hand...and here she was, looking at the ancient remains of what looked to be some gigantic humanoid.

"Absolutely fascinating," Crane said, seemingly mesmerized by the skull. He reached out, and gently picked the thing up in both hands. As he did, Kili could see that a large amount of dirt and debris still clung to it, as well as several strange protrusions that looked like tiny mushrooms sprouting up from the skull's dome. Besides that, and the overall size, it looked identical in every way to a normal human head—though slightly malformed along the brow and bridge of the nose. Kili couldn't quite place what was wrong with it. It just looked misshapen somehow. Warped and swollen.

Ezekiel Crane examined the artifact for several minutes.

"This thing is amazingly fragile," he said quietly, as if the sound of his voice could shatter the artifact into dust. "Ms. Kili, if you would be so kind as to reach into my pack for an evidence bag and tweezers. I'd like to get a sample of this fungus for analysis."

She did as he asked, grabbed the tweezers and the bag, and came around to face him.

"Okay," he said. "Do you know what to do?"

She nodded. "I think so."

Kili opened the bag, and reached out toward the skull with the tweezers in hand. Carefully, delicately, she grabbed hold of a single mushroom bulb, and pulled it from its perch. She repeated the process until she had a total of seven fungal samples, then sealed the evidence bag.

"Excellent," Crane said, turning the skull around to examine its back, but the sound of three shotguns pumping behind them caused him to jerk in surprise. He lost his grip on the artifact, sending it tumbling from his fingertips, and smashing into microscopic pieces upon impact with the ground, like a water balloon that was dropped from a five-story rooftop. The complete implosion of the skull caught them both by surprise... human bones simply did not shatter like that.

Then, the two both remembered the sudden sounds behind them, and spun around; a look of intense anger etched across Ezekiel Crane's brow.

CHAPTER
SIXTEEN

"Thomas Thornton," Ezekiel Crane growled, as he appraised the newcomers with a steely glare. If he had been surprised to see the cult preacher and two others looming behind them with shotguns resting on the crooks of their arms, he showed no sign. On the contrary, it seemed as if he almost expected them to be there...and was furious about it. "You have no business here."

Though Kili hadn't seen Thornton's face the night before inside Bailey's Pub, she had no trouble at all distinguishing him from the two hulking goons that lumbered on either side of him. He was a short, scrawny man with an obvious beer gut jutting from his midsection like a six-and-a-half-month pregnant woman. He wore nothing but black, except for a white collar...a minister's collar. His head and face were covered in a thick, salt and pepper hair and beard...like some sort of priestly Grizzly Adams. But the most stunning feature that Kili noticed was his penetrating black eyes. One stare from those eyes could whither the resolve of any weak-willed person.

No, Kili had only seen one other set of eyes that were more bone-chillingly potent. Those of Ezekiel Crane's.

"I reckon I've got every right to be here, Crane," Thornton said with a sneer. "More so than you anyway. You're the one's trespassin'...not me and my boys. This here's holy ground, and yer desecratin' it with yer presence. With yer Curse." The cultist smiled, revealing a trio of blackened, decaying front teeth, and two sets of diseased gums. "We aim to remove you'uns from the property. Noah McGuffin lets us use this place for worship. I have a might hard time believin' he gave you leave to be here."

Crane took a step forward, reaching into his back pocket, and pulling out the small stick he'd picked up a few minutes earlier. He took another step, reached into his front pocket, and withdrew a small, red pocketknife. His cold stare never leaving Thornton, he began whittling at the stick without uttering a word.

The wind chimes behind Kili clinked rhythmically in the awkward silence.

"First of all," Crane finally said, his voice back to its customarily even tone. He nodded in the direction of their weapons. "Nice shotguns. I've been looking for a match to what shot Miles Marathe a week ago."

The reverend's face went red, but before he could protest, Crane continued.

"Second, I have every right to be here as acting coroner of Jasper County." He pointed to the open grave with the stick, then continued his whittling. "Found another victim. Smack dab inside your little *church* here, as a matter of fact."

Thornton's face shifted from rage red to deathly pale. His eyes widened. Confused, even. He tried to peer around Crane for a better look, but quickly regained his composure. "Don't matter a hill of beans none to me," he said. "We're here to—"

"Third," Crane continued, interrupting the cultist's protest. "You are absolutely correct. This is most definitely holy ground." His knife blade absently sliced a thin piece of bark from the stick.

"But not *your* holy ground. It belongs to the Cherokee people if it belongs to anyone."

Crane took another step toward the motley trio, who in turn took a single step backward in unison.

Still, his blade sliced at the limb almost in sync with the ringing of the chimes, Kili noticed.

Thornton opened his mouth again, but remained silent.

"And finally, are you aware of what this is?" Crane asked, holding up his handiwork. Kili looked at the piece of wood, now pointed at Thornton. His pale face now glistened with a stream of sweat running past his forehead. He opened his mouth again to answer, but Ezekiel Crane cut him off. "Of course, you do," he said, his eyes burning at the cultist. "And I've carved your name —your *full* name—into it too."

The man's mouth fell open, but this time it was not to protest or to argue. His arrogance had drained from him like water from a wicker basket, reducing him to a quivering mass of flesh. His muscle-bound goons on each side were no better off. Tears rolled down their faces as they took another few steps back. Yet Crane did not relent. He merely moved toward them again.

"Please," Thornton said, his voice a shallow whisper of its former self. "Don't."

The chimes seemed to pick up their cadence as a frigid gust of wind blew through the ring of stones. A shiver ran up Kili's spine as if the icy fingertips of a thousand dead hands were caressing the back of her neck.

Crane stopped, held up the piece of wood in one hand, and dropped it to the ground. He then raised up a single boot, letting his heel hover over it. "You have five seconds," he said. "Then, I bring my foot down, and you don't want to be anywhere near here when that happens." The three men turned immediately around and started to run from the site before Crane stopped them. "Oh, and Thornton, one more thing."

The cultist stopped and turned to look at him.

"If you ever threaten Ms. Brennan again...I don't care whose idea it is...well, you know where I'm going with this, right?"

Thornton nodded once, then turned and ran from the Devil's Teeth at a dead sprint. Crane watched for several minutes, chuckling softly to himself, then picked up the stick from the ground, and returned it to his pocket. When he turned to face Kili, he was practically beaming.

"Now, let's get Sheriff Tyler and a crew here," he said, scrolling through the contacts on his cell phone. "Looks like I have another autopsy to perform."

The Crane Homestead
October 15
12:10 PM

ESTHER CRANE RUBBED the bridge of her nose with her thumb and forefinger, then turned another page in her grandmother's old tome. She'd been scanning through her library since Ms. Brennan and Ezekiel had left earlier that morning, trying to decipher the enigma that was the young redhead's unusual talents.

"And you're saying, this young woman can actually hear the Yunwi Tsunsdi?" Granny's apprentice, Delores McCrary asked. Granny had been training the middle-aged woman for a better part of a decade now, in the ways of 'Granny Magick', and was her closest confidant and friend.

"Looks that way, though for the life of me, I can't figure out why."

"I don't understand. Why's it a big deal?"

Granny shrugged. "Because it ain't supposed to happen. One matriarchal Granny at any given time, remember? And it's usually passed down by blood...'cept I had no daughters. Back in the day, I thought Jael would take over the mantle, but after what happened to her brother…well, she just walked away from us. Blamed Ezekiel. Moved to the city and set her mind to science. No interest in this life at all. That's why I've been trainin' you, Dee. To take my place when the time comes."

The portly woman nodded. "Well, maybe theys got plans for her—the Little People, I mean. Maybe they want her to take yer place. Not me."

Granny turned another page in the book, then gestured toward the page. "That's why I've been studyin' this so hard. To see if there's any kind of precedent for such a thing to have happened. My kin have been the Grannies in these parts for nearly seven generations. Everythin' they saw…everythin' they knew, were written down in these books, and so far, I can't find nothin' like what's going on now." She sighed. "Weirder than that, Ezekiel told me he thinks the girl's been seein' his totem."

Delores's eyes widened. "The Raven?"

"Yup. It's all so bizarre." She leaned back in her chair, lit up her pipe, and took in a puff of tobacco. "Don't get me wrong. She's a sweet, kind-hearted girl—though a touch cynical, I think. But she's an outsider. A city girl to boot. She's got no knowledge of the natural world other than what's she's read in her books. None of it makes a bit of sense to me."

"Maybe that's the point," Delores said, tapping her pipe against the ashtray sitting next to her. "Maybe they're—"

Granny cut her off with an upheld hand. "We've got company." She cocked her head as if listening to something, then nodded. "Jimmy Staples is comin' up the drive. He's upset about somethin'."

The two ladies got up from the table they'd been gathered around, and strode to the door. As Granny opened it, Jimmy was standing there, about to knock. Tears were streaking his face. "I can't find my mommy," he sobbed. "She didn't come home last night."

Delores gasped at the news, then looked over at Granny. "Why that lowdown—"

But Granny raised a hand again; the color draining from her usually robust face. "Oh dear." She knelt down on both knees to meet Jimmy in the eyes. "Oh, Jimmy." She pulled him in, and embraced him tight. "It's gonna be okay, sweetie. You're gonna come live with Granny from now on. You're gonna come live with me."

CHAPTER
SEVENTEEN

The Devil's Teeth
October 15
8:50 PM

Ezekiel Crane knelt down at the fifth grave site of the day, and rubbed at the stubble growing across his jaw. The entire site of the Devil's Teeth was now flooded with portable halogen lights, turning the darkness into noonday light, and revealing the most disturbing and macabre scene Crane had ever seen in his life.

Since finding Candace Staples's body earlier that day, Crane and crime scene units borrowed from Harlan and Letcher counties, had unearthed four more recent graves. The occupants, four of the people who'd gone missing in recent days. Unlike Candace, however, most of the bodies had been prepared for burial—dressed in strange black suits that covered them from head to toe. The fabric, an unusual nylon blend, was peppered from top to bottom with the same fungal granules found inside Marathe's body. Or at least, that's what Crane suspected. He wouldn't be sure until he analyzed them in a lab.

"What's going on, Crane?" asked Detective Fred Ward from Harlan County. "This is...this is...just nuts."

After notifying Sheriff Tyler, and sending Kili back to Boone Creek to rest after her trying day, Crane had opted to go above the sheriff's head, and call in reinforcements from the surrounding counties. He didn't know how, but he was pretty sure Tyler had a hand in whatever was going on in the Hollows, and needed to ensure the investigation remained as above board as possible. Besides, since none of these investigators were from around Jasper County, very few were aware of his unsavory reputation, and he found it refreshing to work alongside law enforcement for a change, as opposed to how his investigations normally happened.

"I'm still trying to piece that together, Detective."

"But those bodies? What are they wearing?"

"If I'm not mistaken, they're called 'Mushroom Death Suits'," Crane said. "A new fad in eco-friendly funerary options. From what I've heard, the deceased are buried in these suits, which are sewn with mushroom spores inside them. Once the spores begin to grow, they begin digesting the remains for a cleaner, more environmentally conscious burial."

"Sounds blasphemous."

Crane allowed himself a grim smile. "In this case, Detective, I don't think we know the half of it."

Crane turned his attention past the recently buried body, focusing on a dome-like shape still covered by the moist soil. He assumed, like the other graves they'd uncovered, that he was looking at yet another gigantic skull still interred in the ground.

The giants of legend. Remarkable.

"Crane!" Crane turned to see Sheriff Tyler storming across the moss covered slope. He'd not been happy when he discovered the case had been taken away from him. In fact, even now, detectives with the Kentucky State Police were heading their way. Eventually, they, along with archaeologists and forensic anthropologists from the University of Kentucky, would be taking over the scene entirely. "I need to talk to you. Now." Though still obviously angry, his demeanor had changed since the two last spoke four hours earlier. It seemed as though much of his rage had dissipated, and was now replaced with something more akin to worry.

"By all means, Sheriff." He gestured toward the exterior of the monument, and Tyler began walking in that direction.

Crane followed, and when they were both outside of earshot of the rest of the investigative crew, Tyler continued.

"Okay, I can't do this anymore." Tyler pulled out a cigarette from a crumpled pack, and tossed it in his lips with shaking hands. "Look, I know you're close. I know you suspect that I'm a part of this. It's only a matter of time before everything comes apart."

Crane raised an eyebrow. "What are you saying, John?"

"I'm sayin' I want to confess. Tell you what part I had in all this. I don't know everything. Most of it was kept from us, but I'll tell you what I *do* know."

"In exchange for…"

"In exchange for your word that you'll help me out if charges are filed against me. Testimony that I assisted you. Any help you can get me."

Crane nodded. "Deal." He reached out his hand. Tyler looked at it nervously, then shook the hand.

"Okay. Here's the deal…I don't know how Candy got in there. She wasn't part of this."

"What about the ruse she concocted to lure Ms. Brennan into the bar last night?"

"Well, she did that, but she wasn't part of our little project up here." The sheriff puffed at his cigarette. "She was just so pissed at you, that she jumped at the chance to help us out." He held out his hands, palm up. "And FYI, I had no intention of really hurting the Brennan woman. Just wanted to scare her, is all."

"Spare me. We'll discuss your actions at Bailey's later. For now, go on."

"Fine. Like I was saying, I'll admit, I had a hand in dumpin' those people in the graves. But you gotta believe me! They were already dead when I got them. Just like that Marathe feller. Chest and head popped open like Jiffy-Pop popcorn. We just took 'em, buried 'em, and kept their deaths secret from their families."

"Why? And how, pray tell, did you 'get them' to begin with?"

Tyler shifted on his feet nervously; his eyes downcast.

"Tyler?"

"Please. Don't make me say it."

Crane sighed. "You don't have to. You were doing all this for Ash, weren't you?"

The sheriff nodded.

"But you have one problem, John. I found buckshot in Marathe. He'd been shot. I practically accused Tom Thornton of it earlier today, and he turned white as a sheet."

"Yeah, and he's in the wind too. Can't find 'im anywhere." Tyler tossed the butt of his cigarette down on the ground, and stomped it out. "But he explained what happened...here in the Teeth that night."

The sound of trees crashing to the ground drowned out their conversation...the work of a road crew bulldozing a path to the Devil's Teeth to make access easier for incoming law enforcement teams.

"Care to elaborate?" Crane asked above the noise.

"Says he and a few of his men followed the Doc, Marathe, and Kingston up here that night. They'd already dug up one of the graves. Found those weird giant bones, and were makin' a big stink about it. They were really excited.

"But as you know, Thornton and his cult use this site to worship. If news about these bones got out, their 'holy ground' would be defiled by scientists, news crews, and tourists looking for Sasquatch. Tom didn't want that to happen, so he snuck up on them, and..."

"He tried to scare them off with his shotgun routine, just like he pulled on me today."

Tyler nodded. "Only, that's when all hell broke loose. Tom said that the moment their attention turned to them, this weird green cloud rose up out of the grave, and engulfed them. Kingston instantly bolted, leaving Brennan and Marathe in the thick of it. Then, they just went nuts."

"Who? Who went nuts?"

"Brennan and Marathe. Brennan fell to the ground, screaming. Clutching his head like it was about to explode. Marathe though...the way Thornton told it, the guy just went psycho. Started charging them. Screamin' bloody murder. One of Thornton's boys took a shot—in self-defense the way they tell it. But here's the weird thing, whether you believe it or not. Thornton swears up and down that before the shot was fired, the man's chest busted open and released the same green stuff all around them. His boy couldn't stop in time. He pulled the trigger anyway. Marathe went down. By the time Thornton had time to calm his men down, Brennan was gone."

"What happened then?"

"Nothin'. They just hauled their butts out of the Hollars, and came to tell me what happened."

"Why didn't they bury the bodies in the graves?"

Tyler shrugged. "We hadn't started doing that yet. They never even thought of it. I was surprised as you were when you found the body."

Crane considered all he'd been told, then nodded. "So, the burials...the mushroom suits...how did that all come about?"

"Mushroom what?"

"Those black suits the bodies are buried in. They cultivate mushrooms, using body tissue as nutrients."

"Ah! That explains it," Tyler said. "All I know is that Asherah came to me the night after, and tells me Noah has a new crop he means to grow. A strange new species of mushroom. Said the mushrooms grow best using decomposing flesh, and that they wanted my help. The next day, one of my deputies found the body of Jack Burns—the EMT who worked on Leroy Kingston two nights earlier. I told Asherah about it, and she had me bring the body here for her. She put that crazy suit on it, then had me and a few others bury it in the Teeth."

What are you up to, Asherah?

"Who all are we going to find in these graves, John? I'm already aware of a few of the missing people—despite your attempts at keeping them from me. But I need all their names."

"Well, there was…"

The gentle cadence of the chimes he'd left in the ruins changed with a sudden surge of nerve-grating clashing. The glass and metal clappers knocking against each other with sickening infrequency. Something was here. Now.

The sheriff stopped speaking; his eyes looking past Ezekiel Crane's shoulders. His cheeks grew flush, and he began to emit a piteous little squeal. Crane turned around just in time to see a figure hidden among the trees on the opposite side of the Devil's Teeth. The figure, blanketed in shadow, was a good head taller than Crane himself, and broad in shoulder. It turned, and dashed off into the forest when it seemed to notice Crane looking at it.

Reaching toward Tyler's duty belt, he grabbed a Scorpion high-powered flashlight from its loop, and dashed off in the direction the figure had run.

CHAPTER
EIGHTEEN

The Dark Hollows
October 15
9:24 PM

E zekiel Crane ran deeper into the dense foliage of the Dark Hollows at an Olympic pace, ignoring the clawing brambles of shrubs and trees as he raced past them. He'd lost sight of the figure three times already, but had managed to catch sight of him again each time, and now watched as he bobbed and weaved across the forest floor.

But the figure's night vision was uncanny. Whereas Crane had to stop for a moment every so often to use his flashlight, his prey seemed unaffected by the darkness at all. Instead, he just pushed on and on, never seeming to grow tired and lose his breath despite navigating the rugged terrain. Crane pushed on, however, risking his footing in the deep web of thorny underbrush encroaching his path. Three minutes later, however, he'd lost sight of the figure once more, and was forced to stop to catch his bearings.

Taking deep, intensive breaths, he shined the bright beam of the flashlight all around him, making a complete three hundred and sixty degree turn. A rush of movement caught the corner of his eye to his left. He spun around, aiming the beam in that direction, but whatever he'd seen was gone.

"Blast," he hissed, running his fingers through his sweat-soaked hair. *I can't lose him. Not now. Too much is at stake.*

Carefully, he stepped toward the spot in which he'd last seen the figure, then got down on hands and knees, and began scouring the ground for a trail. He found himself wishing Bear was there with him at that moment, with his uncanny knack for tracking even the most wily of game. But wishes, despite what the townspeople thought him, were not part of his repertoire. Magic or no, he was going to have to do this the hard way.

After several minutes, he found what he was hoping to find. A single toe print. No shoes. Bare feet. Running southeast. His first thought upon finding the print was that it had been Asherah, who compulsively refused to wear shoes. Her reasoning—they disconnected her body from nature. Bare feet allowed her an intimacy with the earth. She drew power, according to her, from the soil itself. But the print he'd discovered had been far too large. Of course, the figure he'd seen had been masculine, and large as well.

Now that he'd found the print, however, Crane would not be as hard pressed to keep pace with his prey. He could casually stalk him. Follow him to wherever he absconded, and get the answers he sought at his own pace.

A rustling in the tree above him drew his attention. He flashed the light toward the sound, and saw the Raven perched on a branch; a mocking glare on its face.

"Well, I suppose you'll be no help," Crane said to it. "You know, if you're going to continue to haunt me for the rest of my life, you could consider making yourself useful at times like this."

But the bird simply stared back at him with unblinking black eyes.

"I thought as much." Crane shrugged, then glanced down at the print again, and calculated his next few moves in the hunt.

Before he could finish his musings, however, a growl erupted from behind him. He wheeled around in time to see a massive form lunging from the woods, and tackling him to the ground. Two large fists pounded down against Crane's head. His ears rang from the impact. The world around him spun uncontrollably, and before he could counter, his attacker struck him again, and again. The attack happened so fast, Crane was unable to get even a remote glimpse of the figure's face. He was merely a blur of motion and rage, whose sole interest was in pummeling him into submission.

After the fifth or sixth blow, despite his dazed state, Crane rolled out of the fists reach, staggered to his feet, and charged at his attacker. Leaping into the air, he came down against his opponent's face with enough force to crack bone. Pressing the advantage, Crane wheeled around, slamming him with a roundhouse kick, that drove him to his knees.

"Submit," Crane said in between heaving breaths. He kept his fists up in a defensive stance, and waited for a reply. But the brute of a man exploded from the ground, hammering a fist against the left side of Crane's jaw. He staggered backward, fell to the ground, and immediately clambered back to his feet, searching for his enemy.

But his attacker was nowhere to be seen. The initial tackle had knocked Crane's flashlight from his hand, and was now several feet away. If he went to retrieve it, he'd be exposed to another attack, and he was unwilling to let that happen.

"Come out and face me," Crane said in a calm, even voice. A stream of blood streaked down his brow into his eyes, but he kept his defensive posture and ignored the discomfort.

He heard more rustling somewhere to his right, and he

trailed the sound from the corners of his eyes to prevent another surprise attack.

"Leave, Crane," a deep, guttural voice said in the shadows. "I have no quarrel with you. Yet. You are not welcome here. This is the land of my people. The land of my brothers. And they are soon returning."

Brothers.

"Come out," Crane repeated. "Tell me about your brothers. Let's talk about this. Help me to understand."

There was a low growl of warning, but Ezekiel Crane couldn't discern from which direction.

"You will not trick us, Devil Crane. Leave. Do not come back. The Yunwi Tsunsdi cannot protect you here."

Then, an explosion of motion erupted just a few feet to his right. The large figure leapt from his hiding place, and dashed away faster than Crane's eyes could follow. The way his head pounded against his temples and blood flowed from cuts to his head and face, he knew he should get medical attention as soon as possible. For now, the hunt was over.

Jasper Travel Lodge
Boone Creek
October 16
11:00 PM

KILI BRENNAN TOSSED under the covers of her bed. Her mind raced through the events of the day in crystal sharp, though confusing, images. She had struggled desperately to fall asleep. It had been such a long, exhausting day—both physically and emotionally. Sheriff Tyler had taken the news of Candace Staples death even worse than Crane had imagined, going into a cursing tirade about the mountain man's evil curse, and about Kili's own involvement in the waitress' murder. He'd practically flipped out when Crane informed him he'd called in help from the state police and a couple of police agencies from neighboring counties. She'd thought the sheriff was going to pop a blood vessel right then and there.

Things went from bad to disastrous for Tyler, however, when news of Candace's death spread throughout the entire state. The second dead body found in two days, more bodies found buried in the Devil's Teeth, and the mysterious disappearance of a prominent professor of anthropology from an Ivy League college, had attracted the attention of several nearby news stations, and the town was now blanketed by news vans from as far south as Atlanta and as far north as Chicago. She'd even seen CNN and FOX news crews scurrying around the town like cockroaches running for cover when the light flicked on. The entire affair was turning into a huge story, and the frenzied circus known as "Corporate News" was finally in town, staking their claim to the next big scoop.

To make matters worse, she'd received a call earlier that day from her boss, Amanda Crosby, who'd apparently been contacted by someone in local law enforcement—presumably Tyler himself—and told that she was interfering with the investigation. As a result, her leave of absence had been summarily canceled. Crosby's orders had been quite specific—leave the search for her brother to the professionals, and return to work immediately. Of course, Kili's boss had given her a choice. She could always forfeit her position with the FBI, which was something that would give her employer great pleasure. It would also dash any hope she ever had at one day becoming a Special Agent.

Then there was Ezekiel Crane himself. The deeper they dug into her brother's disappearance, the more enigmatic and strange Crane had become. She couldn't quite put her finger on it, but she knew he was hiding something from her in this investigation. Something big. And after he'd insisted she leave the Devil's Teeth, and go get some much needed rest at her hotel, she'd lost it. In a fit of frustrated rage, she'd hurled one accusation after another at him; trying desperately to evoke some emotional response that might cause the strange man to slip. To reveal at least some of his suspicions.

But in his usual, and irritatingly calm demeanor, he'd simply smiled at her, said she was naturally tired and that all would be clear very soon.

And of all these issues, nothing quite compared to the now near-incessant squealing of childlike giggling she continued to hear. Only, it had gotten worse. Now, she was beginning to actually hear voices speaking in a strange tongue. A language that seemed so foreign to her, yet so very familiar. A language that seemed burned into her DNA somehow.

The entire affair was enough to give her a complete nervous breakdown. She found herself wondering, not for the first time, if it had been a mistake coming here. If she should have listened to everyone, and just let the professional law enforcement search for her brother. She also began to suspect that the entire episode was merely a horrible nightmare that she was unable to wake up from—which might explain why she was unable to fall asleep.

As it was, however, ever since Kili had had agreed to return to her room, she'd settled into bed around eight-thirty that evening, and had been tossing in her sheets ever since. Finally, two and a half hours later, sleep finally came. But the bliss she'd hoped to attain with it never came. Her mind still raced. Her whirlwind vestiges of conscious thought ricocheted inside her skull like a steel ball in a pinball machine. And then, the dream came.

CHAPTER
NINETEEN

The shrill ring of the telephone jolted Kili awake from her over-soft hotel room bed, her heart pounding furiously against her rib cage. She'd been dead to the world, and the sudden intrusion to her slumber pushed her nerves into overdrive.

She looked at the bright red digital numbers of the clock on the nightstand. Almost one in the morning. She'd only been asleep a couple of hours. Ezekiel Crane had opted to drive her to the motel after leaving Kingston's hospital room—

Wait, that's not right.

Kili couldn't believe she'd forgotten—since leaving Candace's gravesite. She'd pretty much passed out the moment her head hit the pillow after Crane had dropped her off....

Wait a minute, Kili thought. *This seems wickedly familiar.*

The hotel phone rang again, only this time, it sounded less like the customary ring of a telephone, and more like the tinkling of glass on hollow metal tubes cut at various lengths. She looked at the phone. A single orange light built into its cradle glowed brightly, illuminating her darkened hotel room.

Groggily, she picked up the phone's receiver. "Hello?"

There was silence on the other end, save for a series quick shallow breaths. Kili propped herself up on her elbow and white knuckled the phone. "Hello?" Her voice was a little more alert and forceful this time.

A throat cleared. It sounded female.

Candace Staples, Kili thought. *But that's crazy. Candace is dead.*

"Who is this? What do you want?"

"I—I didn't do nothin' to your brother," the woman on the other end of the line finally said. Her speech slurred, and trembling.

Kili felt sure her heart had just paused for a second or two as a frigid chill shuddered through her body. *This is impossible. She's dead.* "Don't let him do..." The voice on the other end of the phone paused, took a deep breath, and continued. "Don't let him do his magic on me or my boy. Please. I didn't do nothing."

The voice that sounded eerily identical to Candace Staples sobbed.

Just as she had the night before. This entire scenario is exactly what happened last night!

"It's okay," Kili said, unsure why she'd said it. She knew she should hang up the phone. Knew she needed to run from the hotel room, and never look back. Knew it was impossible to get telephone calls from dead women who were mutilated, and left buried in the grave of giants. Yet she felt compelled to follow the script just as she had a mere twenty-four hours before. "I won't let him hurt you."

Candace let out a sniffle, then cleared her throat once more. She inhaled sharply again, and Kili thought it sounded as if the woman was smoking. *Yes, Kili,* she thought. *You're thinking she might be smoking weed, and you feel terrible about how snobbish you are. This just can't be happening!*

"Thank you," Candace said with a sob. "But I have to warn you. Yer in frightful danger."

Kili paused at the comment. *This* was new.

"What do you mean?" she asked, bewildered with how well she was taking the fact that she was in the middle of a conversation with a dead woman.

"You know, you really shouldn't be talking to the Dead." There was a different voice now coming from the phone's receiver. It was no longer Candace, but a vaguely familiar male voice. "That's my job…"

Suddenly, she knew who was on the other end.

"Crane?" Kili asked, her own voice trembling into the phone. "Is that you?"

"The Dead are ornery…can't be trusted," he said, not responding to her question. "Besides, there's no need. We already know who's doin' the killin' around here, now don't we?"

"Crane, what are you talking about?" she yelled into the phone. "Who? Who is it?"

There was a soft chuckle, then a pause. An eternity of silence on the other end.

"Hello? Are you there?"

The shrill ring of the telephone jolted Kili awake from her over-soft hotel room bed. She sprang from her bed with a start, heart pounding in her chest. She glanced around the room, panicked.

It was only a dream. I dreamed the entire thing.

The phone rang again.

Kili glanced over at the clock. The bright red digits flashed 11:15 PM. She'd only been asleep a few minutes. She took a breath and relaxed.

She stood there for an indeterminable amount of time, trying to gather her bearings on wobbling, unsteady legs. Her temples throbbed with the tension of being awakened so abruptly from REM sleep.

She stepped toward the phone, her hand hovering over its cradle...

RRRIIINNNGGG!

She took a deep breath, and picked up the receiver.

"H-hello?" Her voice was a mere whisper. She had no strength for anything more forceful.

Silence on the other end. A long, maddening silence.

"Who's there?"

Another pause, then she could hear a rustling on the other end like hands gripping the phone tighter.

A throat cleared on the other end, only this time, she knew immediately that it wasn't Candace Staples. It was too masculine a sound.

"Crane? Is that you?"

Another pause, then, "No, Kiera. It's me."

Kili's breath caught in her throat. Only one person on earth called her by that name...the name her mother had insisted on giving her despite her father's own strange resentment of it. She clutched at the phone as if afraid of losing the connection should she drop it.

"Cian?"

A sigh of relief echoed into her ear. "Yeah, it's me," her brother said. His voice sounded nervous, yet strong. Healthy. "Kiera, look...you are in horrible danger."

For the second time that night, Kili was struck with the unnerving sense of déjà vu. Candace, in her dream, had just uttered nearly those same exact words.

"Cian, where are you?" Kili asked.

"Don't worry about me," he said. "Just leave. Now. Go home. I'll be fine."

She couldn't believe what she was hearing. She'd come all this way to find him...gone through so much...only to have him discard her so easily.

"How can I possibly leave?" She practically spat into the

phone. "I came to this God-forsaken town looking for you! I'm not going anywhere until I know you're safe."

There was a long pause. Too long. For a split second, Kili nearly panicked with the thought that the call had been lost. The crackle of static erupted on the other end—telltale signs of bad reception over a cell phone. Then, Cian finally spoke.

"I know you're worried. So am I," he said. "But things are really messed up around here, Kiera. Really messed up. You can't trust anyone. Not even that bookstore owner you've been hanging out with."

Kili froze. "H-how did you know about Ezekiel?"

Another pause. The seconds ticked maddeningly by.

"Because, I've been watching. Hiding," he said. "I have to until I can get to the bottom of what's going on. Until I discover what exactly is happening around here...to me, as well as prove who murdered Miles..." His voice trailed off briefly, then, "And Candy."

"Cian, let me help you. I'm here to help."

"You don't get it, do you?" There was a distinct bite of venom in his words. "You've always been this way. You've always thought you know better than anyone else. Better than me. You're completely blind to what's going on right now."

"What? What am I supposed to see?"

He let out a frustrated laugh. "What happens if the authorities discover that I'm alive? What happens when they realize that the two people who were closest to me in this town are now dead? Think about it, Kiera."

She did. The truth was, she considered this a number of times before, but hadn't wanted to admit it. Hadn't wanted to even entertain it. But the cold hard reality was that her brother, if found alive, would become everyone's number one suspect. Kili even suspected that Cian had already become the primary candidate in Crane's own investigation, which was the reason he'd been so reluctant to share his theories on the case with her. It was probably the meaning of Crane's strange accusation in the dream she'd just had.

"Don't be absurd," she said, knowing full well how silly it sounded. "Anyone who knows you would know you're incapable of anything like that. Besides, there's a little thing law enforcement needs called 'motive'."

This time, his laugh was a bit more boisterous, if not a little bitter. "Motive? You bring up motive as an excuse to exonerate me?" She could once again hear a rustling sound on the other end, as if Cian was practically strangling the receiver in his grip. "Well, let's start with Miles, Kiera. Did you know he'd been systematically ripping off my work for the last five years? That he was using my own research for his own series of papers he published in scholarly journals? Did you know that?"

Her legs grew more unsteady at the news, forcing her to slowly ease herself down on the side of the bed. Instinctively, she pulled the receiver tighter to her ear. "N-no," she whispered. "I had no idea."

"Neither did I. At least not until about four days before his death. I'd been going through some of his papers, trying to find our research notes on the Dark Hollows megalith. That's when I stumbled on one of his articles." Cian paused, letting out a deep breath. "We had words, Kiera. At the pub. In front of everyone. I lost my cool, cursed him out, and threw a punch. Sheriff Tyler was there and broke it up, but everyone saw it.

"And Candy? Oh God, where do I begin with her? How about the fact that I found out she was trying to get pregnant? Trying to force me to marry her so I would have to take her with me when I left town? Now how's that for motive?"

Kili couldn't bring herself to answer.

"What's worse, everyone in town knows all this. They saw it with their own eyes," he said, his voice strained with panic. "Just wait until they find out about the Steiner Institute…"

"Stop it!" Kili shouted, feeling a wave of anger at the very mention of the place. "Stop it right there. That's well in the past. Ancient history. That was a horrible time in your life."

"Kiera, I was freaking institutionalized!"

"But it wasn't your fault. You were grief stricken. Torn apart. Your wife had just died of cancer..."

"It doesn't matter," he said, his voice suddenly calm again. "It won't matter. If I'm discovered alive before the killer is found, I will be the prime suspect. I have a history of psychological and emotional problems. Disassociation with violent delusions, according to Dr. Keegan. Throw that together with your precious motive, not to mention plenty of means and opportunity—Kiera, what else are they going to think?"

Her brother was right. Things definitely did not look good for him, and the only way to possibly clear his name would be to catch the real culprit behind these horrible crimes.

"Cian, don't you see? This is all the more reason for me to stay in town," she said. "I'm in a perfect position here. I can make sure you get a fair shake. A real investigation...not just some backwoods, redneck lynch mob. I can help you. Ezekiel and I can figure out who's doing this...we can—"

"And you still aren't getting it, are you?" he said, cutting her off. "I told you. You can't trust anyone...including that crazy whack job, Crane. They're all nuts around here, but he's by far the worst."

"Why do you say that?"

He laughed again. It sounded more like a hollow, mirthless grunt. "They haven't told you? You don't know why the entire town despises the guy? Why no one trusts him?"

The all too familiar lump that seemed to be ever-present since this entire affair began reappeared, lodging tight in her throat at her brother's words.

"Not exactly. His grandmother told me a little, but no one else has ever given me a straight answer about it"

"Of course not," he said. "He has everyone so scared, they

wouldn't dare cross him. They are absolutely terrified of the guy."

She couldn't argue with that. The only people in town that didn't seem to be intimidated by him were his grandmother and that park ranger, Bear. Her thoughts drifted to Candace, and the absolute horror that filled her eyes the moment Crane had stepped into the diner. The sniveling mess he'd reduced Tom Thornton and his goons to with the whittling of a tiny stick. The primal fear the man commanded among the townspeople around here was staggering. Then again, a man who is believed to be able to summon Death itself could do that, she supposed.

"So," she said, "why don't you tell me? I know what Mrs. Crane's told me. Now why don't you tell me what you know? What did he do that has everyone so spooked?"

"He murdered his family, Kiera," Cian said in a quiet, cold voice. His tone simply matter-of-fact, as if he didn't doubt what he was saying for an instant. "They say he murdered his parents and six of his brothers."

"I've heard all this before, Cian," she said. "It doesn't mean anything."

"But that's not all," her brother said. "They say he'd made a pact with the devil...kill his family, and receive untold wealth and powerful magic."

It was Kili's turn to laugh. "The devil? Really?"

"It doesn't matter if he really made a pact with the devil or not," Cian protested. "What's important is that *they* believe it. That *Crane* believes it. Whether or not there really was a pact is irrelevant. The thing that really matters is that he killed them. Not his motivations for it."

Kili thought this over for several seconds before a thought struck her.

"Wait a minute," she said. "From what I hear, Crane was just a child when his family was killed. And they died in a car crash. An accident. Not a murder."

"I'd agree with you, but that's not the only time he's been involved in a mysterious death around here."

She laughed again. "Cian, you're being ridiculous. I've heard this too. About the curse. About the mysterious deaths...people dying who've done Crane wrong. Or worse, who he's grown close to. He can hardly be blamed for that..."

"Actually, he can. Kiera, listen to me...in almost every one of those deaths, objects have been left at the scene. Objects used in ritualistic magic. Talismans. Charms. Objects that can be traced back to Ezekiel Crane."

Okay, that was something Mrs. Crane didn't mention, Kili thought, tightening her grip on the phone. Still, it hardly meant Ezekiel had used those things to murder people. After all, there was no such thing as magic anyway, so the fact of the matter is a person can't "spell" someone to death. It just can't be done.

The whole idea was ludicrous. Not only was she having a difficult time swallowing the whole 'magic' angle in this conversation, but Crane, no matter how odd he could be at times, just didn't seem like a killer. At least, not one who would murder in cold blood anyway.

"Cian, I—"

"Look, don't believe me," he said. "It doesn't matter. Just get out of town. I'll deal with this, and as soon as it's over, I'll be free to come out of hiding. I'll be able to see you. I just need you to leave so I don't have to worry about you too."

"I...I can't do it," she said. "I can't abandon you."

She heard him curse into the phone.

"Look, don't worry about me, Cian. I'm a big girl. I can take care of myself. And you know what Dad always said."

He paused briefly, then replied, "Yeah, 'Nothing should ever come between family...not friends, not work, not circumstances'." He sighed after the quote. "Since when did we ever listen to anything that Dad said?"

Kili laughed. "Since my big brother got himself caught up in a murder investigation. Look, you might as well get used to it. I'm staying."

"Okay," Cian said stoically. "Thanks, Sis."

"You're welcome. Now tell me what happened on the night you guys disappeared. On the night Miles was murdered?"

CHAPTER
TWENTY

K ili hung the phone up, and looked at the clock. It was nearly a half past one. She'd been talking to her brother for nearly two and a half hours, and her head spun over all that she'd learned. But she had to admit...Cian had sounded so strange. He had been lucid for the most part, but there were times—well, he just didn't seem like her brother. It was mostly in his word choices. In the inflections of his voice. Occasionally, his voice would grow deeper—almost guttural—before returning to his normal tenor.

Then, there were the wild accusations. The conspiracy theories. They all sounded so paranoid. Of course, what could she expect? The ordeal he'd been through was enough to put anyone on edge. Even a bit paranoid.

Cian had told her what happened on the night of the incident. The night his guide, Leroy Kingston, had practically gone insane with fear, and reduced to a catatonic vegetable in the county hospital. The night her brother's research assistant had been brutally attacked and mutilated. The night her brother had gone missing. But despite the story he'd spun, there were so many pieces missing.

Why couldn't he remember seeing the actual murder? At least we'd have something to go on then.

But he hadn't. He'd only seen the aftermath. Only seen the eviscerated remains of his longtime friend.

They'd all been working that night, excavating near one of the monolithic stones. They had recently discovered the graves and the gigantic remains buried beneath, which was the exciting piece of news Cian had alluded to in his last conversation with her. He had simply been beside himself with excitement. The ruins had a connection with a legendary race of giants and they'd discovered evidence for the basis of that link. Even more amazing, the original British Stonehenge also carried with it a connection to giants. One story depicted Merlin, from Arthurian legend, enslaving a group of giants from the region, and using them to construct Stonehenge.

"Imagine!" Cian told her. "Two similar sites. An entire ocean away and separated by thousands of years…and both associated with a race of giant humanoids."

He'd been nearly giddy describing the find to her, almost forgetting the dark purpose behind the narrative. When she'd reminded him to keep on track, he had seemed embarrassed, if not slightly disappointed in her reaction, but he continued.

He told her about digging into the first grave, and about how their guide had seemed so agitated from the moment they'd found it. Mumbling the old stories of One-Eyed Jack under his breath the entire time they were digging and how the giant Indian warrior would not allow the desecration of Holy Ground to go unpunished. Cian had chalked it up to just local superstition. He'd heard all the stories before in his preparation for the excavation. A number of times, he'd actually wondered if Kingston was trying to milk him for more money.

But all that changed the moment the strange men showed up —he couldn't recall whether he knew them or not—with shot-guns, threatening them to leave. Then, the glowing green haze had risen from the open grave in which they'd been digging. Their guide had freaked out, screaming hysterically as the amorphous cloud hovered around them in a suffocating embrace. Cian had admitted that he'd been pretty scared as well. He'd never seen anything like it. It had been a ghostly orb that had clung to their arms, clothes, and hair like a million invisible hands. Leroy had dropped to the ground, clawing frantically at his skin and clothes, trying to pull free from—well, he'd been yelling that One-Eyed Jack had him. Eventually, in the chaos, her brother had seen Kingston break free from the cloud, and run screaming into the woods like a madman.

Cian had wanted to stop him, but was having problems of his own. He'd heard what sounded like a gunshot, but he'd been too busy fighting off the haze to see what actually happened.

"I can't honestly say that One-Eyed Jack paid us a visit that night, Kiera," Cian said. "But I can't deny that there were ghosts. Hundreds of them, in fact. I could only catch glimpses of them from my periphery, but they were there. I know that sounds crazy. Absolutely insane really. But we were being torn apart by the incorporeal hands of an army of Native American spirits."

She'd needed a moment to take that in. To say this admission had shocked her would have been the understatement of the century. Though they were both raised Catholic, neither of them had ever really believed in anything outside of the material world. They'd often laughed, and made fun of those ghost-hunting shows that were on TV, and the people who watched them. "Brainless zombies," they'd called them more times than she could count. "Desperately needing some evidence of an afterlife to make sense of the insanity we call life."

So when her brother admitted to actual ghosts attacking them in a place ironically called *The Devil's Teeth*, she wasn't sure exactly what to think. Had he been speaking metaphorically? He had assured her no...he claimed to have literally been assaulted by spirit beings.

At this point in his tale, he'd become suddenly solemn. Quiet. He'd seen something else during that encounter, but refused to elaborate on what it was other than to say it looked like an old crone. A witch straight out of a children's faery story. Twisted face. Gnarled fingers. Stringy, matted hair. But that's all he would say. No matter how hard she pried, he would not reveal any more about the ghastly encounter, and the more she pushed, the more agitated he became.

He'd gone on to say that the spectral attack had dissipated almost as quickly as it had materialized. One second they'd been fighting for their lives against an army of ghosts, the next...he was completely alone. Cian had found himself laying on the ground, several miles away from the Teeth. He hadn't been sure how he got there. Hadn't remembered running. Just awoke to discover the hundreds of scratches and bleeding sores all over his body.

Cian wasn't entirely sure how long he'd laid there. He suspected it was actually more than twenty-four hours. Possibly closer to forty-eight. But eventually, he'd awakened, and pushed himself groggily to his feet. Once he'd fully come to and regained his bearings, he'd looked around for Miles. He found him, lying face down in the nearby pot field, dead. He'd been mutilated beyond anything Cian had ever seen before. He'd panicked, unsure of what to do or how to proceed. He knew he had to reach civilization...knew he had to let someone know. In his frazzled state, he'd hefted his friend's corpse on his shoulder, and started the long hike out of the Dark Hollows for help.

By the time he'd almost made his way to the Hollows' boundaries, he'd heard the dogs baying nearby; heard the shouts of the search party as they made their way through the forest looking for them. That's when he realized his predicament. When he became all too aware of what would happen should they find him before finding the real killer. So, he'd dumped the body, and took off, going to ground as best he could, and using old tricks he'd picked up from his knowledge of ancient cultures to avoid the hounds.

He'd laughed mirthlessly at the ineptitude of the search party. "I kept watching them," he'd said. "I can't tell you how many times they passed Miles in those woods, completely oblivious. The dogs seemed to sense him, but it was as if they desperately wanted to avoid the area where his body was dumped. It was the craziest thing."

Kili and her brother had spoken a little longer, but she soon realized that he could offer no more information about that night. Cian had no clue who might have killed his assistant, and was plagued with irrational bouts of guilt and resentment over his death. After all, why would the murderer do such a horrible thing to Miles, yet leave him completely unharmed?

It was this very question that Kili kept asking herself over and over after their conversation ended. Of course, only one answer kept popping up each time she asked it, but the possibility was just too unbearable for her to consider. Impossible. Yet, the great fictional detective, Sherlock Holmes, would often say that once you've eliminated all possibilities, whatever is left—no matter how improbable—must be the answer.

The problem was the only answer that made any sort of sense was just too terrible to imagine.

"Okay, Kili," she said aloud, pouring a lukewarm cup of coffee from the thermos she'd filled earlier that day. "So what other explanation is there? What other possible explanation can you come up with to explain why Miles was heinously murdered, and Cian was not?"

Her brother had told her that Marathe had made no enemies while in Boone Creek. As a matter of fact, most people around there had seemed to like him considerably more than Cian himself. So, the list of human suspects was a complete blank, though his encounter with the shotgun-toting men seemed awfully similar to Tom Thornton's visit with her and Crane yesterday morning. The problem was, they would have to link Thornton to the scene at the time of Marathe's death, and that would be a tricky thing to do if his church used the Devil's Teeth as a place of worship. His DNA would be all over the place.

Her next line of reasoning took her back to the appearance of the ghosts. No matter how far-fetched it sounded, her brother swore they were there and were very real...that they had supposedly attacked them viciously after opening up the grave. If that was true, could it be possible for them to have caused the massive trauma she'd seen to Miles' chest and head? Crane himself couldn't explain what had caused the injuries. He had described them as being almost spontaneous, if that was even possible.

She moved over to the hotel room's writing desk, and scribbled the word "GHOSTS?" on a notepad, but she promptly scratched it out. Kili just couldn't even begin to consider the possibility of a ghostly uprising resulting in Marathe's death. It simply was not an option.

She took a sip of the cool coffee.

"So that leaves only one other possibility," she said. "No matter how much you don't want to admit it."

She scribbled a single word on the notepad, and glanced down at it.

CIAN.

Her pen hovered precariously over the word for several seconds. She contemplated scratching it out as well, but just could not bring herself to do it. No matter how loathe she was to admit it, it was the single best explanation to the whole mess.

Her brother had already suffered one mental breakdown. Eight years ago, shortly after the death of his wife, he'd just lost it—became insane with grief. The doctors had diagnosed him with a very rare form of dissociative personality disorder with violent tendencies. He'd been locked up, confined in that infernal Steiner Institute, for three long years.

Eventually, he'd been released with a clean bill of health, though required to take a regular dosage of medications for the rest of his life. But he'd been under so much stress lately. The incredible discovery of the giantoid remains. His friend and assistant stealing research from him. And the waitress, and her plan to trap him into marriage by getting pregnant. Was it really a stretch to think these things might work together to break him again?

And since he's been living in the wild for more than a week, what about his meds? Is he taking them?

One of the very first things she did upon coming to Boone Creek was to check out his hotel room. Although she found his clothes, some books, and several journals, she'd found none of his medications or toiletries. There'd been no way to know whether he had them with him, and when she'd asked him about it, Cian had simply avoided the question with a rant about the conspiracies that abound in the region. It wasn't looking good for her brother, she had to admit.

No! I can't think like that. There's got to be another answer.

But there was something else that Cian had told her that troubled her. On more than one occasion, her brother had mentioned how the experience at the Teeth had "changed" him. As a matter of fact, he referred to the change almost as if it was an event... with a capital "C". He wouldn't elaborate. As a matter of fact, it almost seemed as if he couldn't. Every time he tried to pinpoint exactly what changes had happened, he'd become frustrated... unable to form a cohesive sentence. Kili had merely decided to chalk it up to the ordeal Cian had been through, and the emotional trauma he must have sustained.

That's the only thing it could be, right?

But no matter what the answer, she now knew her brother needed her more than ever. She had to do something. Anything to help him.

She glanced over the clock. It was only a little after two in the morning. Plenty of time. She could leave, and be back here before Crane came by to pick her up in the morning. She knew she wouldn't be able to sleep anyway. Might as well make the best of her time. She had to find Cian. Had to find him before anyone else. It was her brother's only hope. And for the first time since coming to Boone Creek, she had a pretty good idea where to look.

Grabbing her clothes from the floor, she pulled them on, scribbled a quick note to Crane—just in case—grabbed her car keys, and left the warm confines of her hotel room. She then climbed into her Camry, and drove toward the Dark Hollows with a purpose.

The Devil's Teeth
October 17
2:50 AM

Kɪʟɪ Bʀᴇɴɴᴀɴ ꜰᴏᴜɴᴅ her way to the Devil's Teeth surprisingly easy. Of course, it had been much simpler this time around after Sheriff Tyler, an entire troop of Kentucky State Police, and the swarming news crews had trampled through the woods to the murder scene. They'd actually used a bulldozer to plow a trail to the site, allowing emergency vehicles, and crime scene vans easier access. Kili could have practically driven right up to the ancient ruins with very little problem.

But she didn't.

Before she's returned to her room, Crane had explained how the investigation would more than likely go. The cops would set up a perimeter around the site, securing it from the public. Excavation would be begin, using portable, gas-powered lights mounted on extendable poles. But with such a complex scene, the brunt of the work would have to take place during the light of day. They couldn't risk missing some crucial piece of evidence due to a lack of ambient light. The law enforcement teams would eventually call it a night, leaving a state trooper or two to guard the scene until daybreak. So, at three in the morning, the only thing she had to worry about were the guards on duty discovering her clandestine snooping. So, she opted for a short hike through the woods to keep from being noticed.

Forty-five minutes after leaving the motel, she crept up to the edge of Noah McGuffin's marijuana crop, and peered around. The sky was overcast, blocking out light from the stars and the quarter moon that had already begun to descend past the horizon. In the dim light, she could make out the fluttering strands of yellow police tape that cordoned off the crime scene, but if any officers stood watch, she couldn't see them.

Her muscles tensed as she listened for potential threats.

Nothing.

She thought about that. Nothing. No sound. Not even the incessant voices and laughter of children that had been plaguing her since coming to town. She didn't know whether to feel relieved or alarmed. In the end, however, it didn't matter. She was here. She would finally find her brother and together they'd get to the bottom of this horrible place.

"Okay, Kili," she whispered to herself. "It's now or never."

She took a deep breath, and was just about to step from the shadows of the crop when shouts erupted up on the other side of the megalith. A man, wearing a wide-brimmed Stetson, and a state trooper uniform, stalked into view, followed immediately by another wearing an all too familiar dark hood. A few words were exchanged. She couldn't make out what they were saying, but it sounded heated. The hooded man gestured wildly, pointing away from the ruins. The man in the hat shook his head, stomping his feet furiously.

Then a flash of light, and a bang rang out, echoing across the clearing. The trooper fell over, face first into the soil. *A gun!* The man had been shot.

Instinctively, Kili reached for the holster to her pistol only to remember it had been confiscated by Candace at Bailey's Pub the night before. She cursed silently at herself for not bringing a backup weapon, stepped out from the marijuana plants, and prepared to run toward the remaining figure who was now yelling at someone unseen.

But before she could make her next step, two meaty hands grabbed her from behind, being sure to cover her mouth, and pulled her back into the protection of the crop. Kili struggled to break free, but whoever had grabbed her was too strong. She wrestled furiously with her unseen assailant, but it was useless. His grip merely tightened around her throat, cutting off much needed air...and soon, the world around her grew black.

CHAPTER
TWENTY-ONE

October 17
5:30 AM

E zekiel Crane sped along County Road 309 like a madman. The headlights of his pickup cut through the predawn fog like a razor while negotiating the serpentine mountain road like a professional driver. His hands clutched the steering wheel tight as the truck swerved in and out of the double yellow line to save time. He knew speeding as he was, at this time of day, was dangerous, but it couldn't be helped.

After being patched up by local EMTs after his fight with the unknown assailant, Crane had hurried back to the morgue to perform the autopsy on Candace Staples. Though the plan was to return to the Devil's Teeth in the morning to continue their excavation of the site, he'd wanted to get a head start on the dead waitress since she appeared to be part of a different case altogether.

The results of the autopsy had been staggering. The implications of the discovery had boggled the mind until Crane had enough time to process it. Then, he realized he'd been suspecting similar results all along, though he'd hoped his suspicions to be merely a product of an over-active imagination. But they weren't. The suspicions had been dead accurate, and therefore, increased the urgency for finding Kili's brother as soon as possible. If Crane was correct, Cian Brennan was in horrible danger. And so was anyone that happened upon him unaware.

Crane had called Kili's room immediately after finishing his examination, but had received no answer. When he couldn't reach her on her cell phone either, he'd promptly driven to the motel, and after cajoling the motel's desk clerk to open her door, found her room empty. A note on the writing desk next to the door had explained everything.

As soon as he'd read the note, he'd run to the bathroom sink, grabbed the hairbrush resting on the counter, and bolted from the room in a flash. He'd then hopped into his truck, and headed out to the Devil's Teeth. The place where he knew she was going. The place that was, in a strange sort of way, calling her to it.

"Dang and blast!" Crane growled, gripping the steering wheel tight with one hand while extracting the small rabbit's foot chained around his neck from inside his shirt with the other. Absently, he stroked at the soft fur, praying silently for protection for the rash, young FBI analyst. She simply had no idea what she was getting herself into.

Twenty minutes later, he drove the truck up the bulldozed path, and came to a stop only forty yards away from the ruins. The bright illumination from his headlights cast eerie shadows across the monstrous stones jutting up from the earth. He glanced around briefly, spotting a Police SUV parked casually near a thicket of bushes to his right. A sentry for the murder scene, obviously. The car's interior was dark, and Crane saw no movement inside. More than likely the State Trooper was napping on the job, his seat inclined for more comfort as he waited out the chilly October evening.

Not worrying about interference by the police officer, he slid from the truck's cab, grabbed his flashlight, and a double-barreled shotgun from behind the seat, and jogged up the incline to the megalith.

He came to an abrupt stop near the sacrificial altar of the place, and looked around, casting the beam of his flashlight in a three hundred and eighty degree arc. Except for the digging tools, sifters, and forensic workstation covered in a tarp to protect against the elements, there was nothing there. All was quiet.

Everything is quiet. He spun around again, his concern growing more adamant.

Even at this time of year, there should at least be some activity from the crickets lurking in the dwindling foliage. But there was no chirping of any kind. No birds squawking. No forest animals scurrying about to hide from his flashlight's beam. It was as if he'd stepped into a Dead Zone...which, in many ways, he knew was exactly what he'd done. From what he'd recently discovered, he was sure the animals would have enough sense not to come anywhere near this place.

He took a step eastward, and played the beam along the ground. With the recent investigation, and loads of law enforcement stomping through the center of the ruins, the mossy carpet had been torn to shreds. It was impossible to tell if Kili, or anyone else for that matter, had stalked through there recently.

Then, he caught the briefest glimpse of an unexpected, and gut-wrenching color as he passed his beam left and right. Greens, browns, and yellows were evidently abundant. Perfectly acceptable colors for Autumn in the Appalachians. Even certain shades of red could be expected. But bright crimson? Perhaps. Though not as likely. A bright crimson with a sheen that reflected the illumination from his flashlight? No way. That was foreign. Alien. It just didn't belong. He cast the beam to his left once more until he saw what he was looking for.

A pool of blood. His face remained neutral...unmoved. He

simply walked over to the stain, and crouched down. Gloving up, he tipped his index finger into the pool, and brought it up to the light. Congealed. Which, really, didn't mean much. Blood exposed to air congealed at a remarkable rate. Temperature played a factor, sure. So did the content within the blood itself. Alcohol. Drugs. Fatty foods. Practically anything could affect the speed in which blood would congeal. The same was true for body decomposition, as well. And there was certainly enough of the gelatinous goo to imagine a body lurking somewhere nearby. Somewhere in the shadows. He flashed his light around him, focusing on the nearest stone. Several spatters of blood streaked across its face like some macabre form of wet graffiti.

Hmmmm. High velocity, he thought, stepping toward the spatter. *More than likely, a firearm was used here.*

Which made sense. The moment Crane had stepped inside the ringed megalith, he'd detected the faintest trace of gunpowder clinging to the air.

What happened here? And where was the police sentry during all this? He glanced over at the darkened police vehicle and shrugged, a cold dread spreading through his limbs. He'd need to check on the officer before he left, but that would have to wait for now. He had more pressing matters to worry about.

He turned around, and moved over to the gravesite in which he'd discovered Candace's mutilated corpse. He was pleased to see it had been covered up with another tarp, securely fastened to produce an almost airtight seal. Crane had expressly told the forensic team to do just that when he'd left the site. When their investigation was fully completed, they would have to find a more permanent solution, but for now that could wait.

Pushing the thought from his mind, Crane spun around once more, and made another pass of the ruins with his flashlight. Nothing. The blood was the only sign that some new violence had been committed here, and he could only assume that it had happened after the crime scene crews and law enforcement had already left.

All right, he thought. *I'm getting nowhere fast. It's time I find Ms. Kili and get her out of...*Crane paused mid-thought, staring dumfounded across the ruins at the beautiful dark-skinned woman leaning against one of the monolithic stones. A seductive smile stretched across her face.

Asherah.

Neither of them said a word. They merely stared at each other in silent appraisal.

Then again, they didn't have to speak. They never had. Both had always known what the other was thinking...ever since childhood. And it was no different now. During the six months he'd been home, Crane had managed to avoid Asherah Richardson entirely. Now, he'd seen her twice in as many days, and he knew nothing had changed between them. Even knowing she was somehow responsible for the chaos he was currently investigating, he was drawn to her like a moth to an intense, highly destructive flame.

"Leave me be, Ash," he said coolly. "I'll get to you soon enough. Right now, I have work to do.'

Her smile broadened. "As do I, Ezekiel."

He nodded at this. He should have known she'd be here. Whatever scheme she was playing at had been exposed. She'd be scrambling to cut her losses, gather whatever she could salvage, and disappear in the confines of Noah McGuffin's estate until the approaching legal storm blew over.

"I'm not here to cause Noah or you any trouble," he said. "At least, not yet. Right now, I just need to find my friend and we'll be on our way."

"I would have thought, my love, that you would have given up on 'friends' a long time ago," she said, her smile waning slightly. A flicker of sadness darted across her eyes.

Crane simply stared passively at her, his initial shock of

seeing her finally subsiding. He now found himself once again in control. "Be that as it may, Ash, she's in trouble. I aim to help her. And her brother."

Asherah nodded, and moved away from the stone pillar. "The girl, you may be able to save. Her brother..." Pursing her lips, she shook her head. "I'm afraid it's much too late for him."

"You've seen him then?"

"No," she said, then gestured toward the woods behind him. "But *they* have. The *Yunwi Tsunsdi* have taken a keen interest in the one that's awakened One-Eyed Jack. They've been positively silent with anticipation of late. Things do not bode well for him, I'm afraid."

So, the Yunwi Tsunsdi have been keeping tabs on the entire affair. It was at moments like this that Crane envied the ability of Granny, Asherah, and now, apparently, Kili Brennan to communicate with the little tricksters. They weren't always trustworthy or dependable, but could, on occasion, be a valuable ally should the need arise. But except for two other times in his life, he'd never been gifted with the ability to see or hear them.

"Then all the more reason for you to let me on my way," Crane said, returning his focus to the problem at hand. "As I said, we can discuss *your* part in all this another time."

She feigned being hurt by his words. "My part? Oh, Ezekiel, I'm just a mundane Jasper County citizen, concerned for my safety. All this talk of giant monsters, and what not, just frightens me somethin' fierce," she said, adopting the local dialect for her own twisted amusement. "I'm not responsible for any of this."

He raised an eyebrow, but refused to be drawn into her theatrics.

"I'm serious, Ash. This is no time for your games."

"So be it. After all, you've been gone ten years. I can wait a few days more. You have leave to do what must be done,"

Asherah said. "But just know this...anything I may or may not have done, it's all been for you. All been for our love."

"Please. Don't do me any more favors."

She let out a deep throated laugh, and blew him a kiss. "Now go. Save your little redheaded hussy. But soon, you and I will have to...mmmm...pick up where we left off." And without waiting for him to respond, she stepped away from the ruins, and melted into the darkness.

CHAPTER
TWENTY-TWO

P ushing aside the disturbing thoughts elicited from Asherah's parting words, Crane reached into his jacket pocket, fumbled around for the object he was looking for, and pulled it out—the brush he'd removed from Kili's sink. He then moved past the perimeter of the stones to a nearby Maple tree, plucked a stick—approximately twelve inches long—from a branch, and knelt down on the grass.

After slinging the shotgun's strap over his shoulder, he rifled through the bristles of the hairbrush with his fingers, and withdrew several long strands of Kili's scarlet hair. He then tied them in a spiral pattern around the tip of the stick, and allowed himself a grim smile of satisfaction. The conversation he'd had with the fiery redhead less than forty-eight hours earlier—just prior to discovering Miles Marathe's body—flashed through his mind's eye. She'd chided him on the use of a superstitious tool such as a divining rod. Of course, he'd justifiably denied it. The very idea had been ludicrous when finding a decomposing corpse in the woods was such a relatively simple matter. No need for "mountain magic" for something like that.

But this was different. The circumstances had changed. To his knowledge, he wasn't searching for a body now. Or at least, he hoped he wasn't. Shoving the thought to the side, he pulled out his pocketknife, and deftly carved a series of symbols into the wood of the stick, muttered a brief prayer, and stood to his full height.

Taking a deep breath, Crane held out the rod at a ninety-degree angle from his body, and slowly rotated clockwise. Upon sensing the first tug along his arm, he stopped his rotation, and moved forward with slow, deliberate steps. He repeated this process several times, slowly making his way toward the shadowy confines of Noah McGuffin's pot plants.

Soon, he found himself kneeling again, examining a series of impressions on the debris-covered soil around the crops. Two people. One, decidedly smaller than the other. He crept forward a few more feet, and found more imprints. The larger one had been carefully stalking the smaller. Expertly keeping their presence hidden until the very last minute. He flashed his light a bit higher at the stalks of cannabis that now surrounded him. Several had been broken. Some crushed under foot. Sure signs of a struggle.

Crane stood up, and stretched his legs once more with a relieved sigh. Though the tracks he'd discovered were certainly ominous, there was something there he could take heart in. He knew for certain that Kili, who had obviously made the smaller set of impressions, had never made it up to the Devil's Teeth. Therefore, the pool of blood he'd discovered could not have been hers.

All right, Crane. If you're as smart as you believe yourself to be, then where is she?

A cock crowed somewhere to the south, bringing his attention up to the sky. Dawn was approaching and he could already make out the dark crimson hue breaking over the horizon. Things were about to get a might trickier in the coming hours.

Red sky at night, a sailor's delight, he recited grimly. *Red sky at dawn, sailors be warned.*

The weather would be turning rough very soon, making the task of finding Kili Brennan even more difficult than it already had been.

Running out of time, Crane slipped the rod into his back pocket, pulled the shotgun from around his shoulder, and stalked through the marijuana field as swiftly as possible. His Mag-Lite's beam illuminating the still shadowy confines of the crop, he followed Kili's departing trail with the expert precision of an Indian tracker. Nearly seventy-five yards in, he halted, holding his breath and listening carefully. He'd heard a sound to his right—a distant, muffled shout from somewhere well past the pot field—near Jenkin's Creek, if he wasn't mistaken.

That's when he remembered the caverns. At one point, during the Civil War, the old cavern system had been used as part of the Underground Railroad. A safe haven for runaway slaves making their way to the Northern states. Later, it had become a haven of a different sort—a secret hideaway for boot-leggers running moonshine back and forth over the Kentucky-Virginia state lines. A kind of base of operations in which to lay low when the Feds came sniffing around.

It would also make a fantastic place for a man not wanting to be found to remain hidden for months without the slightest chance of detection. After all, unless you knew the cave was there, you'd never find it. It was near an abundant and clean water source, which would also provide plenty of berries and small animals for food, if necessary.

Encouraged by the insight, Crane bolted through McGuffin's prized crop, zigging and zagging left and right, making as straight a course toward the cavern as he could. Within minutes, he exploded out of the field, and into the thickly wooded forest of the Dark Hollows, heading northwest at a brisk pace. Though the sun now crept higher into the sky, painting a deep purple and orange swath above the forest canopy, visibility still remained poor. Dense fog had rolled in during the early morning hours, which forced Crane to slow his pace through the treacherous terrain. He also still needed the aid of his flashlight, which might unintentionally give his location away should his prey happen to see it. But he'd just have to take the risk, and pray for the best.

Ten minutes later, he crested a small hill, and skidded to an abrupt stop. Crouching low, he thumbed off the flashlight, crept up to a decaying tree stump, and peered down the other side. His keen eyes scanned through the dim light and fog, scouring for the telltale signs of the cave. Jenkin's Creek trickled calmly to his right, which would mean the cavern should be somewhere to his left.

Where is it? I know it's there.

But to Crane's knowledge, it had been nearly fifty years since another human being had stepped foot inside. Like so many places around Boone Creek, the caverns were said to be haunted. A fantastic story to circulate if you wanted to keep people away as the bootleggers had nearly a century before. Over time, the stories had taken a strong hold on the locals' imagination, who grew to see the underground labyrinth as the second most haunted place in the Hollows. Because of their aversion to the place, nature had encroached on the cave's opening over the years, completely deleting it from view from all but the most astute observers. But Ezekiel Crane was no average observer.

He once again pulled the dowsing rod from his back pocket, and held it aloft, allowing its gentle tug to direct his hand. After two minutes of searching, his diligence paid off. Nestled behind the brambles of long dead rose bushes, and a cluster of blackberry shrubs, the dark narrow maw of the cave gaped open. But though he'd found what he'd been searching for, he made no move toward it. Instead, he remained perfectly still. Watching. Waiting.

The sky overhead seemed to darken. Crane glanced up through the trees' spider web of branches to see the monstrous collision of gray-black clouds rolling in from the west. A flicker of lightning streaked horizontally across the darkening haze above him, and he felt the subtle traces of an unusually warm breeze now buffeting him. The storm he'd predicted from the red dawn sky had moved in swiftly, and threatened anyone unsheltered from its wrath.

Though he would have preferred to wait for his quarry to emerge from the cave before making his move, the advancing storm was forcing his hand. Soon, he would have no choice but to seek the safety of the cavern's limestone chambers, and hope for the best. Besides, there were far more dangerous things that could be hiding in those caves than a deranged man, and his unknowing hostage. Black bears had started to reappear in the region, and they would not take kindly to humans invading their dens as hibernation season approached. And wild animals weren't the worst things a person had to fear when treading into the caverns. There were other, more ancient things that made their homes in the dark recesses of the earth—after all, not all the ghost stories were tall tales to keep locals and government agents at bay.

So, setting his resolve, Crane stole forward, creeping slowly down the steep embankment at an angle, and padded toward the cavern's mouth. Holding the flashlight in his left hand, and flicking it on, he rested the double barrels of his shotgun on top of his left forearm, and crept silently into the cave.

That's exactly when the high-pitched screams erupted from the inky darkness before him.

CHAPTER
TWENTY-THREE

The screams were distinctly female—shrill, terror-filled shrieks. Urgent, but also vexing to Crane. The cavern system he was now standing in was vast, with tunnels spiraling octopus-like deep down into the earth. The walls were limestone, slick with slime, traces of guano, and brightly colored fields of mushrooms, which made the acoustics of the tunnels one giant echo chamber. It was nearly impossible to tell which direction the screams were originating.

Slinging the shotgun once more over his shoulder, he reached into his jacket pocket, pulled out a packet of sugar, ripped it open, and poured the contents out into a pile at the mouth of the cave. He then opened a can of snuff, and sprinkled a ring of tobacco around the sugar in the exact same way he'd done when first entering the Hollow two days before.

The reason was simple. While it was said that Yunwi Tsunsdi haunted the woods of the Dark Hollows, it was the caverns and deep holes in the earth they called home. Crane wasn't sure what evils he was about to face as he ventured further into the cavern system, but he knew the last thing he needed was to add the Little People to the list of dangers.

Satisfied with the offering, he withdrew the divining rod, took a deep breath, and allowed his own special brand of 'magic' to do its job. Soon, the all too familiar tug vibrated up his arm, and he stepped forward with his flashlight beam cutting through the darkness before him.

Silently, he crept through the tunnels and chambers with swift, long strides, stopping periodically to get his bearings with the rod, then moving forward once more. As he progressed deeper into the mountain, the terrain changed from solid rock to thick beds of mud, and finally to an underground stream trickling in presumably from Jenkin's Creek outside. Crane moved through the knee-high water, his splashing movements now clearly audible through the labyrinth. It was regrettable, but unavoidable. As the gentle pull of the dowsing rod propelled him farther downstream, he could only pray his quarry had as much trouble pin-pointing Crane's own position as he had with theirs.

After a hundred more yards, he found himself again on solid rock. Pausing briefly, his flashlight scanned the walls and ceilings ahead. He glanced up at the stalactites above, arching his head inquisitively at the sight. Something was wrong here. Something missing. He took three more steps before the answer came to him. Bats. These caverns should have been teaming with them, but Crane could not recall seeing a single one since entering the cavern's mouth. There had been a small amount of guano at the entrance, but that had been the only sign of the flying mammals he had seen. It was as if something dark and malevolent had driven out the denizens of the cave, and refused to allow them to return.

Considering this, he pulled up the bandana tied around his neck and covered his nose and mouth in the same manner as when he'd discovered Candace's body. *In this case, it is* prepared-*ness, not discretion, that is the better part of valor*, he thought as he trudged on toward his destination.

As he moved farther along, the muffled shouts he'd heard upon entering the cave grew louder, more distinct. The cries now seemed to definitely be coming from Kili, though Crane could not make out what she was saying. But it wasn't distance or poor acoustics that distorted her words. It was something else. Something infinitely more dreadful in his opinion, forcing him to quicken his pace. He was running out of time.

Five minutes later, the narrow corridor he'd been traversing opened up into a vast chamber, nearly a hundred yards across and at least thirty feet high. Crane froze in his tracks at the sight that greeted him.

The entire chamber was covered with fields of large, multi-colored mushrooms, jutting up in angles toward the ceiling, like sea of alien skulls peering up from the rocky foundation. It was as if the room's entire floor was carpeted by the strange fungi. Even more unnerving, an eerie green glow seemed to radiate off them, puffing up and out with curling waves of radiance that made his flashlight completely unnecessary.

But the green glowing field of fungi was not the sight that had stopped Ezekiel Crane in his tracks. Nor was, strangely enough, the ring of thirteen large, moss-covered stones that stood like sentries in the center of the chamber. Thirteen massive stones that resembled the jagged teeth of some great giant's mouth opened wide to swallow any unwary passersby in a single gulp. Thirteen twenty-foot stones that matched in every detail to the one that rested at the Devil's Teeth, which, Crane now deduced, was directly above them.

No, the strangest sight of all was directly in the center of the underground megalith. A man and a woman. The woman prone, laying on the sacrificial altar, clawing at the air in pure, unadulterated terror. Her wide eyes were fixed, not at the man looming over her, but at the ceiling above. Her mouth shouting words that Crane could only assume were Gaelic in origin. It was Kili, and though she appeared uninjured, she squirmed unhindered on the altar like a hundred vultures were picking furiously at her flesh.

The man, his back to Crane, stood apathetically over her, muttering something inaudible under his breath. His hair was the same fiery red as Kili's, though cropped very short around his skull. He was tall, at least equal in height to Crane, with massive arms connected to thick, wide shoulders. His clothing was ragged, torn to shreds by his ordeal for the past week and— Crane paused for a second as he examined the man's attire— something else.

His size. There was something wrong, but Crane could not quite pinpoint it. The shredded clothes. The muscular build, which now upon closer inspection appeared disproportionate— as if he'd concentrated his workouts on various muscle groups to the neglect of others. His right bicep appeared the size of an officially sanctioned NFL football, while the one on his left appeared small, if not a little flabby. His shoulders shared the same unequal proportions. Even more unsettling, the man seemed to stoop with a hunch, like Quasimodo free from the dark towers of Notre Dame.

Oh dear Lord, muttered Crane silently as the remaining pieces of the puzzle slipped easily into place. Kili had told him, upon discovering Marathe's remains, that she was certain the corpse was not her brother despite his unidentifiable features. Her certainty had come from the fact that Miles Marathe was decidedly taller than Cian. She'd described him as short, no taller than five foot six with a stocky frame. But the man before him had seemed to grow at an alarming rate, shredding his clothes as he did.

Crane recalled the bones buried in the ancient grave with Candace. The legends of One-Eyed Jack and his gigantic brothers. All the stories…all the myths and ghosts and murders…he understood it all now.

Asherah's cryptic warnings about Cian's condition now made

perfect sense. He only wished that his new understanding had brought more hope than it did. But in fact, if what he now suspected was true, Cian Brennan had very little hope at all. And his sister was in danger of suffering a much worse fate if he didn't act now.

Ezekiel Crane crept forward, tightening the cloth around his face, turning off the Mag-Lite, and slipping it into his back pocket. He then slowly pulled the shotgun around and pressed it tight against his shoulder while taking another step closer. As he did, Cian Brennan's ominous words became more distinct.

"Brothers," he said, looking down at his sister. "It is time. Time to return to the land of the Whites. Time to arise from the Land of Spirits." Cian paused, sobs purging from him in quick, shallow gasps. "I've been alone for far too long, my brothers. Return to me, once and for all."

Crane took another silent step, passing the first monolithic stone into the interior of the ring. He looked over at Kili, still panic stricken, nearly paralyzed, and shouting a string of incomprehensible Gaelic words. It was as if she wasn't seeing her brother at all, which, Crane figured, was exactly the case. If he was correct, she was seeing something much worse. Something far more terrifying. Something pulled straight from her most soul-twisting nightmares.

"*Etnu grasse, mantu ga sebum,*" Cian continued in a tongue Crane wasn't familiar with. "*Garem benura sa grasse menla nor! Etnu hechenom ga sebum loshay!*"

Another step. Left. Then right. He crept closer, the shotgun's two barrels pointed directly at Brennan's head. Crane didn't want to have to kill him. If there was a way to cure his condition...any chance at a normal life after what he'd been through... he wanted to try his best to give it to him. He was fairly certain that, given enough time, he and Granny would be able to find a remedy. But he was wise enough to know that his options were very limited. If it came down to choosing Cian over his sister, he wouldn't hesitate to do what was necessary. He knew, also, that her brother would never begrudge him for that either.

Crane paused, three feet away from Cian Brennan's hulking form. He still appeared oblivious to the interloper's presence in the uncanny drama playing out upon the megalithic stage. It was time to change that. He wasn't there for a fight. He was there to reason with the grotesque figure standing before him. He was there to help both Brennans overcome the nightmarish plague into which they had stumbled.

Suddenly, Crane cleared his throat.

"Cian?" he said softly.

The man didn't respond. He simply continued his arcane tirade to his 'brothers' in short, throaty growls.

"Cian Brennan." Crane's voice was more forceful this time, echoing around the chamber like thunder.

The man's rant ceased, but he didn't turn around. His gaze was still fixed at the prone form of his sister, who in turn, was still writhing on the altar. Then, slowly—excruciatingly sluggish—Cian turned around to face Crane, a faraway look in his eyes.

"Dr. Brennan, I'm here to help," Crane said, lowering the barrels of the shotgun in a show of peace. "I'm afraid you're not yourself. You and your sister both are in dire need of prompt medical assistance."

Cian's eyes slowly adjusted, finally focusing on him. Then, quicker than Crane could have imagined, the large man lunged. His club-like right fist lashed out, grappling the shotgun from Crane's hand and hurling it against the far wall, while his weaker arm came up in a blinding uppercut across his jaw.

CHAPTER
TWENTY-FOUR

K ili Brennan didn't know where she was. More accurately, she wasn't entirely sure she 'was' at all. Instead, she hovered in the emptiness of nothing. Nothing. No sight. No sounds. Nothing solid or liquid. No air, up, or down. Just a void, all around her.

"Hello?" she shouted.

No echo either.

"Is anyone there?"

She knew the answer to that before it had even slipped past her lips. She was alone. Just like always. Just like she'd been since she was a little girl, lost and scared at the King's Park amusement park her father had taken her and Cian to. The park where she'd become separated from her family. She'd wandered the bustling streets for hours, desperately looking for the strong, faithful arms of her dad. She'd never really recovered from that experience. Had always pushed people away after that, determined to never feel the need to 'be with' anyone. She was better alone. Better without anyone in her life in which she would need to depend.

And here she was, on the vast edge of nothingness. Alone. Just like she'd always dreamed. Just like she'd always dreaded.

She seemed to float there, in the nothingness, forever. Nothing moved or changed. Nothing slowed or sped up. Nothing simply continued to be nothing.

Then...

Giggling. Childlike. Infectious. Playful giggling.

Hello? Are you there?

She didn't speak it this time, but she knew *they* could hear her anyway.

Their laughter soon turned into playful shouts, like children pretending to be cowboys and Indians on a playground. Like kids imagining themselves as pirates on the high seas. The voices played. And they drew closer with each passing moment.

The Yunwi Tsunsdi. She finally understood. She'd been hearing their voices all this time.

"Yeeeeesss, deary," came another voice from the void. "You certainly have."

The voice was ancient and sweet. Grandmotherly. And Kili could detect the slightest trace of apple pie baking in the oven. And something else. Honeysuckle. Cinnamon. And something decomposing, like the stagnant putrid stench of swamp water.

"Who are you?" Kili asked out loud.

The laughter had suddenly ceased.

"Just a friend, sweetie. Just a friend. Come to pay my respects."

Kili looked around into the nothingness. Soon, her eyes adjusted, and she could just make out the rather human figure against the blackness. A shadow superimposed on the void. Human, but not quite.

"I've been watchin' you, Kili Brennan," the grandmotherly voice said. "Watchin' the way that liar Ezekiel Crane scampers after you like a lost puppy. Watchin' how even the Little People flock to yer side like there ain't no tomorrah. And I gotta say...I find you downright vexing. Yer puttin' me in quite the little pickle, deary. Quite the pickle indeed."

Kili wasn't sure how to respond. Didn't know if she even should. There was something not quite right about this grandmotherly shadow now speaking to her in the void. Something primeval. Something malevolent. And she found herself wishing to be alone once again.

"Yer dyin', deary. Dyin' a most gruesome death," the shadow continued. "And changin' too. If it don't kill ya outright, it'll definitely nix your soul. That much is fer sure."

"What can I do? I don't want to die!"

"Of course you don't, sweetie." The shadow moved closer to her, extending a dark hand in her direction. "But there's nothin' either of us can do about it. It's up to Ezekiel Crane now. Pray he don't betray you the way he done betrayed me."

"What are you talking about?"

But the shadow didn't answer. Instead, her finger reached out, and drew a symbol on Kili's forehead with a gentle cackle. Kili looked around, hoping to find a mirror in the nothingness to see what had been drawn, but she knew there were no mirrors to be found. Not in the void.

"I now Mark you," the shadow said. "If'n you should survive this little ordeal, yer mine. I claim you for myself."

Then, the shadow began to fade, and the childlike giggling resumed as if nothing had ever happened.

EZEKIEL CRANE STAGGERED backward from the giant's sudden attack, but didn't fall.

"Dr. Brennan, calm down!"

The red-haired man glowered at him, saliva streaming down both corners of his lips in a feral rage.

"Devil!" Cian shouted. "I warned you last night! I won't let you take her from me. Won't let you stop my brothers' return!"

Crane held up his hands, taking a single step back to put more space between them. Cian had been the one to attack him the night before, but he hadn't been nearly this big. Whatever was causing the hypergrowth was working extremely fast. Possibly much faster than a human body could endure.

"I'm not entirely sure what you're talking about," he said. It was only partially true. The pieces continued to fall into place the more Cian Brennan spoke. Whatever delusion the man was going through, he'd taken the legends of One-Eyed Jack and his warrior brothers to heart. He actually believed himself to be Jack, trying to summon the twelve other guardians back into the world. And in his current fanatical state, it didn't look like he'd let anything stand in his way. "Kili never mentioned you having any brothers, but I'm here to help—"

"Lies! I know who you are. *What* you are."

The mountain man gave a slow, deliberate nod; attempting to calm his opponent's rage. "Okay. And who exactly do you think I am?" He took another step back.

Cian Brennan scowled at him, his eyes narrowing. "You're Ezekiel Crane, the Cursed-One. The man who made a pact with the Devil, and became the Harbinger of Death. The Speaker of the Dead."

Crane had not heard that particular string of adjectives used in the same sentence for a very long time, and he'd wondered which of the town's locals had told the anthropologist about them. Pushing the question aside, he nodded once again.

"That's what they say," Crane said. A pained look flashed across his face as he uttered the words. "Whether it's true or not, right now, I only want to help you and your sister." He pointed to Kili's terrified form. At some point, she'd stopped her frantic shouting, and had succumbed to some strange, open-eyed unconsciousness. A disconcerting trance-like state.

Cian glanced down at where he pointed, a bewildered look stretching across his already contorted face. "Kiera? She's merely a vessel." He too pointed at his sister. "The Gateway for my brothers." He bunched his fists up with a growl. "I will not let you stop their return!"

With a roar, he leapt at Crane again, batting him out of the stone ring with a single swipe of his monstrous arm. Dazed from the blow, Crane pushed himself off the ground, and turned just in time to see Cian's enlarged fist flying directly toward his face. Ducking just before impact, Crane spun around, bringing his left leg flying in a spiraling arc. His foot landed across his assailant's jaw in a jumping roundhouse kick, sending the larger man reeling.

Taking advantage of the opportunity, Crane pressed his attack, slipping inside the bigger man's reach, and hurling a series of jabs to Brennan's gut that drew the wind from his lungs. The big man wheezed, taking a step backward, and glaring once more at Crane.

"I will not let you take the Vessel!" he growled, wincing as he clutched his ribs.

"And *that's* not a vessel!" Crane yelled, pointing over at Kili. "It's your sister, and she's dying. You need to let me help her."

Cian glanced back, shaking his head. "No...no...that's the Vessel. The Gateway. My brothers are suspended in the Land of Spirits. I will help them to rise from the dead, like they have so many times in centuries past."

"And with the exception of only one man, the Dead *never* return, Brennan," Crane shouted. "Trust me. I *know* what I'm talking about on this."

Ezekiel Crane stared pleadingly at the big man, who was now trembling with a dangerous cocktail of confusion, disorientation, pain, and fury. "No. It's not true!" Like a serpent's strike, Cian lashed out, grabbed Crane by the neck with his meaty hands, and lifted him straight off the cavern floor. "You're a liar. A deceiver. And I will *not* let you have her!"

The man's fist squeezed tight at Crane's throat, cutting off all airflow through his windpipes. He wheezed, sucking in gasps of nothing while struggling to wrench Brennan's hand free. But still, the grip held tight, gradually closing in even tighter. The pressure to the back of Crane's neck strained at his vertebrae, threatening to crack. In desperation, he kicked wildly, aiming for his assailant's groin. But at the last minute, Brennan whirled him around, forcing the kick to swing wide.

The larger man grinned maliciously. "It's not going to be that easy, Crane. I'm going to suck the very life out of you and you won't be able to do a blessed thing to stop it."

He tried to respond, but could find no air to form the words. The greenish glow of the mushrooms illuminating the chamber suddenly seemed to dim. The world grew noticeably darker past the rim of his vision. *Oxygen deprivation*. Crane had only seconds to break free, or be forced to succumb to the powerful man's fury.

A barrage of images suddenly flashed through his mind's eye. His parents and brothers, climbing happily in the car and waving merrily to a six-year-old Ezekiel, who sat at the window, pretending to be sick. He'd known it was wrong, but what was the harm in staying home from church at least once? The young boy could hardly contain his smile as they drove off, completely unaware of the sly trick he'd just pulled on them.

The scene cut to their funeral—the horrendous pain and sense of abandonment, only amplified by the suspicious stares, and hushed whispers of the townsfolk. Accusing him. Blaming him.

A bright light, followed immediately by another scene. A teenage Crane, kneeling in a roughly drawn circle dug into the earth in the Dark Hollows. A request made. A bargain struck. Hope once again that his family would be returned to him, only to be dashed to pieces month's later when he realized the deal had been a sham. A fool's contract.

Death was a tricky business. The Dead could not be trusted, and they never, *ever* came back. Though they sure had followed Ezekiel Crane around his entire life. His life had been plagued with the Dead for as long as he could remem—

The Dead, thought Crane suddenly, a single skipped heartbeat the only betrayal of the hope that now welled inside him. *The grave. The gigantic bones.* They'd crumbled to dust almost at his touch. They'd been so fragile...so delicate despite their immense size.

With the little strength still remaining, Ezekiel Crane reached behind him, and pawed at the foot-long aluminum Mag-Lite tucked securely in his back pocket. His fingers fumbled around, straining clumsily to secure a grip while the encroaching darkness continued to cloud his vision. The maniacal face of Cian Brennan still grinned at him, saliva oozing from the corners of his mouth, as his one-handed grip tightened even more around his neck.

"It's time to die, witch!" he said to Crane with a snort of a laugh. "Time to get what you deserve!"

Crane heaved for breath, still clawing at the sturdy metal tube in his pocket. Then, just as the darkness enveloped his vision save for a single pinprick of green light, his fingers found purchase, wrapped around the flashlight, and brought it around in a powerful blow to the big man's forearm. With a crack, and several smaller simultaneous snaps, Brennan's arm shattered beneath the thickly muscled hide.

Howling with pain and rage, he released his grip, and hopped around the cavern in a tortured dance. But Crane was unable to exploit the larger man's misfortune at the moment as he struggled to drink in enough air to keep from going unconscious. He fell to the floor, trying to force his atrophied lungs open with each hacking cough.

Both combatants were momentarily incapacitated, racing to regain their composure before the other had time to spring into action. Struggling on the ground, Crane became acutely aware that Brennan's howls were abating. The race was slowly going to the larger man, and Crane knew it would be the end of him if that happened.

Forcing himself to his feet while clutching at his bruised throat with one hand, he hefted the Mag-Lite into the air with the other, and hurled it end over end at the back of Brennan's legs. The flashlight struck true, just at the base of the big man's right ankle. Crane winced at the loud pop coming from Cian Brennan's leg, and watched as he crashed to the stone floor, directly into a cluster of the monstrous glowing mushrooms.

The crushed fungus erupted in an explosion of phosphorescent light—spores shooting out in all directions like a cloud of spectral radiance. Still wheezing, Crane checked to make sure the bandana was still secure on his face, then raced over to Kili's inert frame, and crouched down.

The woman's eyes were rolled back inside her skull while her lips quivered and twitched with slurred, unspoken words. Taking hold of her wrist, he checked her pulse, and found it more erratic than he'd hoped. But then, he should have expected it from the quick, shallow breaths she was taking in.

"Ms. Kili," Crane said into her ear. "Ms. Kili, can you hear me?"

He risked a quick glance over his shoulder, watching as the monstrous green haze expanded slowly toward them, like a drop of ink spreading in a clear glass of water. Crane wasn't sure whether the bandana covering his mouth would ward off the effects of such a concentrated number of spores. But more importantly, he was certain it would kill the catatonic woman if he didn't get her out of the chamber soon.

Crane turned his attention back to Kili, continuing his cursory examination. He could already make out the telltale signs of swelling around her neck and shoulders; and her chest strained against the buttons of her blouse. She was already in the beginning stages of the same strange transformation that had affected her brother.

Quickly tearing a strip of cloth from his shirt, he wrapped it around her face, and then reached down to pick her up off the altar. But just as his hands made their way underneath her, a giant paw clutched at his shoulder, and hurled him backwards— his back striking the rigid corner of one of the stones.

CHAPTER
TWENTY-FIVE

"Stay away from her, you monster!" the thing that used to be Cian Brennan roared.

Arching his back in pain, Crane gasped at the sight of what now stood in the former anthropologist's place. In the few short minutes he'd laid prone on the bed of mushrooms, the man's metamorphosis had taken on a grotesque turn—probably accelerated by the new infusion of spores.

Brennan's wobbling frame leaned on his left leg; his shattered right ankle now uselessly hanging on by skin, muscle, and tissue alone. He now stood nearly seven feet tall, a full six inches taller than he'd been when their altercation first began. His right arm flexed...even thicker, more powerful than before. The left arm was rapidly swelling to the same proportion. But it was his face and chest, more than anything else that chilled Crane to the bone. The rapid metabolic growth was just too much for Brennan's all-too human skin to handle—its elasticity stretched beyond its breaking point. With each heaving breath, his flesh ripped and tore, creating massive lacerations across his brow, neck, shoulders, and chest.

Exactly the same way it had with both Marathe and Candace.

Large hatchet-like wounds split spontaneously over the man's body as he lumbered protectively over the still figure of his sister. Just as Crane had deduced about the deaths of the others, the spores were multiplying inside him at an impossible rate, threatening to tear away at his vital organs, and burst out of his torso in a great concussive blast.

"Cian, listen to me," Crane said. "We have no time for this. Your sister will die if you don't let me take her away from here." He pointed at the green haze that was now snaking its way inside the stone ring. "Away from that. It's what has infected you. It's what has caused this metamorphosis in you, and what killed Miles and Candace."

Brennan's malformed face paused reflectively, as if he was tasting the truth of what Crane was saying. Weighing it against what his own mixed-up brain was telling him.

Pushing forward with this brief reprieve, he continued. "It's the fungus, Brennan. The mushrooms. They were inside the burial site you uncovered...dormant for centuries within the decomposing bodies of the Native Americans entombed there. Once you opened the grave, you exposed yourself and Marathe...and, to a lesser extent, Leroy Kingston to the fungi's spores."

Brennan remained silent, his incisors biting down on his lower lip, producing a cascade of blood that flowed down over his chin in thick streams. Crane couldn't tell if it was from concentration on what he was being told or from the excruciating pain his body must currently be going through.

"The same spores are causing hallucinations too. They're changing your perception. Confusing you," he continued. "I can help her, Cian. Now that I know precisely what I'm dealing with, I'm confident I can discover a cure. She doesn't have to die."

Cian glared at Crane for several seconds before turning his gaze down at his sister. He seemed almost lucid now, despite the physical agony he must be feeling with the sudden increase in body mass. His bones stretching, expanding...his epidermis splitting in jagged gashes...Crane could not imagine the pain the big man must be enduring. Of course, it was this pain that might have helped to combat the hallucinogenic delusions he'd obviously been struggling with since first being exposed.

"She's...she's not the Vessel," Cian said softly, crouching down to brush a strand of bright red hair from her face. He then turned to look at Crane, shock and horror evident on his face. "My God. Candy. I killed her."

Crane shook his head. "No, you didn't. She died from injuries sustained from the fungal spores multiplying inside her. You had nothing—"

"I brought her to the Devil's Teeth!" Brennan retorted, tears now streaked down his mutilated cheeks. "I wanted her to die. Wanted her to feel the pain I'd been feeling. Wanted her to suffer for the misery she'd caused so many people." He let out a slow feral growl. "I'd been watching. Saw what she—and the others—had done to Kiera that night at the bar. Wanted all of them to pay. I stood over her while she struggled, and screamed... watched her face whatever internal demons that haunted her. I exposed her to all that. And I'm as responsible for her death as if I'd put a gun to her head, and pulled the trigger."

Crane stared at him, wanting to console the grotesque man, but fully aware of the green cloud inching its way past his shoulders. They were running out of time.

"Dr. Brennan, we need to leave. We need to get your sister out of here."

Cian continued staring down at his sister, shaking his head. "I killed them. Killed all of them..." He was losing control once more, succumbing to the fungal-induced psychosis all over again.

To make matters worse, the haze hovered past Crane's head, dropping over his shoulder like a cloud of dry ice vapor. Despite Brennan's fragile mindset, he could wait no longer.

Taking a step toward him, he said, "We need to go. Now."

"...my fault. It's all my fault..."

"Brennan!" Ezekiel Crane shouted. "Now!"

The big man turned toward him again, his burning red eyes now glaring at him with renewed savagery.

"Never!" Cian snarled, stepping away from the altar to tower over Crane. "It's too late. Too late for me. Too late for her." He pointed, then laughed viciously. "And too late for you as well."

CHAPTER
TWENTY-SIX

B rennan's hulking mass flew at Crane in a lightning fast
lunge that sent both of them sprawling across the cavern
floor in a tumble of arms and legs. The two grappled, locked in a
frantic struggle to overpower the other...clawing, swinging, and
kicking.

But with Cian's increased strength and speed, it was really no
contest. The larger man rolled on top of the smaller, pinning him
down with his knees pressed firmly on Crane's arms. Despite his
shattered forearm, Brennan's powerful fists pounded against
Crane's face and jaw, sending shockwaves of pain down his
spine, and reopening injuries he'd sustained from their fight the
night before. Blood sprayed from the open wounds, coating the
giant's torso in a crimson bath.

"Not so scary now, are you, little man," the giant roared,
ripping the bandana from Crane's face, and hurling it across the
chamber. "Now to show you what real terror is!"

Ezekiel Crane coughed, a geyser of blood and saliva spewing
from his mouth. His wide eyes glanced around, but he knew it
was too late. He was directly in the thick of the spore cloud

permeating the chamber. He'd already inhaled a considerable amount of the vile stuff and wondered how much easier it could spread with open flesh wounds.

But he had no time to worry about that now. Kili's condition was fast approaching critical, and he still had to deal with her brother. Crane had wanted to avoid doing permanent damage to Brennan, but his options were running thin.

Another swing crashed against Crane's face—ears ringing...brain pounding with each mighty blow. He was losing massive amounts of blood, and inhaling toxic levels of the spores with his elevated breathing. He wasn't sure how much more punishment he could take, but at the same time, wasn't sure what he could do about it either.

"Cian," Crane hissed through swollen, blood-soaked lips. "You've got to stop this." He tried looking up at the big man, but already one of his eyes was swelling shut. He was pretty sure his nose was broken; and the pressure in his jaw told him it was dangerously close to fracturing as well.

Brennan raised his right arm again, preparing for another swing, then stopped. He looked down at his battered opponent —his eyes wide with psychotic glee...blood lust...as he belted out a cackle-like laugh.

"I'm not going to stop, Crane," he growled. "I've finally realized what this is." He waved one arm around the chamber, causing the green haze hovering around them to swirl up in a gaseous arc. "It's the *real* One-Eyed Jack. It's the protector of the Dark Hollows—imbuing those it chooses with immense size and power—and it has chosen me. Chosen me to carry on its work."

Brennan brought one monstrous hand down around Crane's throat, but waited before applying pressure.

"You're a trespasser here, Crane," he continued. The man's face was even more disfigured than before. Fleshy tendrils of skin hung limply around his cheeks and forehead as it continued

splitting in ragged gashes. "As were Miles and Candace. All trespassers. You all deserve death."

"And your sister?" Ezekiel Crane asked, the agony in his jaw
making it difficult to speak. "Does she deserve it too? She came
here looking for you. She came to help you." Still pressing down
on Crane, Brennan turned a glance to his prone sister. Crane
followed the gaze and continued, "She still has a chance. If she
gets out of here now, I know we can cure her."

The big man turned back to Crane, and laughed. "Cure her?
Why on earth would she want that?" he said, bringing down a
bit more pressure on his neck. "She has been *chosen* as well. After
all, *Jacque de L'un Oeil* was not the sole protector of the Hollows,
right? No...he had twelve brothers." He paused, then looked
back at Crane. It seemed as though a lightbulb had gone off in
his head. Understanding reflected back at Crane through the
monster's eyes. "Ah, brothers! I get it now. Siblings, not brothers.
You were right, Crane. I *was* confused. My addled brain was
seeking a return of some metaphysical force connected to One-
Eyed Jack. His brothers. But I had the answer all along. My
sister. Kiera. And soon, the two of us will carry on the tradition
of the giants of the Devil's Teeth, and punish those who dese-
crate the Holy Grounds."

Crane felt Brennan's grip squeeze tighter around his throat.
"But you're right about one thing," the giant said. "She's in pain.
She needs my help, which means I need to stop playing around
with you." Brennan leaned forward, his hands wrapping tighter
around Crane's neck, and squeezed. "Goodbye, Ezekiel Crane."

The big man squeezed harder, once more cutting off all
airflow to Crane's lungs. The strain was almost unbearable as
explosions of white light—artifacts of oxygen deprivation and
pain—ripped through his field of vision. And still, Brennan
continued to increase the pressure...harder and harder.

Then, unexpectedly, there was a loud squeal, followed immediately by cacophony of child-like giggles erupting from some-

where in the cavern. The tinny bursts of laughter echoed in amused merriment throughout the entire chamber.

Hallucinations?

No. Crane watched as Brennan turned his head at the sounds, his mouth agape in confusion. He'd heard them too. Then, just as suddenly as it had begun, the laughter stopped. Crane noticed that the giant hands around his throat had loosened slightly at the sudden alien sounds, easing the pressure and allowing a trickle of air to flow free to his lungs once more.

Then, with no warning at all, a baseball-sized stone flew through the air hard, striking Brennan across the temple. Crane heard a loud crack upon impact, and the large man reeled back in pain, cradling his head in his hands as he leapt to his feet. He wailed in agony, clutching the area just above his left eye.

Seizing the opportunity, Crane rolled out of the giant's reach, pulled his battered frame to his feet, and dove for the shotgun resting casually where it had been hurled only moments before. He grabbed the weapon and spun, pulling its stock tight against his shoulder, and aiming it directly at the howling Brennan.

"Cian!" Crane shouted, keeping the weapon trained on his foe.

Brennan stopped screaming, then gradually lowered his hand from his face. Crane gasped. The big man's head, from his left temple to left cheek had caved in. His fragile bones unable to absorb the stone's impact had simply turned to powder, leaving a gaping, sagging hole where one of his eyes should have been.

One-Eyed Jack, thought Crane with a pang of regret.

Brennan glared at him with his remaining eye, pain still creasing his brow as he snarled. "You summoned the Yunwi Tsunsdi to help you," the big man said with a trembling voice.

Crane simply stared at him—the shotgun's two barrels aimed directly at his head—amazed that the big man was even able to stand, much less form coherent sentences. But he remained silent. Time for talking was over. Kili just didn't have the time.

"It doesn't matter," Brennan shrugged. "They won't save you." And with a roar of rage and pain, Crane's adversary lunged at him, his massive arms outstretched in a feral attack.

Instantly, Crane pulled both triggers of the shotgun, and Cian Brennan crashed to the rocky floor of the cavern with a thud.

CHAPTER
TWENTY-SEVEN

**The Crane
Homestead
October 25
4:25 PM**

K ili Brennan sat up in bed, throwing back the warm blankets and quilts that had protectively covered her for the past week. She was finally ready to stretch her legs, get out of Granny's spare bedroom, and try to enjoy some of the sunlight that still remained before it sunk behind the shadows of the Appalachian foothills.

Well, perhaps "enjoy" was too ambitious a word. Kili was hardly in a position to enjoy much of anything really. She was still reeling from the aftermath of her ordeal in the caverns. Still mourning the loss of her only brother. Still dealing with the bizarre malady that had so changed Cian, and had threatened to do the same to her. And then, there was the strange vision she'd had while under the hallucinogenic effects of the spores. That strange shadow lady. The Mark. A lot had happened to her in so short a period of time.

No, she thought. *'Enjoy' isn't exactly the right word.*

But it was a start. She knew she'd have to move on with her life. She'd have to deal with all of this at some point, and better to get it over with as soon as possible. Getting some much needed sun, and some brisk air would be a good step forward.

Carefully, she swung her feet over the edge of the bed, and set them on the hardwood floor. The room whirled around her, forcing her to close her eyes to adjust to her sudden movements.

"I'm not sure Granny would appreciate you disregarding her orders to stay in bed," came a familiar voice behind her. "She sort of takes her doctorin' very serious."

Kili opened her eyes, and glanced over her shoulder to see Crane leaning against the doorframe of her room. He held a walking cane in his other hand; a necessary evil he had to endure while several of his bones continued to mend from his fight with Cian. She'd only seen him once since he'd pulled her from the cave, and carried her to his grandmother's house for treatment. From the looks of him, he probably needed just as much "doctorin'" as she had.

His face was battered, and bruised. A long linen bandage, anchored by a thin metal strip, stretched across his nose, partially obscuring his raccoon-like eyes. His right arm, bandaged like a mummy, hung delicately in a cloth sling around his shoulder, and she knew that if she could peer past the buttons of his shirt, she'd see even more bandages covering his numerous bruised and fractured ribs.

"Good to see you're doing better," she said with a weak smile. "Granny told me we were *both* touch and go there for a while."

Crane straightened up, limped over to the bed, and sat down on the edge next to her. He let out a soft chuckle.

"Yes," he said with a single nod. "I must admit, I wasn't sure about either of us at one point." He paused, then sighed. "But Granny is an amazing physician, though a medical board might not agree. With the information I was able to pass on to her, as well as a sample of the fungus that had infected us, she managed to mix up a pretty good antidote for the toxins in our system. The rest was only a matter of time. And thanks to Granny's antidote, Leroy Kingston will be making a full recovery as well."

"Oh, good," Kili said with a weak smile.

They both sat quietly for several minutes, staring blankly at the wall covered with old black and white photos of Crane's family from generations past. Then, taking a deep breath, Kili looked over at her new friend.

"So can you tell me what happened? What happened to Cian?" She struggled to force back the tears welling up in the corner of her eyes. "Why he killed Marathe and Candace? And what those mushrooms had to do with it all?"

He nodded once more and spoke. "First of all, it's important for you to know...Cian never murdered anyone."

She glanced at him, cocking her head. "Then who did?"

He shook his head. "No one. Not even Tom Thornton and his goons when they shot Marathe," he said quietly. "He was already dead before the buckshot even struck him. Point is, no human agent killed any of them...not even the bodies we found in the other graves at the Devil's Teeth. I had suspected that would be the case when we first discovered Marathe's remains. His injuries, at first glance, appeared to be chopping wounds similar to something you'd see from a hatchet or a tomahawk. But upon closer examination, I could tell that the force that caused them came from the inside, not out. If you'll recall, I mentioned that they appeared to have occurred 'spontaneously'."

"I remember you saying that, but I thought you were just getting superstitious on me or something," she said. "Thought you were suggesting some ghost had done it."

He laughed at this, and continued his discourse. "Also, if you remember upon my initial examination of Marathe—the examination you insisted I not do, by the way—I discovered several strange granules...something that looked like dust particles and other debris...on the clothing."

"The spores?"

"Exactly. Though I wasn't certain until the lab results came back while autopsying Candace Staples." He paused for a moment, a twinge of regret forming across his brow as he mentioned the waitress' name.

"But I don't get it," Kili said, tossing up her hands. "How could a fungus do all that? How is it possible?"

Crane glanced at her and offered a friendly smile.

"That," he said with a delicate wink, "is one of the most intriguing facets of the case. And one that gave me some difficulty in isolating." Suddenly, he stood up and extended his free hand to her to help her off the bed. "But I think you're right... some fresh air will do us both some good. We'll sit for a spell on the porch and I will continue answering your question there."

Together, the two hobbled through the house, grabbed their jackets, and made their way onto the cozy little porch on which Kili had first met Esther Crane more than a week earlier. Crane helped Kili take a seat on the porch swing, and sat down beside her. His gaze moved across the dying grass carpeting the lawn, past the quaint little white fence, and fixed upon the multicolored leaves of the woods beyond. Reaching into his shirt pocket, he withdrew an old wooden pipe, stuffed the bowl with tobacco leaves, and lit it. Drawing deeply upon the sweet-scented smoke, Crane exhaled, forming three concentric rings that wafted through the air, and out into the open field.

Finally, after several minutes of complete quiet, Crane cleared his throat.

"*Ophiocordyceps unilateralis*," he finally said.

"Pardon?"

With a nod of understanding, he said, "It's as close to what we're dealing with than anything else I could find. Ophiocordyceps unilateralis, commonly referred to as the 'Zombie Fungus' is a fungal species recently discovered in a Brazilian rainforest. Its spores are said to attach themselves to the antennae of ants, creating a sort of mind-control symbiosis that forces the ants to move to an area more conducive for their propagation."

Kili blinked. "A mind control fungus?"

"Well, 'mind control' is a bit of a misnomer actually. It implies sentience on the part of both the fungus and the ant." Crane allowed a brief smile. "In reality, the fungus simply attaches itself to the host, and manipulates the insect's own base instincts. For instance, if the spores need a wet, dank area, it might deplete the moisture from the ant's own body, forcing it to seek out water to replenish itself. After it does, the spores kill the ant, and use its body as a place to grow."

"And this is what the mushrooms in the burial site did to Cian?"

Crane took another puff of the pipe, and gazed out at the setting sun, now cradled just above the tree line of the mountains.

"Actually, this particular fungus is something else entirely," he said. "I'm not quite sure there is a similar species anywhere else in the world." He reached into his jacket pocket, and withdrew a clear plastic bag, sealed with evidence tape. Kili looked at it for several long seconds before taking it from his offered hand. Inside, she saw the remains of what looked like one of the mushrooms that had been the cause of all the turmoil, pain, and suffering she'd been through in the past few weeks. Crane pointed at it and shook his head. "From what I've been able to deduce, that mushroom only grows naturally in those caves near Jenkin's Creek. But it has limited space to grow...to multiply. It needs a spreading mechanism, similar to the way bees carry pollen from flowers. But in this case, insects would be useless. So would small animals such as bats and rodents... they're just too weak. The toxins from the fungus would kill them too quickly. So throughout the centuries, they've relied on humans."

"The Native Americans," Kili said. "The stories of the giants and One-Eyed Jack."

"Exactly. The Cherokee would have been the tribe to have benefited the most from the fungi's unique properties. They would have seen its ability to transform their warriors into giant protectors as a gift from the spirit world."

"And that's why they erected the megaliths, both above and below ground," Kili added.

"Right," Crane said. "Only I think they would have constructed the one in the caverns first...a sort of Mecca, if you will. A place of worship, and possibly a recruiting center for new warriors. The one on the surface was probably built much later...as a sort of memorial. A monument to those who had fallen."

Kili sat up in the swing, and looked at Crane. "That's something I don't understand. I'm not an expert like my brother, but I thought Native Americans burned their dead in a ceremonial pyre. Why would they have buried the giants?"

Crane merely shrugged. "I'm not sure. The important thing is that they did, and it allowed the spores to lay dormant near the earth's surface to infect anyone who disturbed the giants' slumber. Perhaps that was the purpose. Who knows. But when your brother and Marathe uncovered the grave, they were exposed."

"So why did my brother not die from that exposure like Miles? Or Candace?" Her gut ached as she spoke the words. She still couldn't believe he was really gone. Couldn't believe the monstrosity that Cian had become.

"Once again, I'm not sure," Crane said, blowing another smoke ring. "But I think Dr. Brennan was definitely onto something there at the end. He mentioned that the giants of legend were purported to be 'brothers'. That suggests it may have something to do with DNA. Perhaps only a few select humans are capable of adapting to the genetic manipulations that the fungus makes to the body."

"You mean...the gigantism. The increased size and strength."

"The condition is actually called *Myostatin-related muscular hypertrophy*. It usually occurs at birth with certain humans and animals with a genetic predisposition for it. Increased muscle mass, and enhanced strength are the primary symptoms. For the most part, there are very few negatives when the condition is congenital. However, creating the condition in a fully developed adult, the rapid acceleration of muscle and bone tissue growth could have disastrous consequences. For instance, it leaves the bones brittle. Soft. Easily shattered."

Kili shuddered upon thinking of Cian's last few minutes. She could hardly blame Crane for doing what he did, but the thought of the shattered skull as described by Granny, was just too much to imagine.

"And Cian's psychosis?" Kili asked hesitantly. "Why did he lose it at the end?"

"Well, as you and I both experienced firsthand, the spores produce vivid hallucinations...typically amplifying one's own innate insecurities and fears and manifesting them in the form of waking nightmares," Crane explained. "There's no telling what your brother saw within his own mind's eye, but it's clear that his fear of losing his family strangely acted as some sort of catalyst."

Kili sighed, considering her own nightmare under the spores' spell. The loneliness. The sense of abandonment. Worse still, her own desire to push everyone away before they got too close. She and her brother, apparently, were more alike than she ever realized. Suddenly, she became acutely aware of a single tear running unbidden down her cheek. Self-consciously, she wiped it away and smiled.

"Talking about hallucinations," she said in a half-hearted

attempted to change the subject. "Wow, you should have seen mine."

Crane leaned back in the swing, his hands propped up behind his head as he smiled back at her. "Do tell."

"Well, it's going to sound crazy," she said, feeling foolish over the statement. Considering everything they'd recently been through, how could anything sound crazy after all? "But as I was laying there on that altar, I could have sworn I saw...I mean, I was having a conversation with..."

"Yes?" Crane asked, his smile widening.

"Wait a minute," Kili said. "You know, don't you? You know exactly what I saw."

Crane let out a soft warm chuckle at this and shrugged.

"The only question I have," he said, "is if the Little People can still speak in the Gaelic tongue."

Kili returned his laugh and allowed herself to lean back in the swing next to Crane. She was relieved that he hadn't guessed the darker portion of her vision, so she decided it best to keep her shadow visitor to herself for now. She pushed the image from her head, and together, they sat there for a long while, enjoying the setting sun together. The rest of her questions could easily wait for another time.

EPILOGUE

The Devil's Teeth
October 26
3:35 AM

S heriff Tyler's grim face greeted Ezekiel Crane as he limped up the incline to the Devil's Teeth megalith, leaning heavily on his cane. When he received the call from Tyler at three in the morning, he figured there was a problem. But when the sheriff told him there was a problem up at the Teeth...well, Crane had made the drive in record time.

Since being out of commission for the last week, the state police, state medical examiner, and crime scene units from various counties had busied themselves processing the scene without Crane's assistance. The only task that remained was a complete eradication of the fungi infesting both versions of the Teeth. This unfortunate task had been left in the irritated hands of Sheriff Tyler and the Emergency Hazmat team of the volunteer fire department. Using a controlled burn, they'd managed to incinerate most of the area—including Noah McGuffin's marijuana crop, and had blasted the cavern entrance near Jenkin's Creek just in case they'd missed anything in there as well.

"Glad you could make it," the sheriff said, without his usual disdain. This, of course, worried Crane even more. Tyler's attitude toward him had changed drastically since Candace Staple's death, and his unsolicited confession of his part in Asherah's mysterious scheme. He'd become far more receptive. Almost cordial. But this...this was beyond the range of the sheriff's acting abilities. He was sincerely glad Crane had arrived. "Earlier today, I received word from the State Police that the bodies we discovered here went missing from the morgue in Frankfort."

"What?" Crane asked. "How?"

Tyler shrugged. "That's still under investigation. If you ask my opinion, they ain't got a freakin' clue. The place has someone on site twenty-four hours a day. If the medical examiner investigators aren't there, they have morgue attendants to cover as security guards during the midnight shift." Tyler flicked a clump of ash from the cigarette he'd been smoking. "But somehow, when the dayshift arrived around eight in the morning, the bodies of our locals had just disappeared. Security cameras didn't show nothin'. The state's detective was mighty befuddled by it all."

"Apparently, he's not accustomed to dealing with Asherah Richardson and her kind," Crane said. "Did they manage to complete the autopsies before they disappeared?"

Tyler shook his head. "They were backlogged. Hadn't touched a single one of them. The bodies had been quarantined in their decomp cooler. Apparently, they were planning on gettin' to 'em in the next day or so."

"Blast! We needed those autopsy results."

"It gets worse."

Crane felt his pulse rise in his temples. "Do tell."

"Marathe and Candace's bodies...they disappeared too."

Crane sighed. "And Cian Brennan?"

"He was cremated right away, per Granny's instructions."

"At least, there's some good news to all this," Crane said, looking around the ruins. Four bright halogen lamps, raised high in the air by hydraulic lifts, illuminated the megalith in brilliant white light. The work crews, adorned in biohazard suits, huddled together outside the stone rings, whispering among themselves in furtive tones. "So what's going on here? Why couldn't you tell me all this over the phone?"

Crane continued to scan the site, and saw two brown-garbed deputies standing silently on both sides of one of the open graves. He glanced back over at the sheriff and waited for him to answer.

"Well, we're almost finished. We've taken care of the mushrooms just like you told us to," Tyler said. His feet kept fidgeting as he spoke, and Crane couldn't help noticing the lawman's hands shaking too. "The only thing we had left to do was take care of the 'shrooms inside the graves." He inhaled on the cigarette and gestured over to the grave where his two deputies stood. "That's where we found them."

"Them? Who did you find?"

"Trooper Connors. He went missing the night we found Candace. The night you and Ms. Brennan…well, you know."

"I expected as much when I found blood spatter on one of the stones. Saw no sign of the deputy. Figured he'd been killed for some reason, but haven't had a chance to look into it."

"But he wasn't alone in the grave. We also found Marathe. They're both in that grave over yonder." Tyler wiped away a stream of sweat glistening off his brow. "Out of curiosity, we started to dig up another grave. Uncovered the face, and realized it was Tim Crawford." He took in another puff from his cigarette. "Crane, I'm beginnin' to think they're all here. All of the missing bodies from the morgue."

Crane looked back at the jagged stones that made up the teeth.

"Something tells me whatever's been going on up here, Sheriff, isn't over. Whether it's really one of Noah's operations, or Asherah's, I fear things are only about to get worse."

"These mushrooms," Tyler said. "What are they? At first, we just thought it was more product for McGuffin. Some new drug product or somethin'. But if these things are what caused that Cian feller to turn into that...that monster...well, I just don't know what to make of it."

Crane shrugged. "Neither do I. That's why I sent a sample to my sister for analysis."

"Jael? You sent some to her? I didn't think she wanted anything to do with you or Boone Creek."

"She doesn't. But as a biomedical engineer, analyzing this fungus is like catnip to her. She might not particularly care for me, Sheriff, but she jumped at the chance to have a look at a genuine biological marvel."

Crane began moving toward his truck, leaning against his cane over the unsteady terrain. "I'll return here in the morning to begin excavating the graves again. I'll perform the autopsies myself, and I dare Asherah Richardson to steal the bodies out from under me the way she did the state officials."

Tyler followed Crane to his truck. "And what do you want me to tell the state?"

"Nothing for the moment," Crane said, climbing into the driver's side door, and slamming the door shut. "Tell no one about the discovery, actually. Keep as many men on site, guarding it, as possible. At least until I return. Can you do that, Sheriff?"

Tyler nodded as Crane started the engine. "So after we dig these people up again, what's the plan?"

"I really have no idea. But whatever we're going to do, we better figure it out soon."

"Why's that?"

Crane sighed. "Because there's something dark brewing in

the Hollows, John. Something much darker than this fungus. I've seen the signs. Heard the whispers. Another storm's coming soon, and I'm not sure it's one any of us can survive." Having said that, Ezekiel Crane put his truck in drive, and eased forward along the rough, uneven bulldozed path back to Boone Creek.